I Think Olive You

TRISTEN CRONE

First published in the United States of America July 2024 by Lake Country Press & Reviews.

Cataloging-in-Publication Data is on file with the Library of Congress.

ISBN Ebook: 979-8-9902729-0-3 Paperback: 979-8-9902729-1-0

Author website: www.tristencrone.com

Publisher website: https://www.lakecountrypress.com

Editor: Tara Sexton

Cover Art: Vivsketchesss

Cover Design: Emily's World of Design

Formatting: Dawn Lucous of Yours Truly Book Services

Lake Country Press & Reviews

Lake Country Press

Publishing & Reviews

AUTHOR'S NOTE

Thank you so much for giving this book a chance! I want to ensure that you have a pleasant experience while reading, so please find a list below of content that might be potentially distressing. My hope is that it will help you protect your peace and ensure you get to enjoy Matteo and Giuliana's story.

Although on the surface I might not have much in common with these characters, especially compared to those in my previous work, PLAYING FOR KEEPS, Matteo's struggle with mental health is something that I relate to very strongly. Sometimes our brains just suck. Sometimes life just doesn't come easily. I hope that if you've ever struggled in a similar way that you feel comforted in knowing you're not alone.

This story contains the following content that readers might like to be aware of:

- Alcohol consumption and drunkenness
- Anxiety and depression, passing suicidal ideation, panic attacks
- Thoughts of self-harm and negative self-directed hatred during internal dialogue

- Vaping and mentions of smoking
- Mentions of parental death and grief
- Explicit language
- Explicit sexual acts
- Mentions of needles, syringes, and blood

To those of us who've thought we'd never make it this far.
For those of us still learning to give ourselves
the kindness and love we deserve.
It's not our fault our brains suck, but we're still here,
and I'm so glad we are.

New York

The city has a grip around my throat. Lights strobe through the club, slashes of blinding white overwhelming me. This is my scene. It's where I belong. So why does it feel like my skin is too tight around my bones? Bass pumps from the speakers through my chest and the room tilts. This cannot be happening right now. Have the clubs and parties always been this loud and chaotic, or am I losing my touch?

My hands pass over sweaty bodies as I stumble through the crowd. It's incredible how fucking hot it gets in clubs, how thick the air I'm gasping in is.

"Matt!" Brandon shouts above the din and it's tempting to ignore it, but he grabs the back of my shirt. I make out his floppy blonde hair and easy smile in between flashes of lights.

"Where are you going, man?"

"Fresh air and a smoke." I tug out of his grip and forge onward.

It's true. There's no way I'm about to tell him I'm on the verge of panic. The Matt Palmer he knows doesn't have anxiety attacks. What do I have to worry about when I have it all?

There's so much money. It's my cure-all for anything that might crop up to bite me and the first thing people think about when they hear my name. There'll be no sympathy for the poor little rich boy who inherited the keys to a corporate kingdom.

But this is the third time in the last two weeks I have found myself unable to escape into a party's bliss and blinding intensity.

I'm used to being one of the last to leave, living a little too fast and getting too close to ruin. It goes unsaid that if I'm driving, then it can only mean it's a getaway car. The high of a good party extends into the delicious tangle of limbs and lips—heat and hunger. I never seem to find my fill.

Until now.

I rip myself from the dance floor toward the rooftop. The city glints around me—black skies and golden lights. My hands grip rails just too tall to jump over, knuckles aching under the strain as I suck in as much humid, summer air as possible. Still, it's not enough.

Never enough.

My fucking motto.

My vices are many—my pleasures plentiful—and appetite drives me from one fleeting experience to another for as long as it provides joy. But joy comes fewer and further between.

Ah, another night of being a fuck up? When will you realize you aren't worth the name on your birth certificate and give up?

It's my own personal inner asshole. The voice is like a regular lush fighting closing time—never kind, never welcome, and only muted by the slick burn of alcohol. I try to shake it. The delusion is a comfortable lie I tell myself and others. I reinforce it now, repeating it under my breath like a mantra.

"Fuck-ups don't have degrees. Or an open invite to every social event of the season."

No one hears it; just me and the breeze. I pull my vape from my front pocket, sucking it in like a drowning man seeks air—wishing it was something stronger. But there are rules—stipulations to being the Palmer heir.

No drugs. No gambling. No tarnishing the Palmer name. So

far, I've skirted along the edge, unwilling to give up the lifestyle I'm used to. Somehow my father still controls my life, even in death.

White puffs of smoke paint the night air around me and none of my emotions leave along with them. After a minute of heavy drags, I give up and tuck it away. My eyes flick back to the railing and the drop beyond. Dread swirls in my stomach alongside all the alcohol.

"Hey, what the fuck are you doing up here?" Brandon asks, and I wonder how long I've been out here.

"I told you, fresh—"

"Fresh air and a smoke. Yeah, yeah. I mean, it's your birthday party, and everyone's wondering where you are."

Twenty-six years old with a newly-released inheritance. A room full of people wait below—many of whom I don't know. It's not only my money getting me here—well, not all of it. I charm. I smile and laugh and listen. I sow as much revelry as I do trouble.

Because you have nothing else to offer. That fucking voice again.

I work my hands through my dark sweat-dampened curls, anger surging through me and killing what little buzz I have left.

No.

No. I won't do this. I won't succumb to this feeling.

"You sure you're good, man?" Jesus, if Brandon is concerned, I must look more fucked up than I think.

"Yeah. Needed to clear my head, that's all."

"Okay, well. If you're sure... Come on. It's just getting started. We've got a surprise for you." Brandon urges me back toward the revelry.

I take one last lungful of clarity and descend back into the madness of the party—wrap my hand around a drink I sling back rather than savor. The internal voice dulls, my anxiety smothered under the warm hand of inebriation.

The soft body of a gorgeous woman greets me and Brandon makes an introduction I don't hear. She must be my surprise. It's no secret I have a weakness for women. Tall, short, blonde, brunette. Pale or richly dark. Lusciously thick and lithely thin. There's so much to appreciate—every one gorgeous in their own way. Hot lips find my neck, and I bend to return the favor. All I can focus on is salty perspiration, the freshness of mint against my mouth, and the give of a body pressing intimately against mine. This I can do. This I'm good at.

The vibration of her moan tickles my lips as I find a sensitive spot beneath her ear. She offers, and I accept, bodies melting into the dark shadows away from our friends. Time ceases to mean anything. In the repetitive thrum of music and the dire surge of our bodies against each other, we become nothing more than sensation. Nameless—likely faceless by tomorrow, given how wasted I am—she quiets the voice in my mind as I chase the one high I can afford.

New York's vendetta against me continues. Daylight streams in the cracks between the curtains, slicing into the space with relentless fervor. Summer. My phone vibrates on my bedside table and I can't remember how I made it home. As tempted as I am to ignore the call, it's my mother. The part of me that isn't a total asshole swipes to accept.

"Yeah, this is Matt," I croak as I answer—and fight against the bile rising in my throat.

"Happy Birthday!" Too loud. Wincing, I pull the phone away from my ear.

"Thanks."

"Matt, I was worried. I've been trying to reach you since yesterday."

Rolling over in bed, I try to escape the bright light of the window. Ugh, I'm still in last night's outfit. Sweat and come have hardened on the inside of my clothes after our hurried fuck at the party. God, I'm disgusting.

"Yeah, sorry. I had my party and got home late."

There's a sigh on the other end of the line and I know I've let her down. Again. A permanent state of being for me. *Just a fucking disappointment.*

"I wish your father were here to see it all: your birthday, helping at the company, your college graduation. I'm sure he would have been proud."

I bite back a bitter laugh. My father—the illustrious Thomas Palmer—would have been ashamed his son dropped out twice before finishing, only for it to be a fucking liberal arts degree.

"We both know that's not true. Besides, Dad's rotting in the ground right now, so he doesn't get an opinion."

My mother gasps in shock, ready to admonish me, when I apologize.

"Sorry. I'm tired and hungover. That was uncalled for, but let's not pretend Dad was something he's not. He fostered a company, not a son. I'm surprised he even gave me a stake in it when he has a team far more adept than me to run it."

The ceiling is spinning. Ten minutes tops and I'll be spewing my guts.

"You don't have to accept the role of CEO. He gave you a year to decide."

And time is almost up. It's been nine months since Thomas Palmer dropped dead from a heart attack, and everything and nothing changed.

"I don't know why. Everyone knows Alan is champing at the

bit to go from CFO to CEO. He's practically doing the job already. They shouldn't even bother with me."

"Speaking of Alan, he called. Apparently, I'm not the only one who hasn't been able to reach you."

Fuck. This can't be good. My father's former lawyer weaseled his way to the top of the company and is content to pretend he's running the show now.

"What does he want?"

"You need to meet him at the office. It... it didn't sound good, Matt."

Any number of things could be waiting. The list grows in my mind: I pissed away too much money. I fucked around with the wrong person and they're going to sue. A greedy asshole is threatening to expose one of the avenues I've explored to escape my life. It could be any number of things.

"He's expecting you within the hour. So please, show up."

The *for once* goes unsaid, but my inner asshole is glad to provide it anyway.

"Fine. I'll be there." A brief goodbye and then silence from the other end of the line.

I drag myself out of bed, making my way to the bathroom to turn on the shower. Steam fills the room until all I can see in the mirror is a hazy glimpse of my face. There's a brief impression of bloodshot brown eyes and dark curly hair in disarray. I scrub the sweat and vomit and sickly-sweet stench of her—the girl from last night I'll never see again—from my body.

Then I call for a car. A doorman rushes to open the front doors for me and I wait on the corner for a driver to take me into Midtown to the office. Thomas's building. My father's legacy— now technically mine. The business? I'm not sure what to call it anymore.

And up on the forty-sixth floor, my father's—*my*—CFO is waiting.

Offices always smell dusty to me. And this one is no exception. No matter how often the cleaning crew comes or how strong the candle's scent in the corner is, particles sit on the back of my throat and give me the urge to clear the discomfort. But I resist, and I even go so far as to remove my sunglasses so I don't look too rude. Though after ignoring a dozen calls from him, I'm sure it doesn't do shit.

My father's former lawyer-turned-CFO-turned-my-mentor —Alan—puts a lot of effort into trying to look younger. But I remember him balding when I was a kid, and no amount of expensive hair and glue can erase the image. His face is bloated with agents to smooth out the frown and worry lines that come with thirty-some years as a corporate lawyer—and a lifetime of being a tight-assed fuckwad.

"Matt Palmer, thank you for joining me." *Finally,* unsaid but implied.

"It must have been important for you to go to such lengths to reach me." Calling my mom must have *killed* him. I try to keep the drollness from my tone but from the tightening around Alan's eyes, I haven't succeeded.

It's not my fault Alan has so much Botox in his skin he can't frown properly anymore—or that my mother took a huge chunk of money in my parents' divorce—money Alan would have far preferred to stay in the company for his bonuses.

"It is a matter of some urgency, I'm afraid." Alan steeples his hands in front of his lips after he speaks, as if thinking very hard about what he plans to say next.

I stare, waiting. No sense in giving the man a reaction when I'm sure that's what he wants. Since my father's death, I've made it a point to ignore my father's "right-hand man" after what that fucker said at the funeral. No amount of time will get him on my good side.

Alan gives in with a barely-suppressed sigh before pulling out a stack of papers from a drawer.

"As you know, it's been a little complicated untangling Thomas' affairs."

Business and pleasure.

For once, I agree with my inner asshole.

"Yes, though I'd have thought by this point, you'd have handled most, if not all of it," I say. It is his job, after all—the one I'm technically paying for now. Alan convinced the board to let him *prepare* me—the CEO-in-waiting and majority shareholder by a smidge.

Questioning Alan's ability like this is enough to piss him off. I know I don't help the situation when something big passes his desk and I have to come in to sign off. Although irresponsible, I've enjoyed making this "transitionary" process as inconvenient as possible for him.

"And yet what your father left behind grows messier by the day." Alan shrugs and I'm not sure if the double meaning is deliberate.

"Just get to the point." I'm tired of this pissing contest, the metaphorical fencing I have no desire to dodge and dance for.

"You've come into some property."

Not a huge surprise. Not considering some of the other assets and responsibilities Thomas Palmer left behind. My loft is one of those, so I can't see why this piece of property would garner such an emergent response from Alan.

"Okay?" Again, unwilling to give even an inch.

"It's not a sole ownership situation, hence the sensitivity around timing."

"I'm sure you've dealt with enough of these matters in the last year. You should be well-versed in handling this." I shift in my chair, ready to get up. The rough woven thread digs into my palm where I grip the armrest.

Alan flushes slightly, the first indication I've seen on the man's face to imply any genuine unease.

"Am I wrong?" I push, enjoying this moment far more than I should.

Alan sighs, the sound rushed as if he gulps in air out of frustration alone. "No. *Er*, yes." His nostrils flare as he struggles to answer correctly.

"This is not within my purview," Alan says. "This piece of land was purchased before your father started the corporation. As such, I have no authority over any legal decisions. Since you have not appointed me as your lawyer—and this doesn't involve the company—you need to be the one to make the call on this."

No way in hell will I ever appoint this stain of a person as my lawyer. Still, it's a better outcome than I expected. I'd assumed the worst, deservedly, but this is shades better than bankruptcy or a lawsuit. Before the corporation... I struggle to comprehend a time when my father hadn't been in a three-piece suit and five hours late coming home—a ghost more than an example. Strange, his absence doesn't feel all that different in death.

There never seemed to be a time before all of this.

"*Prior* to the corporation?" It sounds stupid repeating it, but I still can't believe it. I've been spoon-fed the PR piece that my father showed up on American soil with a dream and a hundred dollars in his pocket. All bullshit, of course, but it makes for a heck of a byline.

Alan gives a tight-lipped attempt at a smile and nods.

"You mentioned it wasn't solely his," I prompt, interested in my father's business dealings for the first time in years. My father was a lone wolf; kill or be killed. Partnership is the antithesis of what Thomas Palmer stood for.

"Not at all. Not even majority ownership." Alan pushes the stack of papers toward me but I stare at the lawyer in shock, wanting to wring whatever information I can from the man before I turn to the inexpressive legal jargon waiting on the desk.

"Then why?" Why bother? Why even bring it up?

"Despite your differences, Thomas only wanted you to succeed, Matt. You have to know that." Alan's attempt at sincerity is about as believable as his hairline.

"Enough, Alan. You don't need to blow smoke up my ass. We both know my father was disappointed to have sired such a lazy sack of shit. I'm not ruthless like he was—cunning in life or business. I have too much of my mother's weakness in me. He made that evident." I clear my throat of the unexpected emotion gathering at the memory of his parting shot at us—before the movers cleared out his closet, and I heard his Italian leathers clack on the penthouse floor for the last time. The room feels stifling despite the frigid air conditioning covering my skin with gooseflesh. I have to get out of here.

Soon.

Now.

Although this building has been nonsmoking for years, I hit my vape to calm some nerves. Hell, knowing it will piss Alan off sweetens the deal. My deep breath is followed by a plume sent in Alan's direction.

"I'm not so clear on why you're even telling me this. If we—I —*whoever* doesn't even own this property outright, why waste time or resources on it?" It's the most financially-sound point I've ever made. And all of it just to find a way out of the room as soon as possible.

"You could." Alan wafts his hand in front of his face to clear the air and gives me a disgusted look before he pushes the papers closer to me. "Own the whole property, I mean."

I look down at the brief impression of a contract, aging ink faded into the yellowing paper. Old. Older than me.

"Why the fuck would I want to do that?" I ask, sucking in more of the nicotine to calm my nerves. My patience wears thin, my attempt at being polite fraying with every second I'm holed up in this towering metal coffin.

"Jesus, Matt. You know you can't smoke in here. Come on."

I take one last drag before I stash it again and he pushes on.

"Aren't you tired of it? Your father's shadow?" Alan asks, the honesty of it drawing my full attention. The lawyer looks at me with what I consider a genuine expression for the first time I can remember before he urges, "This is your chance. You're not your father. Anyone with eyes and a Forbes subscription can see it. But it doesn't mean you can't be something else."

It sounds important, or like Alan thinks it's important.

"And how do I go about doing that?" *When* his *name eclipses everything you do and no one can see beyond it.*

Alan points at the front page. "In the contract, there's a stipulation, a clause your father put on his investment. Despite being small change compared to what we deal with now, he still had a sound mind for planning back in the day." Alan sounds proud, and I know he loves this job, every grimy moment.

"The clause states if the investor, your father—or you for all intents and purposes—can prove his investment has not been returned or that there's not enough of a success margin... it all reverts to you. The exact parameters are in the contract, which is in Italian, so I leave it up to you to figure out."

"So, I'm going in there for a hostile takeover?" The idea turns my stomach.

"Not hostile. The old partner is dead, same as your dad, and these few scraps won't make a difference to our bottom line. It might be an opportunity to find something... forge something for yourself that doesn't have your dad's name splashed all over it."

Abundantia, the contract reads, the name as far away from Palmer Enterprises as one can get.

"So, you want me to see if this asset is worth procuring? And if I fuck it up, no harm done because it's not tied to the business?" I mean it rhetorically, but Alan smirks and nods, unabashed in his lack of faith.

"Can you honestly say you have something better to do?" Alan asks, and before I can retort he adds, almost gently, "I think you need this. It's a farm of some kind—crops, not animals. Get a feel for a slower pace for a change. You look like shit."

My mind flashes to the sick lurch of the parties—the cramping stomach and the spinning ceilings. Not better. No.

I shrug in response, unable to word what I'm feeling. And not wanting to name the dread that sits in the passenger seat with me and has for the last few weeks—hell, months if I'm being honest.

"What's in it for you?" I ask.

"Less than what's in it for you, kid." Alan pulls another stack of papers from his drawer and chucks them—one by one. Sheets of newspapers, tabloids, and print-outs of online articles land with a thunk in front of me. Weeks of indiscretions pile up and end with last night's exploits.

Playing With Fire! Heir to Palmer fortune spotted

The headline is innocuous, as far as they can be when click-bait rules the day. It's the text below it, the blurry image of me with a half-naked—

In smoking hot situation with Senator's daughter

Well, well, well.

If it isn't the consequences of my own fucking actions.

And far worse than I expected after Alan mentioned the property opportunity. I lowered my guard—my relief too quick.

"But not nothing. The suits aren't happy at all. These are only a few of the articles out this month—some of the more savory ones. There's talk of a vote to remove you from the board before the one-year deadline. Because of your little stunts, we're down ten points and it's a shitshow downstairs."

There it is—the real reason. Alan doesn't have my interests at heart. Not directly, especially not when he lives and breathes this company and I'm messing with it.

"So, this is you unofficially telling me I have no choice?" I ask, wanting it confirmed.

"You pissed off the wrong person. Senator Bridges wants your head on a platter for last night and will take us on to get it. You don't have the experience to deal with someone in power trying to tear this company down—him pushing for certain regulations can make billions of dollars of difference."

So, I fuck the wrong girl and the company eats shit?

"You need to lie low. I've convinced the board to let you tackle this part of your inheritance while things blow over. This acquisition will be the way to prove you have what it takes to run this business. If you don't manage it by the twelve-month deadline, there will be no Palmer in Palmer Enterprises."

Rage climbs up my ribcage, burning up every rung of my ribs.

"This is *bullshit.* Don't look me in the eye and pretend you're doing this for me."

Alan's eyes narrow and he shakes his head, "Of course I'm

not doing it for you. If you had your way, you'd be drinking and fucking your way through the company funds. Mark my words. If you can't get yourself under control in time, you'll lose everything."

I don't have to sit here and take this.

Even if he's right about you? Even if they're all right about you?

The chair groans as I shove it back to stand, eager to escape.

"I do think this would be good for you. Get away for a bit and breathe some new air. Straighten yourself out, for god's sake." Alan's suggestion cools some of my animosity.

It doesn't sound too unappealing. The party scene is wearing me down. If I fuck it up, then the other owner gets it all; a win for them anyway. Palmer Enterprises would be better off, but I won't let Alan have the satisfaction. Not without a fight.

"And where is this new air?"

Please don't be Arkansas or some shit.

"Somewhere in the Puglia region."

Puglia?

I must say it out loud because the incredulity of my question makes Alan's face break into a proper smile or whatever he has amounting to one.

"Italy. Your father's homeland."

Italy... Summer, wine, and food so divine I can gorge myself and still beg for more.

"*Italy*," I repeat with anticipation replacing the anger—snatching the stack of papers and rolling them up to tuck under my arm. "When do I leave?"

"Whenever your ass is packed and ready to go. You figure out the contract. Then gather the evidence you need against the other owner. Prove they're lacking and come up with your business plan to create something for yourself, and then get back to me. But this trip is on your dime. No using company funds, and if you pull shit like this over there"—Alan points at the tabloid shot—"we won't wait until the deadline to remove you, got it?"

I give him a mock salute and put my sunglasses back on. "Capisce, boss."

"Jesus Christ, kid. You realize that's not even real Italian. They're going to eat you alive. Just don't piss anybody off. I don't want the hassle of organizing an international extraction."

"Not your problem. You're not my lawyer, remember? For the next three months, I'll be out of your hair." *Every fake strand.* "And you can all carry on the better for it."

"All I need is for you to sign this agreement saying you're going to honor the board's stipulations." He pushes a paper toward me, pen poised on top.

Despite better judgment—or perhaps due to the lack of fucks to give—I walk over and scribble my signature. Alan slides his business card across the desk and I slip it between my fingers, resisting the urge to flick it back into his face.

"In case you need to reach me via alternate means since I know phone calls are hard for you, that's my email and fax."

I nod and walk out, turning back with the door handle in my grip.

"I'll see you around, Alan. You'll hear from me when I have news."

Alan nods, already returning to his paperwork and emails, and I take the elevator trip down with more air in my lungs than I've had in a long time. Within an hour, I have two bags packed and a one-way ticket to Italy. The nerves eating up my stomach daily are easier to ignore than they've been in a while.

I have all flight long to figure out what the fuck kind of business my dad had in Italy. The man hadn't been back in close to thirty years and he never spoke about his life in Italy except to embellish the sharpness of his rise. Why would a man—one I've only ever known to be ruthless and efficient—bother to keep an investment this old... this insignificant?

The name on the contract says it all, one that's been scrubbed from memory and buried long before my father's body: Tommaso de Palma.

Whatever this is, it's personal.

3

Business class would've been a step down from what I'm used to, but worse still, I'm forced to find a spot in economy for the first leg of my journey to Puglia. It's fine. I booked last minute on a full flight. I'm lucky I have a seat at all. But it's the aisle, and the stewards knock the shit out of my elbow with their cart every time they walk by. There's a screaming kid behind me. Hell, even the little bottles of booze I get with my meal are tiny and taste like spiced petroleum.

Italy. It's worth it, and it'll be over soon. I've had hangovers longer than this flight.

The food cart bruises my arm with its force. The steward offers me two whole meal options and I answer "chicken" through a wince. The swill they serve on this side of the plane is one of the worst meals I've had in a while. The most appetizing part of it is the freaking dinner roll.

Italy. The reminder is more of a mental grimace but it keeps me focused. Overpriced eye mask on, the rush-purchased neck pillow from Hudson News propped just-so, I shove my earphones in to drown out the wailing. I'll land in Naples and then find my way to Puglia—I'm winging it. It'll be okay. Easy. I pop an Ambien and it takes hold—putting me out of my misery for the next few hours.

When I wake, it's with a kink in my neck and my tongue sticking to the roof of my mouth from the recycled air. Disembarking is a crush of people who stand as soon as the seatbelt sign goes off. Overhead bins are thrown open and bags bump anyone unlucky enough to be in the vicinity. The plane smells like sweat and desperation. I count myself among the latter, antsy to get the fuck out of this sardine can. The longer I stand in the press of bodies, the quicker my heart pounds.

Just a couple more minutes.

Once I'm free, I rush to the baggage carousel as if walking will burn off the anxiety of being contained for too long. After a few rotations, my hand wraps around my suitcase handle, tugging. Italy waits beyond the exit doors.

Steeling myself, I step out into the Neapolitan breeze. The air is different here. It's not a stretch when New York carries its own personalized scent, but here it whirls around in my lungs and calms the calamity in my chest. Stepping away from the doors, I wait on the sidewalk as cars pull up and depart just as quickly—witness to sweet reunions and hurried rideshares.

Naples is apparently the best place to get authentic pizza— my first taste of Italy. This might be the turn I've hoped for. Things are looking up. I google the top-rated pizzeria in Naples and order a taxi to get me there.

Other tourists mull about, stuffing their faces with red sauce and cheese. Spots dot the crust, blackened where it's risen too close to the flame. I'm thankful Naples is such a tourist town when I'm able to place my order in English. Thomas Palmer immersed himself in the American Dream so fully you'd hardly guess he was Italian at all. That left me with a severe lack of knowledge and almost zero language skills.

I people-watch while I wait and let the city's energy settle around me. Woodsmoke and bright tomato; the smell hits me before I see it. The waiter sets a piping hot pizza down in front of me and it pains me to wait for it to be cool enough to touch.

The moan following the first bite is easy to excuse. After a rude awakening to suffer through another terrible plane meal, it's only expected. The second and third bites feel downright sinful. Flavor bursts along my tastebuds—sauce sweet and salty in the best way. The dough has a rougher texture on the bottom where they've either floured it or added something to stop it from sticking to the base of the oven. Fresh basil lends an earthy and sweet distraction to the richness of fresh mozzarella, torn off into bubbling balls of decadence.

Jesus Christ. Did I just fall in love with a pizza slice?

I force myself to take a break from devouring food to look up my best option for travel—no direct flights from Naples to any airport in Puglia. The train is an extensive journey, which leaves *buses.* I'm very tempted to find a driver who will take me all the way, but the rolled-up contract in my backpack hangs heavy.

I haven't looked at it yet. Seeing my father's birth name on it left me with a feeling I didn't want to examine back in New York. It can wait a little longer, right?

Takeovers and dismantling corporations can't happen on an empty stomach. This has nothing to do with me being scared shitless and wondering for the first time what I've gotten myself into. Looking before leaping might have been a good idea. How the hell am I going to manage this in three months? Part of me is unconvinced I want the CEO title, but that was when I had time to decide. The board forced me into a corner and I can either rise to the occasion, or...

Be the fuck up everyone expects you to be.

I don't have much going for me, it's true. But perhaps this can be my chance to do something outside my father's scope. Thomas Palmer was well-known in New York. But here... here my father was Tommaso de Palma and his only legacy is rolled up into an agreement close to thirty years old.

I could make it mine, could find a space where I fit without having to self-medicate and plaster on a smile. This could be fulfilling. At least I might have something to fall back on if I fail at being CEO—besides vices.

Sucking it up, I book the bus ticket. Matt Palmer hasn't taken a bus before. He's a spoiled asshole whose only talent is finding trouble. Today, and for the rest of the summer, I'm determined to be more than just Matt Palmer. What that means remains to be seen.

A handful of sweltering hours later, I step off the crowded bus into a town called Taranto. The sun-kissed edge of the coast glistens in invitation. My first impression of Puglia is sunlight and sensation. Heat leaves my limbs languid—the daylight baking onto my skin—and the wind offers a kiss to temper the bite. The air tastes different here, unburdened by smog and fumes. A summer breeze dances around me, laced with freesia and the hint of rich, tilled earth. It's like a fucking postcard, and all I can think is I've had all this waiting for me and never knew. So close, yet so far.

In Puglia at last. I finally pull out the contract. *Abundantia* stares up at me like an accusation. I find precious little on the internet when I look up the name. There's an old article about the farm in Italian that Google is trash at translating. The rest is about some ancient goddess. The address of the law office where the contract had been drawn up is in Gravina—a good fifty-some miles away, and after a full day of travel even I can't ignore my body's need for rest. As desperate as I am to get started on this whole endeavor, I'll be useless without sleep. So, at the very least I can find a place to spend the night here. As much as it pains me, I ignore the contract and see about trying to find accommodations.

After a frustrating exchange of broken English and piss-poor Italian I have a room, a hot shower, and the sinking feeling that there's a very strong possibility none of this will be as simple as I intended. Sleep drags me under almost the second my head hits the pillow and when I wake in the morning, I feel halfway human. I take a moment to enjoy an espresso and some breakfast, staring out at the sparkling waters of the Ionian Sea. Sunlight catches the ripples in the water of the gulf, seagulls squawking overhead, and it feels so far from New York I might be dreaming.

But then one of those fucking birds shits on my luggage and I'm reminded of the pigeons back home. Birds are assholes everywhere, it would seem. Scrambling to find something to clean it with, I take it as the omen that it is to get going. I swear if I could make eye contact with that little asshole his beady eyes would be saying "get out of here," like he's from a bad mafia movie. So, I get my ass in gear and hope this isn't an indication of how the rest of this trip is going to go.

I approach a ticket window at the bus stop, pointing to the town's name on the contract and hoping for the best. The man behind the partition only scowls as if I've personally offended him. His bushy brows bend down into a severe frown. The impressive mustache he's sporting emphasizes the downturned brackets beside his mouth. He could be anywhere between thirty and fifty. His swarthy skin holds few wrinkles but his demeanor screams grumpy-older-man.

The attendant dismisses me with a backhanded wave and shakes his head. Through broken English and unintelligible Italian, I glean there are no buses for the rest of the day. My confused expression must soften the man because he sighs, hands me a pamphlet for Vespa rentals, and gestures to a building across the street with his thumb.

My phone's power is on the brink of uselessness. I've forgotten to buy a converter at the airport, and the idea of being stranded sends anxiety rocketing through me.

Just get to Gravina. We're so close.

The rental is about to shut for riposo but I flash a wad of

euros, and fifteen minutes later, I wobble out with a sunny yellow vehicle. Handlebars in my grip, ownership papers for the Vespa in my backpack beside the contract—I push it out onto the street. It doesn't make sense to rent one when I have no idea when I'll ever get back here.

I strap my bag to the luggage rack on the back of the bike and straddle the seat. Engine sputtering, the sound jumps from a mild grumble to a roar when I twist the throttle and take off. Wobbling at first, jerking the handles in an attempt to keep the Vespa upright, it takes a minute for me to get used to the feeling of driving. Once I'm sure I'm not going to tip over spontaneously, I follow the rudimentary verbal directions I've been given (thanks to a now-dead phone) and eventually the road signs.

Gravina comes into view, its ancient aqueduct rising proudly. The town rests like a fortress on a hill—a remnant of the Middle Ages. My amazement grows as I venture deeper into town and traverse the twisting streets. Vendors display a wide array of products, fresh fruit, and other oddities. Another road is littered with small groupings of tables and chairs—people sipping wine. The music of rapid Italian and laughter follows me as I pass. How have I never known about this? How did my father walk away from all this life and beauty for the gridlocked, heart-attack-inducing misery of corporate New York?

I can only speculate. There's no way to ask what it must have been like for him thirty years ago—how he grew up and if it was difficult. I might never get the chance to know now he's dead and gone.

There's no time to ruminate on bitterness over the past, not when the Vespa veers on the road a little as I try to soak it all up before it blurs past me. The airport was standard, the bus as I imagine most others. It's here, in the country, further from the hub of tourism that I feel wonder start to spread through me. How long has it been since I've felt excited? Months? Years?

I can't wait to trade vodka for limoncello, kale salad for homemade pasta, and American kisses for the famed fire of Italian women.

All I have to do is find a hotel. No big deal. I'm a big boy—Italian by blood, if not by culture. If I have any chance of taking over a piece of property on this side of the world, I better start learning how to navigate. Hence the Vespa and the shirt buttoned lower than I usually would. Wind whips through my dark curls under the helmet, mussing them, cooling the sweat from my body beneath the linen shirt.

Cobblestoned streets send uneven bumps through my arms, and I round a corner I'm *sure* has to lead to a hotel. I've been up and down this area multiple times, and this is the last street I haven't tried. Too preoccupied with looking up at the few signs I can see up above the entryways, I hear her yell just in time.

My hands crush the brakes in my grip. The Vespa's tires screech loudly, echoing against the buildings on either side of the narrow street. The roaring of my heart fills my ears, dulling the world around me until her voice pierces the fuzz.

"Che cazzo stai facendo!" she shouts, not even three feet from my face. Rage twists on her face but she's beautiful in her fury. Pushing her hair back in frustration, she huffs out an angry breath. The lustrous silk of her dark strands distracts me from the fact that I've very nearly hit her head on. How do women get their hair that shiny?

"I'm sorry," I whisper, senseless for what must be the millionth time in my life, though rarely over a woman.

"American?" she accuses more than asks. Watching with amusement, I wonder if she's going to spit at the ground in my general direction. Her demeanor gives off that vibe. She's justified. I deserve it.

"Yes. Again, I truly am sorry. I'm lost and I was preoccupied."

The words feel clunky leaving my mouth. As she stares me dead in the eye, my usual charm evaporates—brain empty.

"Typical." Gesturing at me, she mutters under her breath and bends to gather up the canvas tote bag she dropped in her haste to get out of my way. I'd be a fool and a liar to say my eyes don't catch on her generous curves as she retrieves what she can. It's a lost cause, though.

Oranges roll down the street, and whatever bottles were in there have crashed to the road. Thick syrupy liquid drips from one corner and onto the cobblestones below. The other corner spreads red wine like a bloom of blood, soaking the fabric.

"Please, let me make it up to you."

Why haven't I shut up yet? There's no way she wants anything to do with me now. As far as first impressions go... near-death isn't the most endearing start.

Bag retrieved, she breathes deep and releases it slowly before looking at me. I catch myself watching her lush chest rise and fall.

God, stop being such an asshole. You almost killed her and now you can't stop checking her out?

"It's not necessary. I think you've done *enough*." Ire colors her voice and she turns to leave, stumbling slightly.

"I feel terrible. At least let me reimburse you for the mess I made?" Maybe if I keep trying? Something in my chest flutters, uncertain. Why does it matter to me at all?

"I appreciate the offer but," she says over her shoulder, a frown carving into her tanned skin as she waves me off.

"Okay... Honestly, I do want to help you, but it's for selfish reasons. I'm so far out of my depth here. I'm afraid I'm going to have to find the nearest fish and catch it with my bare hands to avoid starving. My phone is dead. I don't speak a *lick* of Italian, and I'm a little desperate." My stomach gives an impressive gurgle as if to punctuate the direness of the situation.

"You *must* be desperate since we're an hour from the coast and it's a long way to travel for a lone fish… especially with how you drive."

She's joked back, her eyes softening, and the knowledge spreads through me like a shot. The color is dark spiced rum, and they make my chest burn the same way. Her lips tilt up into the ghost of a smile and my own stretches against my cheeks.

"So, what do you say?" I venture—feeling like a kid—giddiness bubbling in my chest. I try to make it sound cheeky, even throwing in a wink for extra measure.

"I say… only if you follow my rules." It's stern. Her tone is grave though her eyes glint with amusement.

"Name them."

"No questioning what we eat." She ticks it off on her index finger.

"No comparing it to American food." A second finger now.

Stopping to think for a second, her expression turns pensive, and I know I'll do as she asks if it means I can turn that frown into a laugh.

"And lastly?"

"Lastly…" A smug smile curves up her mouth. "I drive."

"Drive? I just bought this thing!" I protest halfheartedly.

"Those are my terms. Take it or leave it." She shrugs, but I can tell she's enjoying this little exchange almost as much as I am.

"I don't even know your name."

"Giuliana Santoro." Sticking her hand out for me to shake, I shift my hold on the handlebars to respond in kind. My hand swallows her palm. The touch is a juxtaposition of velvet skin and calluses on the pads beneath her fingers. Given how small her hands are, I wouldn't have pegged her for having calluses, but her grip is firm, and her introduction friendly.

"Matteo de Palma." I offer.

Why didn't I go with Matt Palmer the way I do back home? There's no need to use my government name out here. It's not the goddamn TSA line. Maybe I want to convey I'm not a total stranger—not a mere pathetic tourist—but possibly something more.

"Okay, Matteo... move back on the seat and get ready for the ride of your life."

Hanging her ruined bag from one of the handlebars, Giuliana settles herself in front of me and I have to tuck my legs around her in order to fit us both.

The Vespa surges beneath us and somewhere between my hands around her waist and the thundering of her heartbeat against my chest, I might have pulled an Icarus... because Giuliana's skin burns so hot against my hands, I wonder if I'll have any fingerprints left when I pull away from touching her.

To say Giuliana knocks me off balance is an understatement. I'm used to women. Hell, I spend a lot of time with women—mostly in a state of undress—as the recent articles can attest. But, I realize in rising alarm, precious little of that time consists of talking.

I'm sure some of the women I'm acquainted with must be smart with sparkling wits, but I can't speak to it. Not when the conversations we share lie in the sway of hips and the seductive curl of a smile. They want something from me and they know how to get it. It's a mutual respect of desire.

Giuliana has far less guile. I don't want to say she isn't like the other women because that's condescending. But pretending to be Matteo has me wishing I was a better person. Had I been back home, my mouth would've sampled the divot of her dimple by this point. I'd be halfway drunk on straight spirits and her kisses—though I'm not sure she'd allow it. This lady takes no prisoners. Instead, she pulls over outside a little store and I follow like a lost puppy.

"What are we doing here?"

Giuliana gives me a look over her shoulder, eyebrow raised with an unsaid 'What did I say about questions?' before strutting into the shop like she owns it.

"Giuliana?" The cashier asks, confused. Eyes darting between us and the ruined bag dangling from her fingertips, he purses his mouth.

"*Mi è caduta la bottiglia. Posso avere dell'altro vino rosso?*" she asks.

The man springs to action, grabbing a clear bottle from under the counter and turning to the wall behind him—lined with tapped casks. Maroon liquid drains into the bottle and swirls around the inside.

"What is this place?"

Innocuous from the street, I'd have assumed it was a bar except there's nowhere to sit and drink.

"It's called *vino sfuso*. You bring in your own container and they fill it with local wine priced by quantity. Unfortunately, my bottle broke." It's so pointed I can feel her words pierce my skin. "Dario is kind enough to give me one of their bottles instead since I'm a regular customer."

Dario perks up at the mention of his name and gives her a sheepish smile, his cheeks staining as red as the wine being poured. The bottle clinks as he sets it down on the counter and rings her up for a second time today, I assume.

"So, you said something about making it up to me?"

"I did..." Please don't let this come back to bite me.

"You can start here. I had dinner plans and those got thrown out, so we get to rebuild them together."

I pull out my card and hold it out to Dario, only for Giuliana to give me a little "Uh, uh. Cash only for totals under ten euros."

My fingers are clumsy as I fumble to pull out the money and pay. Fucking Italy and no one wanting to take credit cards for small purchases. Eventually, I manage, and Giuliana greets Dario with a cheerful little "ciao," before she struts out the way she came and sits her delectable ass back on the Vespa seat.

"Where to next?"

"Down the street to the salumeria. I'll grab us a few things and then we'll head to one of my favorite spots."

And that's how we end up on a tiny, precarious set of stairs winding down beside the aqueduct bridge. The ravine below looms far too close. Giuliana walks without fear, a new bag of goods clutched in her hand—including different kinds of alcohol and food items. She even talked a shop owner into giving us dinnerware for our impromptu picnic.

"Are you sure about this? Wouldn't it be better to be on the bridge rather than beneath it?" Now might be a good time to tell her heights aren't my favorite. I try to forget the moment on the rooftop of my party a few nights ago.

"Matteo... trust me. Up there, it's tourists taking pictures, far too busy. Down here, we can take in the ravine—admire the old ruins and the city on the other side."

She ignores my grumpy noises behind her, forging on until the stairs turn into a metal walkway connecting us to the bottom half of the aqueduct. Giant arches rise above us. Trees and rock slope up on either side of the ravine, and I follow her to the center.

"Are you sure we won't get in trouble for this?"

"No offense, but based on your driving, you don't come across like the kind of guy that worries about trouble."

Mouth gaping as I sputter, I can't help but admit she's right. Giuliana sinks onto the stone walkway and unloads our feast. There's no choice but to join her, I suppose. Tummy gurgling in desperate hunger, I settle down beside her, and she hands me a drink she's poured into our borrowed glasses. Far be it for me to turn down a drink, but one mixed on a bridge is a little suspect.

"It's to open up the palate and whet your appetite," she explains, taking a sip of her own. The bright orange liquid is a compliment to the fiery sunset lighting up the horizon. We sit side-by-side, staring up at Gravina and her grandeur, and for the first time I can remember, I don't have the urge to outrun my own mind.

The anxiety abates for now. There's a novelty to sitting

down for a meal with someone instead of being alone and forcing myself to soak up some of the night before. The new experience sends a fizz of something I can't name to my insides. Yeah, I've heard the term butterflies, but can they apply to a situation as a whole and not just the rush of desire I'm used to?

I take a hefty swig, a bitter taste coating my tongue. Despite trying to stay cool, my face twists in disgust, and she laughs at my dismay.

"It's an acquired taste. If you'd prefer, I can pour you some of the wine?" The unlabeled bottle from the *vino sfuso* dangles from her fingers and I accept with gratitude.

"I am sorry to have disrupted your day," I say as she fills my glass, a sheepish smile punctuating my apology.

"And almost killing me?" Rolling her eyes, the answering smile she gives is radiant.

"*And* almost killing you. It won't happen again." I solemnly cross my fingertip over my heart.

"Of course not. You're not driving that thing again until you've learned how."

Giuliana picks up the keyring from her side and dangles them. The metal clinks together before she closes the keys into her fist and tucks them into her pocket.

Since the shock of our initial meeting, I've had time to get a better look at her. And what I see sends a heavy feeling into the pit of my stomach. Giuliana is arresting. Long lashes over big brown eyes that would be demure if not for the wicked glint in them when she teases. Her dark hair is thick and slightly wind-blown from our ride. The bite of the breeze and the tease of alcohol give her cheeks the slightest blush.

If I were a better man, my assessment would stop there, but I'm not. I note the way she fills out her jeans, and the dip of her soft waist where I'd love to span my hands again. This time I want to trail my fingertips along her sides and see if she's ticklish.

Two parts of me are at war. Now, it's not the voice inside my head drowning out reason—it's the spiral of desire snaking down and settling low in my abdomen. I want her, but perhaps, for a change, I want to *know* her a little too. If I'm going to turn over a new leaf, I might as well start here. So, I figure I'll enjoy whatever I can get.

Gathering the bits she's procured along the way, Giuliana puts together a few helpings of bruschetta. I pop a piece of bread topped with tomato, cheese, and balsamic into my mouth in one bite—starved.

"You Americans always get the name wrong. The 'ch' in bruschetta doesn't make the same sound in Italian. There is no 'sh' sound. It's '*SK*.'"

I only raise my eyebrows, urging her to say it again, enjoying the warm tone of her voice—like daylight... but the kind that makes your body lazy and turns your skin a shade darker without the hurt.

"Broo-sketta," she emphasizes.

I repeat and she gives an almost proud nod, as if it's her sole duty to inform ignorant Americans of their faux pas. More items emerge from the bag, and soon I sample the second most delicious thing I've tried since I arrived in Italy. Although the prosciutto crudo is scrumptious, it doesn't quite compare to the pizza I tried. She gets even more determined when I tell her about my pizza Napoletana experience.

"Local food is as good as what you can find in the cities. Even better because it is so fresh, sourced from farms in the area. You tourists always choose the dishes closest to your American fare and miss out on a proper taste of Italy." She bites into her own delectable morsel of cured meat and cheese, her expression darkening as irritation sinks between her brows.

"Are you saying real Italian pizza isn't good?" I challenge, guessing it'll get a rise out of her.

"Of *course,* I am not saying that," she scoffs, "only, you miss out when you limit yourself."

"Well, trust me when I say I'm not missing out right now." My voice drops slightly, trying to convey how diverting I find her company.

"It's just a taste. Pace yourself."

I wonder if she's aware of the effect she has. Probably—she seems comfortable in herself, not fazed by me at all. My glass of wine stays topped up and between the two of us, we drain the bottle. Throughout it all, she talks to me about the history of the aqueduct and the ancient Roman influence on the city. We snack and drink, and I soak up her words like parched earth enjoys the rain. It's refreshing to see someone so at home in their skin.

I like to talk a good game, and my swagger is a maintained front to see me through my daily interactions… but Giuliana carries herself like someone who knows their place in the world and has worked to get there. I think again about our handshake, the calluses on the pads beneath her fingers.

"What brings you to Italy?" she asks, fist tucked under her chin as she leans her elbow on one of her knees.

"I'm here to find my purpose and discover more about my roots in the area. Vacationing in between." I shrug, unsure how to be concise about being here to secure my future by fucking over someone else.

"Ah, so nothing big?"

Tilting her head, she examines me and gives me a little smile. What can I say? Coming here to find my path is the biggest step I've taken in my whole life. But things with her are light and easy, so I respond with a smile and a shrug, trying not to dwell on how big this contract thing might be. Focusing on her instead...

God, I haven't had such an enjoyable conversation in quite a while.

"It does make sense then, why your name is Matteo."

"And why I look like a Roman god?" I say it with a cheeky smile and my insides warm up when she laughs.

"And why your ego is as awful as your driving. All that Italian machismo pumping through your veins along with the marinara."

"You've got me pinned. Half Italian, half toxic." *Fully over-whelmed by how much I want to touch you.*

I lift my wine glass and she clinks hers against mine in response, drinking to what is a true statement. There's something about the fresh night air. Early summer floats on the wind and stirs the ends of her hair, sending her scent swirling around me. The heady taste of good Italian wine and the lingering essence of food feeds my soul. It makes me feel like I can be better than I've been, better than everyone back home believes me to be. Because I want to be that man—I want my confidence to be real, my body to be honed by work, and my mind to be quiet.

Our plates are nearly empty, our glasses of wine dangerously low, but my chest aches with the prospect of our parting.

"Tell me about yourself. Do you have any deep dark secrets? A boyfriend? A nickname only certain people get to call you?" I ask, eager for whatever bits she deigns to share before the night's over.

She shakes her head at me. "No. No boyfriend. No nicknames. I don't like them very much. It's always been Giuliana."

I know then, at least for the rest of the night, I'm going to try and squeeze in at least one nickname or endearment—even if it's to push her buttons and see if I can get her fiery again. Like she'd been when we almost collided. She carries on though, unaware of my plans.

"My job has been killing me—financials getting in the way—and although it's necessary, the numbers are soul-sucking. I needed a break, so I thought I'd treat myself to some downtime before things pick up at work. Gravina is a world away from my troubles, but unfortunately, tonight is my last night here. I figured I'd bend my own rules and take a chance on a man who looked as lost as I felt." A sad sigh leaves her and there's an air of something different. The hollows beneath her eyes are shadowed and when she isn't smiling or laughing, her expression settles into something weary.

Swirling the last bits of wine in her glass, she stares at the liquid as if it might provide her with something she needs.

"Lot of pressure?"

"*Oh*"—she gives a dry chuckle—"too much. But I never shy away from a challenge." Her mouth is a resolute line, softening only when she lifts the tiny whirlpool in her glass to her lips and swallows.

"And I've run from almost every single one of mine. Totally opposite, you and I."

I lighten the conversation, attempting some self-deprecation to make her smile—which works. Sort of. It's a wry smile, one that makes me reach both hands out to touch the one she has resting on her crossed knee.

I turn her hand so it rests palm up on my own, tracing the lines with my fingertips—skimming over the rough edges of her skin and the lifeline carved deep into her skin.

"You wear hard work on your hands." I glance up to check Giuliana's reaction only to see her lids lowering, absorbed in our touch. "And walk like you command the earth. As if it will mold itself to your step." I tease my touch against her skin, and she curls her fingers into her palm to stop my light touching.

"My maternal grandmother is English and always hated how my hands looked and felt. She thought it was 'unladylike and uncouth.'" Her grip tightens into a fist, and I lift it to my lips, placing a kiss on her knuckles and coaxing her fingers open again to thread between my own.

"Is that why your English is so good? Your grandmother?" I ask and she nods, stuck somewhere in her mind, so I keep talking. "Personally, I think it shows strength and perseverance. I think there's something beautiful in a physical manifestation of effort."

She squeezes my hand in hers, but I can tell she doesn't believe it from her face. I know what it feels like to believe the worst in yourself. Perhaps she experiences that to some degree.

"Yes, she stayed with us for a few years when I was younger, around the time my mother—" She breaks off and I wonder what it is that taints those spiced rum eyes with sadness. "—and we see her every Christmas. She insisted on us learning. And about my hands—you're sweet for saying so, but you don't have to work so hard to give me a compliment."

"No one has ever accused me of working hard in any capacity but one." My voice is husky—mind muddied by the food, the drink, and her. I let the insinuation linger, knowing I'm being forward while not having the luxury of my reputation to do the work for me. New York is soulless, but at least the name Palmer gives me a head start there.

"And you feel the need to prove yourself to me?" Her gaze softens, heat filling the space where our skin touches.

"You don't seem like the kind of woman who is easily fooled. My words wouldn't be enough, I fear."

There's precious little space between us, our bodies canted toward each other. It's not until she takes a deep breath and it tickles my cheek that I take in the closeness. I wait, perched on the edge of something desperate.

Initiating these kinds of affairs isn't new, but I've never felt the need for it this keenly. Something about her calls out to me. It's as if she won't merely dull the demon within me but instead bring it to heel. Selfishly, I try to convince myself she might benefit from our encounter as well. Giuliana looks stressed when she isn't joking; she said she was here for a break. And I am the king of distractions.

Night swallows Gravina and the glittering lights within the buildings above us lend an intimacy to the air that hadn't been as evident at sunset.

I wait, watching as she mulls it over, hoping beyond what I've allowed myself for a long time for this moment with her.

"Actions speak louder than words, after all," Giuliana whispers and we close the distance between us until our lips meet in a tentative kiss.

Although I want nothing more than to devour her, I keep my attention light to enjoy the tart taste of her mouth. Giuliana deepens the connection, threading her hand into my hair as the kiss turns greedy. I can't say how much time passes when my heartbeat is too frantic to count and she's pulled me so deep into her orbit I can think of nothing but her.

"Matteo?" Giuliana whispers against the shell of my ear.

And god, if that doesn't make me fucking clench my jaw, muscle there jumping with the strain. I have to remind myself not to tighten my hand, not when hers is within my grasp and my other cradles her cheek. Is it a denial? An invitation?

"I don't have a place to go for the night yet..." Had the mood been anything but hungry, my statement would have been innocuous. But our appetites aren't sated yet.

"I have one for tonight. But I leave for home tomorrow," she warns and stands, tugging me up with her. We make quick work of our meal, tucked back into her bag. The steps are harder to find this time.

I hold onto her free hand as she leads me toward the Vespa.

Settling my body around hers this time is different. The smoldering ember from earlier turns to flames licking at me, driving me to distraction. She tucks away the kickstand so my shaky leg is the only thing keeping us upright. The keys slot into place as my mouth finds the sensitive skin at her neck and I trail a blaze of kisses down the side. Giuliana sucks in a gasp that stretches her ribcage, its sharpness evident in my arms. The bike ignites, rumbling beneath us. My fingers skim over her soft stomach—thumb tracing the underside of her breast.

"Matteo." It's a warning. It's a plea.

I heed her. For now.

I wrap my fingers around her hand instead, feeling her turning the throttle. I lift my leg and she sends us surging down the street. Giuliana gathers herself enough for me to go back to my exploration, and the bike wobbles a little when my thumb finds the hardened tip of her nipple straining through the thin fabric of her shirt.

"*Ti ammazzo*," she growls, her tone irritated, and I know I'm in trouble. But I can't quite bring myself to care, not when I can feel how tight she's wound.

The need to have her, to sample her and feel her body relax, is a physical ache. I'll be sure she gets to let go. Tonight, I want to give her pleasure. She's already helped me escape, helped me forget, without me having to sink into her body. I'll repay that kindness.

The Vespa winds through town—Gravina much quieter now. The air blows cooler and fraught with what sizzles between us. We pull over outside of town, a small place that looks more like a home than a hotel but could be an Airbnb. I'm beyond caring. It's doubtful I could even scrounge up questions with my cock pressed to the generous curve of her ass.

We stumble from the bike, mouths on each other as soon as

our feet are on solid ground. Feasting on her lips, I gather her close. Giuliana winds her arms around my neck. Deft fingers weave into my dark curls, devouring me with as much intent. She walks me backward until my back hits the wooden door with a light thud. Her hands snake down my body as she tries to extricate herself, pushing against my chest for me to release her.

The growl coming out of my throat when she breaks our kiss is shameful—insatiable.

"Keys. I'm trying to get inside." It's a frustrated grumble as she digs through her jean pockets for a keyring—upset when she remembers it's still in the bag dangling from the handlebars.

Inside. Inside is good.

"They're in my bag," she pouts.

I eat up the distance between the door and the bike with angry strides, back at her side between the span of a few breaths. She rifles through the bag and I've never been happier to hear the jingle of metal clinking.

Unlocking the door is taking too long and I poise myself behind her. Pulling her body flush with mine, the hardness in my jeans presses flush against the dip of her lower back.

"Not fair," Giuliana complains, but the key turns and the door swings open.

"I don't play fair. Not with this." It's a rough whisper against her neck. Body aching with desire, I pack away the little something in my mind that feels suspiciously like a conscience.

Then we're inside, and Giuliana's leading me toward a bedroom. The windows are cracked open, curtains dancing with the wind. Kicking off my jeans, Giuliana tugs at her shirt in between kisses. The fabric of our clothes joins in a pool on the floor until we make it down to our underwear, and I can't hold back any longer.

Pulling her tight against my body, my hands cup the voluptuous curve of her ass as I walk her backward to the bed. A gentle push and she's splayed out in front of me. Standing between her legs, I watch as she's bathed in silver and starlight —her hair fanned out around her and her breathing ragged. God, she looks fucking phenomenal.

Her breathless laugh lets me know I've said it out loud and I shuck my underwear before I sink down to my knees at the edge of the bed.

"What? What are you—?" is all she manages before my lips find the soft flesh of her thigh. Holding the outside of her legs, I urge her hips up to ease her underwear off.

"Matteo?"

"Tell me to stop now, gorgeous, and I will," I command as I pull the fabric down her legs and kiss my way back up, goose-bumps rising on her skin in response. She doesn't protest the endearment, rather my actions.

"I don't want you to stop. I want this. I want you. But you don't have to... I know guys don't really like—"

"Giuliana, the next time you open your mouth better be because you're moaning my name."

Slotting my mouth over her heat, she arches up against the bed at the contact. My hand presses into her belly—holding her in place as I lick, and suck, and savor. The taste of her essence is slick and sweet, and I wait until she can't keep still before I test her.

Finger sinking in with ease, Giuliana hisses and moans at the friction.

"So hot," I say, sucking on her clit until I feel her relax around me. And then I add a second finger, curling them up to rub against the textured wall deep within.

"You're so tight." It's little more than a moan against her thigh, my cock weeping with want for her. If I touch myself now, it'll be over. I'll spill all over myself like an untried teenager.

No one has driven me higher, pushing me closer to the brink without even laying a finger on me. If Giuliana wrapped...

I grunt at the thought, my hips jerking.

No. Focus. Focus on her first.

"Matteo..." It's reedy, almost a whine, and she rocks her hips so my fingers sink deeper inside of her.

"Yes, beautiful?"

Giuliana reaches her hand down and her fingers snake through my hair, playing with the springy curls. My thumb brushes against her clit and her hand tightens in my hair.

"*More.*"

There's nothing to do but obey. I stroke and tease and feel every inch of her quiver. Thick thighs tighten around my head as she chases the high, on the precipice of falling. And then she *does* moan my name, a guttural, almost pained sound as she crests. Clenching around me, her body's rhythm strong, she pulls me in deeper before she finally melts.

Giuliana's body goes lax save for a few twitches when I kiss her—when my tongue laps up the proof of her desire. I tug my fingers from her wet walls. Fingers coated in her essence, I wrap them around my cock and squeeze—not trusting myself to move. Not until I'm sure she's pleased with me. Not until I've earned it.

Her breath shudders out of her with a sigh, and she lifts up onto her elbow to look at me—her eyes glassy and half-lidded. Fuck. Staring up at her from my knees feels like a high I've never reached before. A giggle passes her lips before she flops back down. "I feel like I don't have any bones. That was... so good."

Rising up, I stare down at her dopey little smile. She looks as relaxed as I hoped she'd be. I stalk onto the bed, kneeling between her spread legs, and press my lips to the pulse at her neck. "Oh, Giuliana, that was just an aperitivo. I was preparing my palate and whetting my appetite. Now the real feast begins."

Don't fuck this up. Don't embarrass yourself. The reprieve from my own mind is at an end, and it angers me, tainting this experience. Sure, I kind of agree with the sentiment, but the self-loathing accompanying it tampers my desire to a manageable level. It's enough of a cold splash that I remember to get a condom first. I need to recover some of my wits because lord knows I discarded them somewhere between her breast in my hand and her orgasm on my lips.

"Come back," she commands, leaning up on an elbow, her hair falling over one shoulder, and I want nothing more than to feel the silky strands run over my fingers before I grip them.

"Condom." It's all I can manage, hissing as the cold silicone engulfs my overheated cock.

"Hurry." It's almost a pout, and if I were anything other than fucking delirious with want, I might've found our rudimentary conversation funny. But all it does is serve as proof of us being beyond words.

"Protecting you."

Because this cock has been in far too many places and you can't promise that you're safe. Not until you get yourself checked out.

The self-hatred starts to spread but then Giuliana lifts up to wrap her hand around the back of my neck. The time for thinking is over. Her fingertips trail down my muscles and I twitch in response to her exploration. Featherlight touch changes to feverish and she drags her hands down my chest and abdomen until they wrap around my girth and position it against the promise of bliss.

Leaning forward, I sink into her as slowly as I can manage—teeth bared against the exquisite agony of our joining.

"You take me so well, gorgeous." Whispering the praise into the crook of her neck, I fight against surging within her and losing my mind. Giuliana arches in response, impossibly taking me deeper and I'm grateful to be this clear-headed.

Sure, we've been drinking, but the food soaked a lot of it up. Time and the cool breeze did the rest. This is the most lucid I've been during sex in a while, and holy fuck does it feel better than any other escape I've sought out.

Rotating her hips under mine, Giuliana tests the feel of me inside her. I can hold back no longer. Driven by the force of how badly I crave this, I drag against her on the retreat and push back with abandon. It has a bite to it—a frenzy I should try to keep at bay, but I'm beyond it. And Giuliana meets me thrust for thrust.

My hands grip the curves of her hips as I move within her, leverage for my oblivion. The nails she rakes down my back keep me grounded. Moans catch at the back of her throat and spur me on. Giuliana takes what I offer and she enjoys it with relish. So, any regret I may feel for taking my fill—for consuming every shuddered breath and grunt—fades away. I drink from her lips and the sound of her... every whimper and shiver are a taste I'll never get enough of.

The sharp-edged knife of the high fast approaching builds within me. So close.

But then she stills me in place. Sharp nails dig into the flesh of my ass and her legs hold me locked inside so I can't move. I pull away from tasting the salt of her neck to stare down in confusion.

A wicked glint in her eyes has taken over—a certain satisfaction in her expression and she looks like a fucking tempest. Fear rises in me, though this time it's not fear of myself or the darkness in me. This time it's the promise I see on her face—the knowledge that she intends to ruin me as thoroughly as I've tried to ease her.

"My turn," she promises and plants her foot against the bed to flip us over.

Air whooshes out of me at the delicious feel of her sinking down all the way, her wet heat flush with me. The muscles of my stomach are taut with anticipation. The first undulation of her hips against me has white noise buzzing across my vision, then she leans forward to kiss me.

Her breasts drag against my chest and the friction of her body against my nipples borders on perfectly painful. It's a slow ride. Torturous. Clearly, she's not as affected as I am since she has the capacity to pay attention to my breath hitching. Giuliana waits for me to build, listening for the ghost of a moan as an indicator to stop. And then she pauses, stunning chest panting above me, and starts all over again. Each time she delays my pleasure is more tormenting than the last.

Driving me to the edge and then calming, over and over—infuriating. I can't understand.

"Why?" I ask—beg. Cupping my cheek in her hand, her expression softens. Giuliana strokes the pad of her thumb against my swollen lips and opens her mouth as if she's going to explain. Instead, she digs her fingers into my pecs and raises up, slamming herself down onto me, and I honest-to-god think I'm going to die.

My cock is so sensitive, but she's dragged me to and from the edge so many times I fear I'll never cross it. It's coiled tight in my insides; my limbs so tense I worry they might seize and never relax. Giuliana fucks me—taking me into her body with fervor. The punishing pace she sets has her breasts bouncing, and her muscles burning, I'm sure. All I can do is hold on, grip the dip of her waist and the strong muscle of her thigh, and pray to a god I don't believe in for relief from the most agonizing pleasure I've ever known. Because it's too much.

Every nerve ending is on fire. It's a damn shame I've never felt this alive—this in touch with my body—without the help of some kind of substance. And I hate it and I love it. Trembling, I yearn for release; at the same time, I never want it to end.

"Take. What. You. Need." Voice husky and rough from the moans that have been ripped from her own throat, she commands me.

One of her hands lets go of my chest and she nestles it between her legs. The edges of her knuckles brush against my abdomen as she teases her fingertips against her clit. Head thrown back, her cunt flutters around me. And it unleashes something in me. Gripping her hips, I push into her from below —already planted so deep, every thrust serves to remind me how wholly she's consumed me.

This time when her breasts bounce, it's from my fraught rutting. It's an animalistic demand I can do nothing but acquiesce to. Fingers dancing across her clit, the sounds of our wet flesh meeting and her enjoyment push me to a fever-pitch. My chest feels like it's being pried open as my heart thunders against my ribs and my muscles burn from the exertion, but I don't care.

I don't give a single fuck.

Because she moans my name like I'm her personal savior and then clamps down around me—her moan turning to a ragged scream. My hips jerk once, twice, three times. Teeth bared, thorns of desire rake down my spine like shards of glass. Too much, too much. Too good. Not enough.

I can't. I want. I... fuck.

Fuck.

Fuck.

Giuliana leans forward, draping herself over my chest as her body trembles. The shiver of her cunt pulsing around me begs me to join her.

"*Yes*," she whispers into my ear. Licking up the side of my neck and sucking, adding another level of sensation I'm helpless against. I wrap my arms around her back, imprisoning her against my chest and I fuck up into her, over and over.

"*Matteo. Per carità.*" It's a moan against my neck between drugging kisses, and I lose the battle.

It cleaves into me, this pleasure I have no name for. This release is guttural—beastly.

A cry wrests itself from my throat, drowning and desperate. Giuliana's fingers tangle in my hair, pulling painfully. I respond by biting the curve where her shoulder meets her neck, something I've never done before. My cock releases spurt after spurt, jerking gracelessly into her body.

The voice is quiet. Everything is suspended in this moment of tangled, sweaty limbs, depleted and shaking. We collapse and her grip in my hair turns from punishing to comfort. Giuliana strokes down my twitching muscles and I want to stay buried in her heat forever.

We break apart once our hearts have calmed to a normal rhythm and breathing doesn't feel like a gasp to fill our lungs. Holding her against my body as our sweat cools with the breeze from the window, my fingertips trail against her soft skin. Goosebumps raise where my touch has been.

We've made no promises or said anything about what happens when the sun rises tomorrow. Giuliana made it clear this was a one-time thing—which suits me just fine. Do Italian girls expect nighttime cuddles and a sheepish exit in the morning? I've never been sober enough to care before.

Propriety churns in my stomach, foreign, and I feel the need to get out right now. The peace I've found with her tonight is replaced with something else in the aftermath of her destruction. Something sinister and greedy. So, once sleep claims her and her body settles into another layer of relaxation, I pull myself away carefully.

Picking up my clothes, I sneak out of the room. The fabric against my skin feels wrong. All of it feels wrong. I shouldn't be doing this. Giuliana deserves better. Hell, they all did, every woman I've done this to.

What a fucking asshole. The inner voice accuses and I agree.

This night has been strange and wonderful. A wicked first date—not that I've ever taken anyone out on a real one. There's never been a need and I've never wanted to revisit a night of oblivion with the same woman again. But this is clear-headed. No drunken high dulls my senses and I want to go right back in there to immerse myself in her—lose myself in her body and never resurface.

Sleeping with her once isn't enough. From the pleasure we shared and the way her wit was sharper than my own, I don't think a one-time fuck could ever be enough. Giuliana's thrown my careful, cultivated routine into disarray.

And it's terrifying.

I find a hotel, eventually. Wandering back into town, I stumble onto one a few blocks from where I nearly hit Giuliana. Making my way over—no longer keen to explore—I hope for the best. I unstrap my bags from the back of the Vespa and head inside. The proprietor's English is limited but decent. Between that and my gesturing, I get through the room booking process.

The man types as if he has a personal vendetta against the computer, irritated by my late appearance. His eyes are crusted with sleep and his cheek pillow-wrinkled. After I pay, the proprietor walks me up narrow steps carved out of the ground. I duck my head to get into the doorway. The light bounces against walls that feel too close. They appear to have been built or rather formed out of the edge of the mountain. It would've felt cave-like if not for the big window letting moonlight and fresh air in.

They have USB charging ports. Oh my god, I could kiss the fucking floor. I failed to consider the world doesn't cater to American whims. The converter plays a big part in that. Definitely my biggest mistake thus far.

Your biggest mistake was leaving without saying goodbye or giving her your number.

Shut up. I can't afford to think about her. Sex got me in this mess in the first place. If I'm going to save my skin, I can't get caught up like that again.

That wasn't just any old sex. That was amazing. She was amazing.

Shut up. It's better this way, for both of us, no matter how mind-blowing what happened between us was.

The proprietor shuts the door behind me on the way out and I collapse on the bed, exhausted, raw. Sleep drags me under without mercy.

When I wake, it's with restlessness and a hollow ache going further than the surface—past skin and muscle. Something about last night shakes me, rattles me. I did the right thing... didn't I? Giuliana is better off without me and it's best we leave it as what it is: one glorious night and nothing more.

But you do want more, which is the problem.

I know Giuliana's name—nothing else. Without her phone number or address it's useless, and she said her stay in town is a temporary reprieve from work. She's probably already left back to her corporate bullshit in the financial sector, I think it was? It's better I buckle down and focus on the task at hand—the very reason I came here in the first place: the contract and my inheritance. I have to cast her and her stunning body, and those little mewls in the back of her throat when she came, from my mind.

Good luck, asshole. Good luck trying to forget that.

I pull the contract from my baggage, unroll it and set whatever I can find around the room to use as a paperweight on the corners. The contract's in Italian, because of course. Nothing about this is going to be easy—that much has become obvious. I pull up the translation app on my phone, point the camera at the first page, and try to make sense of the mangled interpretation of legal jargon. All I need is to figure out the location of the property. The rest can wait.

There's a journal beside the bed I decide to pilfer for myself (never know when the writing degree I fumbled through might come in handy). For now, I transcribe what I understand to be the address onto a pad of paper. Flipping through each page of the contract until I reach the end, I stare at the sprawling signature that used to belong to my father. Grand even in death.

The press of ink to paper was heavy and sure, the swirls of his name signed with flourish and confidence. It's longer than the one I've seen most of my life. Tommaso seemed to have taken his time to sign, to consider. Thomas scribbled the same quick flick of his wrist onto so many papers, indiscriminate.

What stands out from my pathetic and quick translation attempt is two things: first is the address. It's easy enough to make out even in Italian and, according to another Google search, not too far from Gravina. Lastly, Alan made it sound like my father waited for the endeavor to fail so he could sweep in and take it for himself. It's the very thing Alan encouraged me to do, but nothing in the glimpse I've taken at the contract leads me to believe it was my father's first intention. Tommaso invested a good sum of money into the venture, and he held a stake in the company. But the language suggests it was an investment for something other than profit.

And that's the biggest shock of all. Thomas Palmer lived and breathed the bottom line.

With him gone, I have no way of knowing if any of this was true—if the man I glimpsed in this contract could truly have been the father I knew. And if so, what changed him so drastically? What drove him from this place?

All I can do now is try to find answers. I want this chance to make something of myself and learn about a life that could have been mine had a few things been different. So, I change into clean clothes and ready my belongings, phone charged, and the contract safely tucked into my backpack.

Breakfast is a quick pastry though it's practically *lunch* at this point. Since I've slept so late, I ponder my next move as the sun arcs across the sky. My vape is almost dead, and the adapter isn't the only thing I've forgotten in my excitement and haste. I'm fucked with no charger packed and no vape shop I can find in the vicinity. Should I turn back toward a bigger city? It's an hour in the opposite direction from the farm. Is it worth it or a waste of my time? I don't want to need it, yet the itch under my skin spreads as I panic a little.

My crutch gone out from under me.

But I'm here for a reason, and the longer I put it off the more bullshit is going to grow in my brain and stress me out. Might as well rip the band-aid off. I opt instead for nicotine patches from a local pharmacy, too vain to consider cigarettes. The smell alone would put anyone off, and stained fingers and teeth do not appeal to me at all.

At worst, I'll make the drive into one of the cities once I've found the farm.

The address is about twenty minutes outside town, roads curving along the landscape. The Vespa rumbles down the streets of Gravina—the fortress where my own stone walls have been compromised, and I ache at the thought of Giuliana back in that bed in town. I wanted to stay, curl my body around hers, and indulge in her again until my brain finally calmed. But I'm not meant for...*intimacy*. It'll hurt us both if I try.

I follow the twisting roads, up and down hills between vineyards and groves, and the sweet summer breeze teases my senses. It varies with each turn—the fruit and earth and flowers. Why did I never open my eyes to everything outside New York? All I've done is ignore what the world has to offer, which was a mistake. I've missed out on so many small delights while I hid in sharp-edged pleasures.

How can a life of excess be so deprived?

By the time I make it to the address, I have a fair layer of dust and sweat on my skin from where the asphalt turned to hard-packed earth and summer made her presence known. The

Vespa comes to a stop and I look up at the sign arching over the road. Half a mile to go according to the GPS, straight ahead, but when I get there the name is missing from the sign. There's no mention of *Abundantia*. The arched wood has been sanded, or painted over. Something there has been scrubbed away, yet to be replaced.

Still, perhaps I can ask the owner about it. It's possible I've taken a wrong turn.

The bike jerks, bouncing on the uneven ground of the one-lane road. I make it to the top and the view snatches my breath away. Not just a farm. Rows upon rows of olive trees, gnarled and reaching, leaves vivid in the sun. In the valley, I see a glimpse of a stone building with a terracotta-tiled roof, surrounded by overgrowth with no path. On the other side, there's a larger home. White and villa-like in appearance, it's where the road I'm on ends.

I follow, taking in the scope of the property as I continue. My driving slows as the pebbles under the tire make the ride difficult. A woman steps out into the road ahead, waving her arms for me to pull over, the cloud of dust behind me choking.

Sun-bronzed skin glints with sweat and her smile is bright and open when I stop. Her dark hair is pulled back and she has wrinkles spreading out beside her smile.

"*Buona sera?*" she greets me and I feel like a total ass. I haven't even bothered to learn basic greetings before coming here.

"Hi," I finish, turning the key to silence the sound of the Vespa, and giving an awkward wave.

"*Ah*, Americano?" Her eyebrows raise in question.

"Sì," I say, the only fucking Italian I know besides goodbye.

She claps her hands together in glee and gestures for me to follow her. "*Vieni,*" she urges, pointing toward the white villa I saw on the hill.

I dismount and push the bike alongside her. I can tell she wants to talk to me—she keeps looking over—but the language barrier is something I have to work on and fast. Frankly, it's embarrassing and in poor taste. I can't expect everyone to cater to me or my language. Especially not if I'm going to take over here. But she does speak.

"You here to help? America?" she asks, trying to bridge the gap.

I nod. Because yeah, in the truest sense I am. It appeases her and she gives me another smile, nodding as if she's happy with the state of events.

Are they expecting me? Maybe there is no new owner after my father's partner died. I know it's foolish to hope, but there's a chance this may go perfectly. If they know I'm coming or want me here—it'll be what I need to make my new start. This is my opportunity to forge something, to grow away from my past.

The walk up the hill is a little strenuous when one contends with the weight of a bike and bag I've strapped to the Vespa, but any exertion is forgotten as I take in the scenery around me. By the time we make it up to the villa I'm filled with the urge to walk the land and marvel.

The lady urges me to stay and wait as she goes inside. Biting back a laugh, I watch her try to command me with gestures and body language alone. Still, it's effective. Even though she looks like she's trying to calm a rampaging bull, I stay put.

I can hear faint voices—raised and angry—from the house and behind me in the grove are others. Some laugh, some talk. Birds sing with unfamiliar calls as they swoop from tree to tree, and I watch with fascination as one dives down to peck at the ground. These don't look like American birds—the plain and small sparrows or the lazy pigeons I've grown up with. The bird flitting between ground and sky is a beautiful combination of light blue and green. Vibrant.

I'm so caught up in taking it all in. The trees sway with the wind, leaves rustling as the branches arch and flex in the air. Voices of those within the grove carry on the breeze. I'm so transfixed I don't notice my guide's return. She beckons me and I set the Vespa down, kickstand out, to follow her inside.

As we walk inside, a man around my age storms by us and shoulder checks me—rushing out of the house with a sheaf of papers fisted in his hand.

Weird. But my guide doesn't wait for me to consider what that might be about.

Fans spin in almost every room we pass to circulate the air and combat the heat absorbed by the house. My guide rushes me through the hall and I catch glimpses of the interior of the house. There's a vague impression of cream and dark furniture, high-contrast. Even within the design of the house—the light walls throw the beams across the ceiling into relief, emphasizing the dark wood lending support to the roof.

At the end of the passage, I see an office. The wall I can spy through the doorway is mostly taken up by windows. A large mahogany desk sits centered in front of the windows, facing outward. The chair behind it is turned toward the windows as well—as if whoever works here wants to be able to see the grove while they do and cares little for greeting people who come through the door. The farm is more important than business, clearly.

Whoever sits at the desk now is unaware we've entered the room.

"*Signorina*?" my guide asks, presenting me to the room.

A female voice sighs before she speaks and a shock of electricity edges through me. There's no way.

"Oh, our American friend? I'm glad you made it, although I must admit, we weren't expecting you so soon." Papers shuffle on the desk as if she's preparing herself and her things before turning. "I'm so grateful you signed up to test out the volunteer program for us. I'm hopeful it will signal a big change for the grove; one you will benefit from as well."

Her voice clangs inside my head again. It couldn't be, could it? The warmth of the voice fills my mind and mingles with memories of tangled limbs and heat. But before I can focus on the possibility, I'm struck with confusion. Clearly there's been a mix-up, or at least a case of mistaken identity. The last thing I'm here for is volunteer work. I'm here to see about a transition into power, to step into the spot carved out for me by my father's name and turn it into something wholly my own.

I open my mouth to explain the confusion and clear the air. My tongue works to ask where the hell I can find *Abundantia*.

But then I see it on the wall—off to the side—an old wooden sign not dissimilar to the one being replaced above the road. Only this is weathered and scarred with age and the elements. *Abundantia* had been carved there. The paint which made the word stand out against the woodgrain is chipped and missing in places, but it's unmistakable. I'm here. I'm *here*.

I pivot in my mind, trying to find the words to explain *why* without fucking up the first impression that will determine my future here. Clearly, she's running the show, if not an owner, then a foreman or something. The last thing I need is to alienate her before my claim is substantiated and unshakable. I step forward into the room, wiping my hands on my shorts to dry the clamminess covering my palms, in order to shake her hand.

The chair starts to turn and I take a deep breath, bracing myself for what stands between me and what I'm coming to believe is my destiny. I've deluded myself into thinking it might be Giuliana. There's no way she's here. By her own admission she lives a world away from Gravina and works in commerce. It's my mind being a dick again.

I steel myself, schooling a charming smile onto my face

and letting the facade slip into place. She stands from her chair, looking down at the papers in her hand for a split second. But in the space of that second before she tilts her head upward—a breadth of a moment—I feel my stomach plummet to my feet. The world spins, and I wonder if this is what it feels like to have the bends, to ascend or drop so fast your body revolts.

No.

No.

Life is fucked up but it can't be this cruel.

She looks up, large dark eyes shadowed, hair tied back but the dark silk unmistakable. Giuliana's fragile smile dies on her face, her eyes locked on mine in a way that screams louder than anything she might have said right then. I drink in the sight of her like only she can quench the thirst inside of me.

"*Patrizia, lasciaci, per favore,*" Giuliana says it without breaking my gaze, without moving a damn muscle. I want to rage at her composure because it feels like I'm being torn apart.

I ran from her and chose to be a coward because knowing I might want more from her than one night of oblivion scared me. And because the universe has some *sick* sense of humor it brought me back to her regardless.

My guide departs, shutting the door behind her, and I wait poised to see what Giuliana will do next.

"*You.*" It's a whisper—a curse. Her hand tightens on the top of her chair, knuckles white. A familiar twist of rage mars her beautiful face. Giuliana takes a step toward me before stopping herself.

"You left. How can you show up here after—" Anger moves through her body like a rippling wave. Her expression cracks into something sad for a moment. Plush lips tremble and her eyes widen in shock before she packs it away and transforms it into a cool mask of indifference.

"I... I didn't know..." I say, lamely. But it's true—I had no idea.

"It doesn't matter now." Brittle words drop like stones between us and she finds her body. Unnatural stillness gives way to her pacing in front of the desk.

"Giuliana, I'm sorry." It's inadequate.

"It clearly didn't matter to you so just leave it. I don't want to talk about this with you."

She turns her back to me, staring out at the windows as if the matter is settled.

"In my defense I had no idea you *owned a farm*, let alone this one," I hiss. "You said you worked in finances far away from Gravina."

Whirling around, Giuliana pins me with a glare. The anger peeks through again and I watch in fascination as the fiery woman from yesterday stuffs her feelings down with a handful of breaths. Her words are professional and calm by the time she speaks again but I can see the faint mark of where my mouth kissed a bruise into her neck last night.

"The grove *is* a world away from the city. And farming *is* a business. I needed an escape from the pressure, not a therapy session. Sorry for not imparting my life story to a stranger and —forgive me—but you didn't exactly nudge much further than my bedroom door." It's haughty. Her defense is almost comical to me given how upset she was at my appearance. Hypocritical.

Giuliana carries on regardless. "It's in the past and we both need to forget it ever happened." Waving a hand at me, she dismisses me and last night as if it *did* mean nothing.

"But," I protest, the truth poised on my lips. There's been a giant misunderstanding between us.

"But nothing, Matteo. You made no promises to me. You took what you wanted and left like a thief before sunrise." A bitter laugh from her throat crumples my resolve. Giuliana smooths a hand over the silky hair I splayed my fingers through last night.

The memory leaves me hot and aching, and I picture the strands of her ponytail wrapped around my hand as I pull—

"It is what it is. We had no idea and it's unfortunate. But if this is going to work, we need to keep it professional." She is still talking. Fuck. Get it together. "No one can know what happened. Not. A. Soul."

The words lash against me—almost desperate in their ardor—and I'm confused. I know why it's a problem for me. This entanglement complicates my situation. But what's causing an issue for her? Besides the fact that I was an asshole and skipped out on her. Is it to salvage her pride?

Giuliana must read the question on my face and she launches into an explanation—one I grip onto with both hands.

"I need this volunteer program to work. This season with you has to be a success, and that *cannot* happen if..." She trails off, looking at me—really looking—until she shakes her head as if to clear it of all traces of last night and starts pacing again. "It is unprofessional. If word comes out I was *involved* with one of the volunteers the program will be in the ground before it even starts."

"The program?" I ask, unsure what she's talking about.

"Training a volunteer and having them work the summer in exchange for room and board. We're starting small until this can grow into volunteers, plural, helping with the harvest and learning the trade. It means nothing to you, I'm sure. But I'm trying to clean up the mess"— her voice cracks a little and she clears it before she continues, wiping away her tears before they can fall—"left behind after my father died earlier this year. The volunteer program is step one of my business plan. I understand if you don't feel like you can carry on with this anymore, but I *implore* you. Don't let this venture fail because we made a drunken mistake." Her feet still again, this time she stares out at the grove, her hands gripping the top of her chair.

The words careen around my mind like rogue bullets until they find a target. "Drunken mistake" turns out to be it. The word echoes within—settling into the marrow of my bones and covering me like a cloak.

Yeah, that about fucking sums it up. Drunken Mistake. Heck of a title but you live up to it, don't you?

In my hurt I can't formulate anything to say, not when I'm in turmoil inside. Giuliana thinks I'm here as part of a pilot program to draw interest in the farm and drum up business? She's under the misapprehension I'm here to be her *savior*. The irony sits on my throat, choking me.

The universe has handed me the opportunity to get *exactly* what I want.

Guilt stings what little conscience I have, because she's still grieving and I'm about to rip the rug right out from under her. According to the bit I glimpsed of the contract, for me to get control of the farm she will have to fail. I have to prove her efforts futile and lacking.

In doing so I lose whatever chance I might have had with her as well. There's no way to have both. Not unless she opens herself up to me now and gives me a reason to believe it could be possible. The truth has to come out, now. Her dismissal in the face of what we shared hurts and that aching side of me wants to raze the place down around us. The part yearning for more of her hangs suspended, testing.

"Drunken mistake?" I whisper, my brain unable to conjure up anything useful.

She turns to look at me, the regret on her face plain. I feel my hope curdle.

"Matteo, please. Be reasonable. I've taken out loans and put everything on the line to see this through. The farm is lost to me if I fail. This place is my whole life." She gestures around her, unknowingly holding the grove in the palm of her hand from this vantage point.

"I cannot be distracted by casual sex. Will you still help me? I know it's unfair to ask but it would mean a lot to me if you stayed and finished what you came here for." Her eyes plead and I feel the nerves in my stomach—the ones that sprang to life at seeing her—hardening into a stone.

She inadvertently makes the choice between her and my mission for me. Handing me the keys to my success, she tells me in the same breath last night was nothing but a meaningless distraction.

Fucking brutal when the shoe is on the other foot, no?

My inner voice stokes the anger roiling within. Fine. I'll finish what I came here for and I'll give her what she wants. Distance. My father's voice rings in my mind, a reminder this is business. Not pleasure.

And like that, I choose the coward's path again, swallowing the truth that tastes like bile on my tongue. My plan forms. Under the guise of being her volunteer I'll get to see firsthand how the business works and what kind of rough shape it's in. When the time comes, I'll take what's mine.

"Fine. I'll do as you ask." The anger in my voice is palpable and her face shutters. The open woman from last night—so sure of her place—tucks her emotions away again as she nods at me. Is she pleased to have gotten what she wanted?

"I'll show you the ropes tomorrow, and we can go over what the season will look like. Since you arrived earlier than expected, I haven't carved out the time to do so today. For now, I'll take you to your room." There's no waiting as she walks ahead of me—not looking back to see if I follow. I rush forward, climbing the steps scant feet from her body. If I reach out, I can touch her. If I touch her, I can pull her against my chest and prove last night was more than a mere distraction.

Rounding the corner, she opens a door. Giuliana's careful not to enter, taking a step back when I come forward. Her hand grips the doorway as tightly as she clutched my back last night. I look down at her, at the smooth expression she has trained there. Her lips thin—the only sign of emotion, and she nods.

The luggage I'd strapped to the back of the Vespa has already been carried inside and placed beside a desk. A double bed is centered in the room and the covers are an inviting shade of blue. Light fills the room from the window and it lends a cheerful air—perfect for a volunteer to live and learn in.

Perfect for me to orchestrate her ruin, and my own truth be told.

I know what has to be done, but whether I can go through with it is a different story.

Hardening my resolve, I clamp down the hope that surged in my chest for the split second when I saw her again, and turn back to her.

Giuliana shuts the door, closing the channel between us and cuts off the part of me that wants more of her. The part of me that might have wanted to help and had some grand delusion of being a better man fizzles out into nothing.

No, she's made it clear what's most important to her, and for a moment... for one minute of insanity I almost forgot what I came for in the first place. If I fail at this the business and this grove will be lost to me. I can't believe I nearly lost sight of what is most important. *Abundantia* will be mine. I'll be sure of it.

Peace is an illusion and what she offered me last night was a falsehood. It's time to get down to business.

Guess you are a Palmer after all.

With dawn comes renewed purpose and the bitch-slap of jet lag. Although I managed to put it off until now, adjusting here will be harder in more ways than one. Someone wakes me up with a quick rap on the door. A note slides under the gap, and I drag my ass out of bed with a sigh. My sleep patterns have never been the best. But there's a huge difference in forcing myself to try and sleep because it's nighttime in Italy, and waking up at what would be my normal bedtime.

Still, I promised myself I would see this through. It won't do any good to quit on day one. I have reconnaissance to do and a trade to learn. Somehow, I have to try and intercept the *real* volunteer at some point too or my cover will be blown and I can kiss my future goodbye.

I slap a new nicotine patch on my arm and pull clothes out of my bag. Dressing in the early morning light peeking into the room, my linen shirt is as rumpled as I feel. I have the presence of mind to remove the contract from my backpack. Crap, it looks so rough from my constant rolling and unrolling. Foresight would have been good—foresight would have meant a folder to place it in to keep it pristine. But that's another one of my shortfalls.

One of many.

And so, the magic of being in Italy can no longer contend with the relentlessness of my inner voice.

As if a shiny new location would change anything.

But it does. I will make sure it does. This is my opportunity to get out from under what's been suffocating me in New York for the summer. New York leaves me listless, aimless... apathetic about life. All I needed was a purpose, and now I have it. Someday soon I'll stop thinking these things because I'll have something to show for myself, something to console myself with when my thoughts take a turn toward darkness.

I tuck the contract between two large books sitting on the desk, and slide them into the desk drawer. My insides contract, curling in on themselves. A sick sort of lurch swoops through my stomach at the physical proof of my deception—the continued attempt to hide my intentions.

No risk, no reward.

I haven't gotten anywhere so far by skating by. Thomas got shit done, even though his methods had been less than stellar. I'll have more success in life if I take a page out of the Palmer playbook.

A dry swallow grates down my throat as I stuff down the uneasiness rising in my esophagus. I'll worry about the morality of it later.

I bend to retrieve the folded note, fingertips stroking over the sure indentation on the paper. The handwriting is hard and confident, sloping as if written in a hurry.

Meet me in the office when you're ready.
I'll be waiting.
Giuliana

It's fucking foolish to think she means it the way I want her to mean it. Because I *am* ready. I'm halfway to distraction thinking about her and the possibilities her desk provides. But she made it clear it will never happen again—it was a mistake.

Just like you.

"Fuck off," I whisper to myself and leave the room behind, creeping through quiet hallways to find the office again.

Giuliana leans her ass against her desk, watching the door when I eventually find my way through the house. The sun pinkens the sky behind her into pastel flames, illuminating the sprawling grove.

"I appreciate your discretion yesterday. It's been a hard shift for the workers and I don't want anything to jeopardize the trust I'm building. Some of the men in particular might have a problem with it."

Some of the men you're involved with?

Shut up. What a fucked-up thing to think. What she does with her time away from work is not my concern. But my curiosity is a hard thing to ignore.

"The man I bumped into on my way in?"

I shouldn't be asking. It's none of my damn business. All I need to worry about is getting the information I came for.

"It's complicated."

"Despite appearances, I'm sure I can keep up." My smirk has the intended effect and I can tell she's fighting the urge to roll her eyes. Instead, she closes them for a moment and a shuddering breath leaves her chest.

"We worked together, yes. Umberto was my father's foreman and we had a sort of... relationship."

Ah.

"So, the no dating the volunteer rule—"

Only applies to me.

"Came about because he didn't care for 'his woman' telling him how to do his job. Umberto assumed we would marry and the grove would be his to run after my father's death. I didn't take kindly to him deciding our lives before asking me what I wanted. He left with half of my workforce and decided to show his face yesterday to throw around some new threats."

"Threats?"

Warring sides of me pipe up. Giuliana is understaffed and Umberto's threats could prove useful—I should reach out to him to gather proof. But the other part of me is strangely angry that someone would threaten her at all.

"It's handled. Or it will be. As long as this harvest goes well the threats won't matter. That's why I need this volunteer program to work... so if another man decides to undercut me, I won't be on the brink of ruin because of it." Giuliana's expression is dark with resolve and I feel a frisson of fear. Heaven help me when I'm on her bad side. The only way to do what is required of me for now is to be *nice.*

"I didn't mean to cause trouble for you. From here on out I will be a model volunteer. You say jump, I'll scrounge up a trampoline." I try to inject some levity into my response, a half-smile curling up my face despite the guilt slithering around inside of me.

Whether I mean to cause trouble or not, it comes regardless.

And you have no plans of stopping it now.

"Do you have experience with farming of any kind?"

"No, uh... I'm a city boy, trying out a new adventure to get away from the suffocating vibe in New York."

Giuliana reaches around to grab a notepad off her desk, scribbling in that sure handwriting of hers.

"This is perfect. It will give me a chance to gauge how intensive we need to make the program in order for a newcomer to understand the process."

Something about the way she phrases it has my breath catching in my chest. Newcomer—not a stranger, not an outsider. It feels open. She's welcoming me—a freaking Trojan horse—into her home and showing me the family business. All I can do now is play my part.

"We have less than three months until the harvest. Future volunteers won't stay as long, if anything they'll likely only help out with the harvest itself...." Giuliana carries on almost as if she's talking to herself and not me. She bites the back of her pen as she considers things, then goes back to the scratch of ink to paper. Sunlight crawls deeper into the room, shafts of light in window shapes reaching in to heat the floor, and casting specks of dust into glitter in the air.

"But if I teach you—give you a crash course—we can figure out what the most important things to know are and I can model the program around that!"

Giuliana pushes off from the table to pace in front of the desk and I fight the laugh sitting on my throat. Seeing her talk herself through the process, watching her mind turn in real-time is strangely entertaining.

Stay focused, asshole. Stop thinking about how cute she is when you're going to fuck up her life.

"We'll go over the cultivars, explain how they impact taste and what we use each for."

She ticks it off on her index finger. So much like our first meeting. Hurt blooms inside me for a split second as the memory of her skin flits through my mind. Giuliana plans out the next three months of my life and I watch her—hungry and exhilarated. I'll have to figure out how to set the bits of shame I feel aside. No room for that now. Which means I'll have to keep her off my scent and lean into the image of the useless playboy I am.

"And will I get a final grade for all this? How do I know if I pass?" It's meant to be a joke but Giuliana takes me seriously.

"You raise a good point. I'll give some thought to incentives.

Perhaps each volunteer could get their own personalized bottle of olive oil at the end?"

One with the Palmer logo on the front?

It's a traitorous thought and I know it'll be a long few weeks dealing with the discord inside of me.

"Anyway, let's get some food in you before we start the day. Nonna will never forgive me if I deprive her of getting to feed you."

My rudimentary Italian knowledge helps me with that one.

"Your grandmother?"

"Yes, on my father's side." It's a little abrupt, as if she's done enough talking about her personal life for today.

Giuliana stalks ahead of me down the corridor, expecting me to follow. Once again, I'm rushed through the house, toward an eat-in kitchen. The tantalizing scent of strong coffee hits me first (thank god), followed by the homey feeling of a kitchen abuzz with activity.

An old woman with more salt-than-pepper in her hair is trying to wrangle a girl—no older than seven or eight—who's hurling rapid-fire questions while bouncing on the balls of her feet. I don't need to understand Italian to read the tired frustration on the old woman's face, or to sense this is a regular occurrence in the household.

Giuliana's entrance breaks the spell, the sudden quiet in the room leaving me uneasy.

I glance around at the arches over the doorway and windows. The warm walls suck up the early summer sun and radiate it around the room. Handmade tiles serve as a backsplash behind the stove, and they glisten with teal accents.

"*Nonna, Chiara... Questo è Matteo.*" Giuliana gestures toward me and I give an awkward little wave. "Matteo, this is my grandmother, Isabella, and my sister, Chiara."

"Nice to meet you," I say, a little shy I can't say it in Italian. But they don't mind.

Chiara chatters at me in English. "Why are you here? Are you Giuliana's boyfriend? Why aren't you speaking Italian?"

My mouth is agape as I consider each question. "I—I'm from America and I'm here to work for the summer."

I'm not going to touch the question about being Giuliana's boyfriend. Best to move right past that.

Isabella urges me to sit, placing a plate of fresh bread and a pot of some kind of jam. "*Pane, burro e marmellata.*" Isabella confirms and sets a steaming cup of cappuccino in front of me.

"Chiara..." Giuliana warns but I'm not paying attention because I'm caught up in the breakfast in front of me and the woman who served it.

Isabella gives me a scrutinizing look and I fight the urge to squirm under her gaze. The older woman only breaks her perusal to look at Giuliana but settles back on me, as if something in my face gives away more than it should. But it melts into a small, guarded smile after a moment.

Taking the seat beside me, Giuliana leans over to whisper conspiratorially, "I apologize for their enthusiasm. We don't get many new faces, especially not young men."

"I don't mind. It's kind of nice." It's the truth. I should keep it guarded. But having someone fuss over me is poignant in a way I hadn't expected.

Wow. The bar is on the fucking ground. An old lady gave you toast and you're ready to weep over it? Pathetic.

"Yeah?" Giuliana asks, pulling me from my thoughts, her smile bashful. Her professionalism drops for a second, her eyes softer than they've been since I showed up at the grove.

"Yeah. I don't have any siblings."

That you know of.

Ugh. SHUT UP.

"My family isn't super domestic," I say, "so this is a welcome change."

We turn back to the scene, and Chiara jumps into our conversation.

"Did you have to fly to get here?" Her brown eyes are large with curiosity and I wonder if she's had the opportunity to fly anywhere.

"Yep! From New York and it took hours and hours. I even slept a little bit on the plane."

"All just to be here? How long are you going to stay?"

I open my mouth to try and answer but realize too late I'm not too sure, imposter that I am.

Thankfully Giuliana intercedes. "He's going to be here until the harvest—at the latest the first week in October. And we're going to help him settle in. And we're *not* going to bother him with all our questions. Sì?" She gives the little girl a pointed look until Chiara grumbles her agreement.

Harvest could continue into October, but for the purposes of the program I don't need to stay longer than then. It'll be plenty of time to get a feel for the process.

Chiara's questions are stilled by Giuliana's hand, an unspoken command to quiet herself and eat. Chiara pouts a little but perks up when Nonna tells us she's going to make *torta colonne* for dessert tonight. And then all is forgiven, and we turn to simple sustenance to provide us with the energy we'll need for what lies ahead.

Despite it being early in the day at the start of July, the sun pelts us with heat. Summer is well underway, and I have three months to make this happen—whatever *this* is. It's hard to think about what I came here to do surrounded by her family, with the sweet tartness of homemade jam dancing on my tongue.

Once we're sated and ready for the day, Nonna shoos us

away. Even though I don't understand the words, the sentiment comes through: you're wasting time, get a move on.

"Your family is great." It hurts to think about—to consider if I carry through with my plan, I'll be leaving them out in the cold.

They're not merely a name on a contract or some intangible thing. Giuliana, Chiara, and Isabella are lovely ladies who are forging out a life despite loss and grief.

"They are. I'm lucky to have them even though they drive me up the wall most days." Giuliana chuckles to herself and her smile does something to me, my mouth stretching in response even though I'll never be in on the joke.

I have no grandparents I've met. No younger sibling to pester me. Loneliness was a construct to me before, something which felt less acute in New York with all my vices to distract me. Here, faced with the real thing, it's sharper.

I'm tempted to ask her about some of those instances, to hear about what it was like. Giuliana looks up at me with an open expression on her face. It's like she's relaxed incrementally back into the woman I first met—the one unhindered by expectation and duty. But then it's gone as quick as it came.

"We'll walk some of the property today so I can give you a feel for things and explain more about the cultivars we use." Professional Giuliana is back.

Good. Makes it easier to screw her over when it's business and not personal.

Still, I can't help but think back to our first meeting and consider all the ways I'd like to unravel her careful exterior to peer back at the woman who knocked me on my ass. It's going to be a *long* three months.

The grove stretches further than I expected. From the stone courtyard, I can see expanses of trees like soft waves cresting against the horizon. Giuliana stands beside me, gesticulating as she speaks, explaining the breadth of the operation.

"The grove isn't quite small enough to constitute a 'family farm' but we don't produce the volume to compete with larger, well-known groves in the area. What has set us apart so far is the particular cultivar my great-great-grandfather introduced to the area. They changed it again in between but my father brought it back and it has grown for over thirty years. It was considered a very old-fashioned move, but so far, it's paid off."

My stomach jumps, questioning whether my own father had any hand in that decision. What did Tommaso think about taking a risk here? Was he a silent partner or did he walk the same paths, stare over the same treetops as I do now?

Giuliana walks me through some of the rows, pointing out how to tell if a tree is young or old. She touches on the basic timeline but promises to go into more detail when we start our hands-on experience. All the while I think about what she said at the courtyard.

"Why old-fashioned?" I ask, surrounded by trees that, by all accounts, are comparatively young, if I'm understanding her correctly.

Giuliana's gaze moves over to the side, set away from the

rows of trees. Off to the left of the big house I see an older stone structure, the one I saw on my drive in, and behind it trees that are larger than some of the ones closest to us.

"I'll show you."

The walk to the old farmhouse is quiet, broken up by the snapping of twigs and the crush of small rocks under our shoes. Birdsong breaks up the silence, serene and unusual to me. It's a far cry from blaring horns and the shuffle of feet against asphalt I'm used to. Heat sets my temples to sweating and I wipe my brow with the back of my hand once we traverse a slight incline. The view of the grove from this vantage point is just as stunning, only the trees here were planted in a more haphazard way.

Instead of a neat row, they take up space of their own. Trunks and branches twist and stretch in the openness they've been afforded. The fruit is visible, if a little small. But what strikes me is how old the trees look, in particular one near the crest of the hillock.

"My great-great-grandfather planted these trees. They had a bad harvest one year. A prolonged cold followed by too much rain left it unsalvageable. A lean year followed, one which made him consider some of the older varieties he'd grown up eating. Even though they were less favorable for high quality olive oil, it was worth a shot. They weren't as easy—if harvested at the wrong time they were far too bitter. But he figured he couldn't be any worse off than he was to begin with. The cultivar everyone lauded had failed him."

She must see some confusion on my face because she answers my question before I can ask it. I absorb her every word —every little sigh of information she's tucked between the dusty corners of her life.

"A cultivar is a variety of plants, in this case olives, that have been bred to be a certain way. Sometimes they're hybrids created by crossbreeding, sometimes by accident. But it impacts things like taste, texture, and how long it takes to ripen."

Walking up to the large tree, Giuliana raises her hand to stroke one of the sage-colored leaves. Her thumb trails over the curve of one of the developing olives. I don't dare speak, can't interrupt her when faced with a history I long for. My grandparents were strangers to me. I never even knew the names of their parents, let alone great-greats. Time and separation have erased them, and I'm left with a jealousy sitting sour in my stomach. Generations of her family have worked this land. What do I have to show for mine?

"They had a modest harvest, and my great-grandfather kept this strain—cared for it, and his son after him. By the time my grandfather took over, it carried him through for a few years. Not profitable enough, so after a while, it became something purely enjoyed by my family. My grandfather improved his methods and the original cultivar took precedence. Until my father..."

Giuliana isn't looking at me—she's barely looking at anything at all. Her eyes are lost, faraway in a memory I can't touch.

"What was his name?" It's a stupid question, one I already know the answer to, but I want to call her back to this moment. It's selfish. But what else can be expected from an asshole like me?

"Lorenzo," she says, soft, the word cradled in hurt.

I want to ask more—want to delve into the story of a man I didn't know but who has handed me a chance at something new. But I don't want to push, not so soon.

Giuliana gathers herself, clearing her throat before she carries on.

"By the time my father took over, the cultivar they'd been using was massively popular, the market overrun. He had two options: sacrifice prestige in order to sell a mass market product. It would have meant keeping the operation as it was but geared toward making more oil of a lower standard. Or he could start small, with the certainty of a loss for the first few years, and introduce a different cultivar—new trees to the grove."

There's no need for her to fill in the gaps. I can guess what comes next. Lorenzo opted for the latter, securing his success with the support of a backer. The perfect lines of younger trees cement the story.

"I assume he went small, aiming for something to set him apart?"

Giuliana confirms it, opens her mouth as if she means to say more, but shakes her head.

"He remembered the lesson from my great-great-grandfather. Although it's a different cultivar than these old trees it has a similar taste profile, and would fare well. My father was a very stubborn man but, in this instance, it paid off. At least then. That was thirty years ago, and the trade is different now." Giuliana sighs.

She has to innovate in her own way, to keep up with the world at large.

"And are you going to put your mark on the grove, the same way your father and great–great-grandfather did?"

Giuliana looks at me with incredulity, scoffing. "The grove put its mark on me. I'm just here to be its caretaker. Who am I to spit in the face of tradition?" The words are bitter, as if she's thought about this a lot and is dissatisfied with how it panned out in her mind.

"I don't know," I say. "You're doing the volunteer program. There was a mention of a multi-part business plan. It sounds like you've got ideas for something different."

I'm not trying to push; really, I'm not. Giuliana is just too damn compelling and it's not even about absorbing information at this point. If only I can get the frown on her face to melt away so her mood matches the pleasant warmth radiating from above.

"It's something. We'll see how well it goes." Giuliana shrugs.

"No pressure, Matteo." I chuckle at myself, trying to lighten the mood and I see a smile playing on her lips. Giuliana could have protested and tried to appease me, but she got enough of a taste of my humor the other night to know I can handle it.

"Yeah, don't mess it up for the rest of us, Matteo. Nonna has placed a bet on you. I may have joined the pool." She drops the words with a small smile fading when she catches herself teasing.

Why her cold professionality bothers me, I can't say. But Giuliana walks back toward the big house, leaving me to ponder what the exact terms are.

"Hey! Hold up. You can't drop that little tidbit and rush off."

"I have no idea what you mean. If I'm hurrying, it's because I have a lot of work waiting for me at the office." It's terse, and I can't help but persist.

"Come on, I know you're not the boring businesswoman you're making a show of being. We'll always have red wine and Gravina. No amount of pretending otherwise can change my mind. You're a firecracker and we both know it."

"It was a joke, Matteo. Leave it be." Her pace is quick, bordering on a jog and I rush after her.

"Seriously. Don't make me chase after you. Tell me the bet and I'll leave you be."

"Or what?" Giuliana throws it over her shoulder, the ghost of a smirk, and her pace picks up to a near jog.

"Wait!"

The pathways are unfamiliar to me. Weaving in between the trees to try and catch her, my shouted warnings are met with footfalls and the whisper of her breathing. I skid to a stop to try and get a handle on her position.

"Giuliana, what exactly did you guys bet on?" I shout after her.

"Can't tell you. It might mess with the results!" Her voice comes from further than I expect and before I can launch after her people start to fill into the grove.

"I'll corner you later, I swear!" I whisper-yell, hoping she'll hear me without me having to embarrass myself in front of the other grove workers.

"Don't threaten me."

Her voice comes up right behind me and I startle in surprise. At least it breaks her facade and she gifts me with a laugh. My heart pounds with fright, and something else.

"The only thing I'm threatening you with is a good time." I turn, giving her my signature cheeky smile but she doesn't take the bait. The teasing cools from her face into that professional facade I'm starting to hate.

"I think, Matteo, it doesn't matter what the bet is. Her expectations and mine are irrelevant. All I want is for you to learn from this experience. How you choose to use what you've gained here this summer is up to you."

Her words stir up uncomfortable feelings in my stomach, the sentiment hitting a little too close to home, but before I can say any more her phone rings.

Giuliana reaches into the back pocket of her linen pants and raises it to her ear, rapid-fire Italian following. The words are tinged with anger and I wonder what's going on. It's hard to tell but I think I hear her say the name "Berto."

Midway through a response she covers the receiver and whispers, "I will see you at dinner around seven. Feel free to explore the grove for today. Something else has come up. If you are hungry before then tell Chiara and she and Nonna can help you with food."

All I can do is nod and watch her walk away, the curve of her hips as she struts back up toward the house leaving my mouth dry. Giuliana is an enigma, soft and serious. Reluctantly joking and sharp. The woman holds multitudes and frankly, it's a little scary. It's better I get some time to look around unsupervised.

Walking for what feels like an hour, I get lost in the grove. I won't wander back to the house before I've gleaned something from the time out here. How the hell am I going to pull this off? Should I even keep trying?

Her family is here. They're letting me sleep in the same house and feeding me. Sure, I reacted badly when Giuliana shut me down, but it makes sense? Kind of? If I was a professional and one of my one-night-stands showed up to the Palmer building the next day, I'd have HR on that in a heartbeat. It doesn't have to go this way. If I can figure out how to get it to work for both of us...

I make it back toward the main gate, the small road stretching over hills back toward Gravina, before my phone vibrates in my pocket.

Alan.

What does that fuckwad want now? I consider hanging up but it might be important—even though I haven't screwed anything up yet.

Haven't you?

I answer, trying to keep the sigh from my voice. "What do you need?"

"Hello, Matt... *how are you*?" he says, the way one would remind a child of their manners, but I don't give a fuck.

My mind's already swirling with everything that's happened within the last few days. Another complication is the last thing I need.

"We both know you're not calling to exchange pleasantries. So yes, I'm in Italy. I'm at the grove."

"You're more resourceful than I expected. Good job. I'm

surprised they welcomed you with open arms." Alan scoffs, as if my charm is in doubt.

I could have made it work even without the mix-up. I might be an asshole but I'm an asshole with a pretty face.

"Apparently, they were expecting an American volunteer for the summer. I arrived before him and assumed the role. They're going to show me the ins and outs of the whole operation."

And somehow, I'm going to have to figure out what the hell to do about the real volunteer, if they ever show up. My ruse could be over in a second.

I try to ignore Alan's malicious chuckle and how slimy it makes me feel inside.

"I underestimated you. Looks like you have some Palmer in you, after all."

Like father, like son. Both willing to screw people over for their own benefit.

"Alan, I'm not so sure about this. Even though the owner died, his family is still here running the place. Plus, they are capable and care about their employees from what I can tell."

"Please don't tell me you're going soft on me. How long are they expecting you to volunteer for?"

"Until October-ish when we do the harvest."

Feeding information to the enemy... Wonderful.

It's easier to paint Alan as the enemy, rather than to face knowing I'm the one who poses the biggest risk to Giuliana and *Abundantia.*

"Plenty of time to catch them slipping," he says.

"This feels underhanded and dirty. I don't like it."

"You don't *have* to like it. Just do it. Now is not the time to get sensitive. There's more at stake than you know," Alan says, as if there's something I'm missing.

"What else is at stake?" I pace between the rows of trees, trying to avoid running into any of the other workers. But I'm far enough from the main house that I should be safe. Plus, whoever I run into might not speak English very well.

"Your father hoped you'd rise to the occasion yourself…"

I can almost picture Alan, spinning his chair away from his desk to stare out of the floor-to-ceiling windows. The city would be sprawling around him—glass and steel, sharp and unforgiving. Alan would have a little constipated smile on his cheeks, the one where he knows he has his audience's attention but the Botox won't let him celebrate with his whole face.

"What does that *mean*?" I grit out.

What did this fucker do now?

"You're aware of the expectation that you take over as CEO of Palmer Enterprises within twelve months of your father's death—"

"Or I lose my stake in the company. I know."

"There's more. I didn't only send you out there to prove you have what it takes to assume the role. Or to cover up your indiscretions. The truth of the matter is, your father wanted to make sure you were successful and not resting on your laurels."

"Tell me, Alan, for fuck's sake." My strides eat up the earth and I can almost feel the walls of an invisible office closing me in.

"If you don't prove yourself worthy as his heir—either by taking over his business or another one—your entire inheritance is forfeit."

Rage, white hot and piercing shoots through my body and I'd kill for a fucking smoke right now. Of course, my father had another little 'fuck you' lined up after death. Me getting an English degree instead of my MBA must have enraged him.

It's not only the threat to my livelihood, it's the fact—

"And *no one* thought it was important to tell me that little detail?!"

"You weren't supposed to find out. Like I said, he wanted you to rise to the occasion on your own. Thomas wanted more for you than to waste away in a haze of alcohol and parties. You need to *grow up*, Matt. You're not a teenager anymore. So, suck it up, and get shit done. Or you might not have a way of getting home come October."

As if I want to come back to that hell hole and face you after you gleefully screwed me over.

"Is that a threat, Alan?"

"It's a promise. You have a little over two months. If you don't have something for me by the end of September you are officially disowned."

"I need more time! How can I gauge their profit margin or anything important if we haven't even made it through harvest?" I'm desperate now, clawing for some other option, anything to buy me the time I need.

"Not my problem. It's decided by the anniversary of his death. I don't give a fuck about the harvest and neither will the lawyers. You'll figure it out." Alan hangs up, silence on the other end of the line and a sick swirl in my gut as I think about what just happened.

Two months.

Two months until I either ruin Giuliana's life or my own.

Fuck.

M

My walk is enlightening, but not in the way I hope. Instead of gaining insight into the grove or Giuliana I find myself teetering on the edge of life as I know it. I don't like to throw around the word *hate*. It has too much power, too much of a hold over people. But at this moment, the ground crunching underfoot as I make my way back to the house, I feel it well within me.

There's hatred for my father and for the lackey who enjoys carrying on Thomas's legacy... hatred at myself for being like them, unable to sacrifice or give up the comfort money provides.

Giuliana is tied up, dealing with the business or more fallout from Umberto's departure. Chiara roams the grounds somewhere, and Nonna... well, I'm not going to seek out the shrewd-eyed old lady. The way she was watching me at breakfast... studying me, as if she can see under my skin into the person beneath, is deeply unsettling.

So, I close myself off in my room, pulling the contract out from its hiding spot and poring over the words that have the possibility of changing my life forever. It's slow going translating it all—and Google isn't the best for it—but I get the gist.

The clause was put in place near the end of the document, stating Tommaso fronted Lorenzo's decision to change the cultivar. Per the agreement, Tommaso would pay for the planting costs and float the farm until they could produce a satisfactory harvest. Lorenzo would then either have to pay the investment back over ten years, or relinquish the majority share.

If the company (under Lorenzo's management) didn't produce a consistent profit for at least five continuous years after the initial payback period, Tommaso took it all. The grove was collateral.

The way my father left things alone until now leads me to believe either they met the first part of the agreement, or my father stopped caring.

I flop onto the bed, staring up at the ceiling—at a total fucking loss.

If he was still alive... none of this would be an issue. Of course, my father is more involved in death than he'd been in life. Thomas Palmer was a cold son of a bitch. Not the kind of man who showed up to parent-teacher conferences, or graduations. The company that paid for our lives was the child he fostered into the success it became. I'm just a loser who does a disservice to the Palmer name.

I check my phone, having ignored the calls and messages since my impromptu plane ride. The only one I answer is my mother to let her know I've made it here fine and will be staying for the summer. The rest are a shitshow. Some are invitations to events, parties and the like. A *lot* of them are "friends" sharing multiple articles of me with the senator's daughter.

Brandon even went as far as to rank a list of my past hookups by level of scandal.

The Palmer Playboy. So original.

Chucking the phone onto the bottom of the bed, I cringe a little when it bounces and hits the floor. A shout of frustration builds behind my breastbone and I fight the urge to let it loose. None of those people give a damn about me as a person. I'm a headline, an in to another party. Hell, for some it definitely *is* the appeal of my money. What kind of asshole can't even conjure up one real friend?

What do you expect? If you smell like shit, act like shit... then you're definitely a piece of shit.

Shut up. For one fucking day.

I wish the voice in my head would give it up for a little while. Reminders are unnecessary since I'm painfully aware. The inside of my cheek is raw where I've taken to chewing on the flesh when the nicotine patches don't do enough to diminish my cravings. Never thought I'd end up quitting, but leaving the grove for something as small as a vape is stupid. At this point, I've taken it as a personal challenge to piss the voice off and prove it wrong.

I don't *need* to smoke. I am more than my vices.

But there are no true friends I can turn to, no one I can unburden myself to who would understand. They all see a charmed life. The business waits—and the grove if I have the guts to go through with it. I should be grateful. Instead, I feel trapped, destined down a path I never intended to walk in the first place.

My eyes fall on the journal I took from the hotel, the contract beside it. If I get some of this out of my system, my mind won't hate me as much. So, I sit—tucking the contract back between the books in the drawer—and open the journal. Flipping to the first page, it calls to me blank and waiting. I find a pen in the top drawer of the desk and start writing.

Italy is more than I ever thought I'd experience. It's the soft kiss of the wind against my face, the earthy scent to the air. It's the ends of Giuliana's hair catching fire in the sun. I feel sick with how much I want this, with how desperately I might need it. New York would have killed me, one way or another. Italy feels like I can breathe again for the first time in years. I don't deserve the kindness, Giuliana's her family's. But I soak it up the same way the ciabatta drinks the olive oil they make here. Matt Palmer I have complicated feelings toward Matt Palmer. But Matteo de Palma could be someone I don't despise.

Either way, I'm going to take it all in. I'm going to learn as much as I can. Even if I lose the grove, it might be worth it enriching useful for once in my life.

I shut the notebook, not daring to reread the words I've purged onto paper, and go in search of food. Bread and olive oil sounds pretty damn good right now.

Giuliana doesn't rest. She functions at a level I envy and loathe. Up early each morning followed by a quick breakfast with more strange looks from Nonna, and chatty Chiara, before we head out toward the grove for lessons. Giuliana sets out with a bag draped across her shoulder and I follow her like a lost puppy, excited to learn but mostly basking in the opportunity to be around her.

A few rows into the grove, Giuliana sinks onto her knees, hands splaying into the dirt.

"We test the soil acidity with a meter. My father used to dig up with a trowel and collect samples for test strips, but it's more streamlined now. We like to keep our soil between 5.5 and 7.5 and we increase the pH using lime or decrease it using sulfur if it's less than ideal."

She hands me the meter she's brought along in the bag, urging me to stick it into the earth she's uncovered.

We wait for a moment, the device beeping with the results and she smiles when the number hits 6.4. Wiping her dusty hands on the front of her coveralls, she looks more adorable than she has any right to.

"We'll test at multiple points in the grove. Thankfully it's just maintenance at this point. Years of soil conditioning have paid off. The other thing we need to keep an eye on is rain and water levels. Since the trees are bred to withstand the hot summer, at this point we have to make sure the soil retains its humidity. Rain and supplementary water are far more important in the spring and autumn."

Walking from row to row, we alternate between checking the soil acidity and feeling it for moisture. I didn't think testing dirt could be tiring, or understand *how huge* the grove was.

Not big enough to be considered a large grove, my ass.

But my skin starts browning under the warm sunlight and my hands roughen from working with the earth. I fall into a routine quickly. By two weeks since that first day in her office, I have it down.

Mornings start with a soft knock on the door and Giuliana's attempt at a whisper forcing me from bed. I can swear I hear her mutter something about alarms before she walks off. Dressing doesn't take very long, though I'm running out of clothing suited for time outside, doing physical work. Down to my last clean linen button-up t-shirt and shorts, I shove my feet into incredibly dusty sneakers and head down the stone floors of the house toward the kitchen.

Chiara explains to me one morning why the floors are made of stone. "The big house was built a long time ago. It's from before Giuliana and she's *old*. So, Papa built it like in the olden days to keep the house cool in the summer."

I don't want to contradict and say it must be miserable in the winter. Not when she pads barefoot over the cool stone floors, a huge buck-toothed smile on her face.

The little girl is a shadow, quiet until you notice her and once you do, she becomes a whirlwind of words. I don't dare bring it up to Giuliana—don't want to project my own damage on the situation—but I recognize the frantic energy of loneliness in my brief conversations with Chiara.

"What do houses look like in New York?" Chiara asks.

"There are a lot of different kinds, same as here. I live in an apartment at the top of a tall building. It has lots of windows and I can see plenty of the other skyscrapers around me, most of them long and skinny."

She considers this for a moment. "Is it scary to be up so high?"

"Sometimes, but you get used to it. My father's office is even taller and I hate going there. It feels too far up. But sometimes the views can be very pretty. People and cars look like little ants on the ground."

Her mouth rounds into a "wow" of wonderment and I can see she's about to launch into another question, burning curiosity behind her eyes.

Giuliana steps in. "Chiara, give Matteo a break from questions. We have a lot of work to do today. You should try to find some time to play or read."

Nonna tuts, grumbling at Giuliana in Italian. She even

throws in a pointed "Giulia." Giuliana bristles and I wonder if it's one of the nicknames she doesn't like. The cycle of scolding continues until they're all grumpy but put in their place.

Once we walk to the grounds again, I work up the urge to ask.

"So, I can't help but pick up some tension between you and Isabella..."

Giuliana gives a big sigh before she levels me with an annoyed look—and one which would have had me pulling back if this was a normal situation. But there's nothing normal in living with your boss (technically), especially after having slept with them.

"You picked up on it?"

"Hard not to. I may not speak Italian, but I'm not a total idiot. I know what that tone of voice means, *Giulia*."

My assumption is correct because she huffs at the name. "No. No Giulia. It's *Giuliana* to you."

"I'm teasing, you know. I'm not trying to piss you off."

I stifle my smile and she softens a little, sucking in a shuddering breath before responding.

"It's okay, just... I don't want the workers to think I'm too cozy with you. I'm still dealing with the fallout of the mess with Umberto." Her halfhearted shrug tugs at my insides, and the word "cozy" and all it implies settles inside me like molten honey. But I can't slip into that, so I deflect instead.

"Only in private. Got it." I nod, knowing I'm pushing my luck.

Giuliana gifts me a chuckle that's half-sigh but lets my comment slide in favor of explaining the situation with her family.

"Nonna wants me to spend more time with Chiara. I understand, but I have responsibilities here. Chiara is fine when it's not summer and she's going to school. The rest of the year she gets to be around others her age but now... it's isolated out here. I remember from when I was a girl her age. Except I had both my parents. All she has is me and Nonna, and acres of land."

"How young was Chiara when you both lost your mother?" I hold my breath. It's a difficult and personal question, but I've been wondering. Lorenzo's death was not a surprise to me, but I have yet to find out about Giuliana's mother.

"Childbirth. She had complications. They tried for many years, hence the difference in our ages. The doctors warned against it, but my father wanted a son to carry on the farm, so they kept at it until Chiara."

"Jesus."

Giuliana nods and her dry humorless chuckle lets me know I've said it out loud.

"I know my father loved my mother, and she him. I sometimes wish they loved each other a little less. If he'd cared less, he might have moved onto someone else who would give him the son he craved. If she loved him less, she might have stopped putting herself in danger for the sake of legacy." Her words are bitter, sharp. I can almost taste their tang in the air.

"I'm sorry," I say. It's all I *can* say.

"So, yes. There is tension between me and my nonna. She wants the best for the both of us and she won't be around forever. It's all to make sure Chiara and I have each other for when that happens."

"It still doesn't mean she should give you crap for it almost every day. What are you supposed to do while you're putting a roof over everyone's heads?"

A tiny voice in my heart pipes up that my father had been doing the same and I resented him for it.

"Nonna believes in 'destino' and claims no matter how hard I work, if it isn't meant to be it will crash down regardless. She says it's better to surrender to life as it comes and take time with those most important to me. Nonna says a lot of things."

Giuliana blushes for some reason and starts walking away, as if this conversation is over.

My hand shoots out, grabbing hers and stilling her.

"Your work counts. I see it and the workers see it. Don't let her convince you otherwise. You can't be everything to everyone. Sometimes it takes sacrifice."

Nice words, asshole. What do you even know of sacrifice?

Giuliana looks down at where our hands are clasped together, the contact lasting a little too long and I feel a frisson of energy shoot up my arm. Her skin is soft and warm, familiar. Unbidden images of the feel of it spring to mind and I drop her arm like it's burned me.

"I'm sorry. I'm overstepping."

"No, I appreciate it. I don't have too many friends anymore. After school most moved away, and the few who stayed near town got very tired of me canceling plans to work or take care of my sick father. The person I thought would understand turned out to be a huge mistake. So, it's nice having someone outside of my family to talk to. I'm sorry we got off to such an awkward start."

My mind wanders to our night in Gravina, our bodies entwined and it's a double-edged sword of desire and pain. I wouldn't call it awkward. Not at all. Though I'm not sure what name to give it. One-night-stand sounds cheap, incorrect somehow. There are too many muddled feelings involved for it to be so simple.

"I'm sorry about your father. I'm sure the two of you were close." *Unlike me and my progenitor.*

"In some ways, but we had a difficult relationship. When Mama died a lot changed in him. He lied about being sick and avoided going to the doctor for a long time which might have made a difference—lies that only hurt in the long run. But he needed me and by the end we had made peace." Her eyes are a little glossy and she clears her throat of the building emotion there.

"Anyway, I think we better get back to the task at hand. I have to meet with the mill owner next week to check in and set our harvest date. He will be able to explain the process to you, but first I'd better explain some terminology since his English is limited." She walks ahead, gesturing for me to follow.

"The fruit still has a few weeks of growth left. By the time we harvest, the branches will hang heavy with some overripe fruit dropping to the ground and getting in the way underfoot. But those olives are just as important. As they decay back into the ground, they feed some of the little animals, keeping the ecosystem of the grove balanced, and enriching the soil more."

I reach out for one of the olives, the outside firm and smooth to the touch. It kind of blows my mind how something this small creates a multi-billion-dollar industry.

"We have a big showing for the first day of harvest, and then a party to celebrate after. There's still more to do after but the bulk of it happens on that first day. Once we've gathered up all the product, we try to get it to the mill as soon as possible. You'll learn more about what happens after the harvest once we get there. It's kind of an involved process and it will be easier to explain if I can show you."

I follow behind her, our shoes leaving footprints in the dusty earth, and seeing it makes my stomach flip—closeness, even this slight.

The sun catches on her hair, ponytail swishing with her decisive steps as she walks ahead of me. Giuliana pauses to talk to the workers as we go. Every few rows she bends down to inspect the ground, rapid Italian to the workers followed by a brief explanation to me once the conversation is over.

"They're worried because too much of the ground has eroded here, exposing the root system and making it vulnerable to animals. We'll get some additional soil to add here. After we've got the pH balance right, it'll be added to this spot."

It carries on for hours and I breathe it in, soaking up every minute with her—watching. The workers treat her with respect, deferring to her expertise. Giuliana's not afraid to get her hands dirty and by the end of the day she's sweaty and tired. We both are.

She cares. It hits me square in the chest. Yes, she's sassy and smart like the woman I nearly hit with the Vespa but she's also so much more. She's kind and firm—serious. But when she smiles and laughs, it bubbles up from somewhere deep within so you know it's real.

Giuliana is genuine. In a world where everyone I've ever known is so focused on appearances and getting ahead at whatever cost necessary—Giuliana is without guile. She treats me as an equal even though I don't have a smidge of knowledge on any of this.

I want to be who she sees—someone worthy of sharing things with, knowledge, experiences. Giuliana makes me want... more.

I t's mill day. I never thought I'd be excited about a fucking excursion but here we are. Over the last few days, we've worked the ground and finished testing the soil. I've tasted how revolting an unripe olive is and started to enjoy this whole thing. Today is when I get to tour the mill they use to produce the olive oil and I feel like a kid going on a field trip. My shower is brief, clothing tugged on and breakfast scarfed down. Giuliana has been out since sunrise, preparing the workers for her absence, and I decide to take a walk around the grounds while I wait for her.

From my vantage point near the top of one of the hills a plume of dust rises from the road, a car heading this way. The sign still hasn't been put up, so if anyone is looking for *Abundantia* they're going to have a hell of a time without GPS.

Weaving between trees toward the main road, I stumble my way downslope as fast as I can. By the time I make it down the car is almost upon me. Stepping out into the road, I flag it down with a wave of my arms. The car skids to a stop beside me—gravel and dust kicked up by the wheels clinging to my skin and irritating my throat. The window gives a soft whirr as it disappears down into the door and a friendly face smiles up at me.

"Hi, you don't happen to speak English, do you?" he asks in an American accent, my relieved sigh leaving my body in a huff. Shit. What if he'd been Italian? I keep taking people understanding me for granted.

"Yeah, I do. How can I help you?"

This is fortuitous for him considering my own arrival and how subsequent weeks have been comprised of a lot of broken Italian and English, and hand gestures. It never occurred to me I might miss hearing a familiar accent so soon.

"I'm looking for *Abundantia*."

I lean my hand against the top of the car, looking down into the window to try and get a read on him. He's around my age, perhaps a little younger, blonde with freckles dotting his tanned skin. Something about him screams West Coast.

"Well, you've found it. I'm heading back to the house myself, mind if I catch a ride with you?"

A smile spreads across his face and he leans over, opening the passenger door for me to hop in. Once I'm seated, he reaches out a hand for me to shake, and I take inordinate pride in knowing mine feels work-roughened where it meets his smooth palm.

"I'm Cameron."

"Matteo, nice to meet you."

The car rumbles down the drive, swirling dust trailing us and I can't help but wonder if rain will settle it soon or if the whole summer will be this dry. Rainfall never concerned me before but all Giuliana's talk of the soil and growing conditions is at the forefront of my mind.

"How long have you been on this side of the world?" Cameron asks.

"A few weeks. I'll be here through the summer."

"No shit. Same here."

Huh. I mean if he's college-aged he might be backpacking for the summer break. But something sits uncomfortably at the base of my stomach. "What do you think of it? Italy, I mean."

Cameron's mouth tilts into a lopsided smile and he looks me over, as if to decide whether or not to share.

"Italian girls…" He shakes his head. "Man, it's been wild. I would have come sooner but I couldn't turn down the opportunity." Smirking now, his implication leaves little to the imagination and I give a breathless chuckle as we pull up to the house.

Cameron wastes no time getting out of the car and unease bubbles up inside me. Why exactly is he here?

"Are they expecting you?" I follow behind him as he forges into the house without a second thought. Perhaps he's been here before?

"Yeah, I'm working here this summer, though I suppose I'm a little late. But Umberto assured me it's not a big deal I was… delayed."

Umberto, huh?

Heat rises in my stomach. Anger, I realize. This man deterred plans he'd agreed to—plans Giuliana needed him for —just for a fuck and it bothers me. It's hypocritical of me to care since my trip started in much the same way. Seeing it reflected in him and hearing it from someone else's lips—it pisses me off.

"I'll let them know you're here," I grit out, trying to keep my composure.

Fuck. How the hell am I going to get rid of him? One word from him and Giuliana will know I lied.

Can't believe you missed it. You should have known he was the volunteer. It's not like this place is crawling with Americans.

Perhaps I can get ahead of it if I explain…

Yeah sure. Just tell her 'Sorry, Giuliana.' Explain how you've been lying for weeks. She's been housing an imposter who's here to steal her livelihood from her. That's going to go over so well, asshole.

Giuliana is at her desk, bent over her work with eyebrows furrowed in concentration. It takes me clearing my throat for her to look up. Blush stains her cheeks and she gives me a sheepish smile.

"What time is it?"

"Not sure." I swallow heavily. "But there's someone here to see you. His name is Cameron and he's under the impression he's working here this summer. Apparently, he's been in contact with someone named Umberto, or was sent here by Umberto. It's not very clear."

I'm almost sad when her little smile hardens. The stone of nerves in my stomach does the same. Heaviness and dread hang low and my anxiety rises higher than it has since my birthday party.

Cameron walks closer down the hallway and the fact he's followed me in without invitation incenses me. Footsteps echo in the suspended breath between me and Giuliana, until I can feel Cameron's presence behind me.

I should say more. Before it's too late.

"Thank you, Matteo. I'll be out soon, if you'd step aside for our guest." 'Guest' sounds anything but welcome falling from her lips and I see Cameron's swagger falter for a moment as he steps past me into the room.

"If you'd be so kind as to shut the door behind you on the way out," Giuliana bids me and I obey.

I should wait out front, and afford them privacy. But as usual I'm shameless. Pressing my ear against the door I pray for a miracle.

"I have an agreement with the owner—with Umberto. He organized for me to spend the summer and learn about the olive grove. I need practical experience for the last semester of my agricultural degree."

Ah, college student. I was right.

"Well, Cameron... *I'm* the owner, not Umberto. And he no longer works here. So, whatever agreement you might have had before is null and void. When was the last time you spoke to him?"

"This morning. He knew I would be a week or so late but he

assured me it wouldn't be an issue if I was. I got the impression it was preferred. Umberto mentioned the program wasn't ready yet and to give him time to get it together. I assumed I'd be reporting to him…"

Well shit. Seems I wasn't the only one trying to sabotage Giuliana and her venture. Umberto had his own ulterior motives and plans. Is Cameron a plant? My brain jumps to a stupid quote about having a nickel for every time this has happened…

Giuliana would have two nickels, which isn't a lot but it's weird that it's happened twice.

"I can't *believe* he would stoop so low." She mutters, her voice getting closer and closer until it sounds like she's right beside the door. "Your services aren't needed. And you can tell Umberto the next time he tries to fuck with my business he better have the balls to do it himself! I am done talking."

Anger colors her tone and I'm glad to be on this side of the door, away from what I'm sure is her stunning wrath. I take a few steps back, in case.

The door swings open, thudding against the wall. Gesturing for him to leave, Giuliana stares him down until he gets moving. Cameron sputters, his freckles disappearing behind the redness creeping up his face, and some part of me takes malicious joy in seeing it.

"You can't—this is bullshit." He stalks toward Giuliana and looms over her.

Oh no, he better not even think about it. I open my mouth and Thomas Palmer comes out. "This is *business*. She said she's done talking. Now get off her property before I call the cops."

My hand is in my pocket, pulling out my phone as if to emphasize how serious I am about this. Inside, I'm shaking.

"What the fuck am I supposed to do now?" Cameron spits at her but Giuliana doesn't look up… doesn't even move a muscle.

Her glare is filled with ice and I can't believe his audacity—I'd have withered by now.

"You're a college boy, you're smart. Figure it out. Away from here. If any of the workers see you here again, we'll have you arrested for trespassing." I try to inject as much authority into my voice as I can, channeling my father, my brows drawn down into severe slashes to bring it all home.

Shoving past me, Cameron shoulder checks me and I stumble back a step. Cursing echoes down the hall as he storms out and I hope Chiara isn't nearby to hear it.

"I—I'll be outside in a moment." Giuliana's voice breaks through the focus I'm putting toward burning holes into Cameron's back with my eyes.

"Are you okay?"

The anger from earlier has drained from her body and her cheeks are pale. Those rich brown eyes are lackluster and her breath catches in her chest as she inhales.

"No. To be honest, I'm not okay. Umberto is like a thorn in my side that I can't get out. Thank goodness you arrived early or his imposter volunteer might have messed everything up. Can you imagine if he got here first and I sent you away mistakenly?" She sighs and guilt burns up the back of my neck along with the flush. Giuliana has it backwards but I'm not about to correct her.

"We're running late though, and Arturo is not going to be pleased if we waste his time by making him wait. The last thing I need is to piss him off before harvest." Giuliana runs her hand through her hair, those silky strands falling back into place ever-so-slightly mussed, and I'm struck by just how much I love her hair. But she's stressed and now is not the time.

Pushing is a bad idea. So, I nod and fight the urge to gather her into a big hug.

"I'll be waiting outside whenever you're ready."

Truthfully, I'm relieved. Somehow, I escaped my fears around this situation—around my duplicity.

By the skin of your fucking teeth.

The weight sitting on me these last few weeks, since the start of my ruse, eases. Not all the way. I know I'm not in the clear, but at least I can stop looking over my shoulder for someone to shout that I'm an imposter.

The wait is minimal but Giuliana gives me a tired look when she sees me leaning up against her little Fiat. "Well, get your butt in the car."

Settling into the passenger seat, I try not to think about how close we are in the tiny vehicle. Our arms are scant inches away from each other. It would be nothing for me to rest my hand on the inside of her leg. Or to brush my thumb over her lush thigh.

"Do you have to stare?"

It's clipped, irritated, and although she's right—I have been staring—I don't want to admit what's on my mind.

"I don't *have* to. I like to."

"*Matteo*..." A blush creeps up her neck, and her mouth is soft around the shape of my name.

"Yes, gorgeous."

Her head whips over to me, my prodding pushing her out of her shell. The red seeping into her cheeks spreads to the tips of her ears as she blushes. Whether in anger or embarrassment I don't know. I relish it all the same.

"What have I told you about that? We're supposed to be colleagues and this is a professional relationship. Gravina was a one-time thing."

"It's not my fault it's the only way I can get a rise out of you. You're in work mode *all the time* and that asshole fucked with your mood. I just want to make sure you're getting a little dose of fun and teasing outside of it all."

She sighs, the fight leaving her body—her knee brushes

against mine and my stomach flutters. Although Giuliana stares ahead as she drives, I catch the way her hands tighten on the wheel and she worries her bottom lip between her teeth before she speaks—as if deciding whether or not to speak at all.

"I wish I was free to tease—regardless of if I want to or not, I can't. It's important that this season goes well. It's my first harvest without my father and all eyes are on me—waiting for me to fail. It's an insane amount of pressure. Sorry, I'm just trying to do my best. Teasing isn't high on my list of priorities."

Giuliana doesn't look at me as the countryside blurs past us. I wish I could reach over and cover her hand with mine, pry those clasped-too-tight fingers from the wheel so the skin around her knuckles isn't quite so strained. And then I'd kiss every individual knuckle until I heard her breathe properly. She's so intense—taut. I worry that all it will take is one wrong tug and she'll fray.

"I understand, and you're doing a great job. I just kind of miss how sassy you were with me on our first day."

This time she turns and I see just how close she looks to cracking under the pressure. Her brows are puckered, her lush lips downturned. Fuck, I wish she wasn't a punch to the gut every time we latch eyes. Giuliana Santoro makes it so hard to try and stay focused.

"Well, you're going to have to keep missing it. I can't afford to fuck this up, Matteo. Please."

There's more to it. I know there is. With the open road stretching between us and Arturo's mill, I take a chance. "You said there's eyes on you waiting for you to fail. Are you talking about Umberto?"

Her eyes stay locked on the road and the impression of Italy moves past me without notice—just a haze of blacktop and sunny fields.

"Umberto got used to being my father's right-hand-man. I

got used to him being around. When my father's illness worsened too much to ignore, we ran the grove together and grew... close. It wasn't until after I inherited that his ugly side came out."

Every time she shifts gears on the car the back of her hand brushes against my leg. I try to ignore it to pay attention but I'm a weak man. It takes a few deep breaths before I'm able to speak unaffectedly.

"His ugly side?"

"My father borrowed money from him... money I knew nothing about. When it became clear he wasn't inheriting anything or getting to the grove through me, he demanded repayment."

Between her father lying about being sick, borrowing money, and Umberto lying about his intentions, it's no wonder Giuliana is trying to keep herself aloof.

"I was able to get a loan by using part of the grove as collateral. At least the bank won't try to salt my land or plant spies."

"He tried to salt the land?" My outrage bursts through my lips.

"When I broke it off and made it clear I wouldn't let anyone, under any circumstances, dictate how I run the grove... especially not a small-dicked coward who exploited my father during his illness and crawled into my bed to control me."

White-knuckled, the leather of the steering wheel creaks under her grip. Still, despite being upset she's got it reigned in enough that she's only going slightly over the speed limit.

"One of the workers who stayed found him drilling holes into the roots of a few trees and pouring a heavy salt solution into them. The salt stress would have taken a while but it'd ruin the harvest and kill the trees within a few weeks. He ran off and by the time the police came he was long gone. Unfortunately, it was too dark to guarantee he was the culprit and with no physical evidence tying him to the attempted sabotage, the police couldn't do anything."

And here you are to sabotage her. No better than Umberto.

Fuck off. It's not the same. It's not personal. I'm not trying to hurt her.

Seems pretty personal when you're drooling over her half the time.

"What was he doing at the grove the day I arrived?" I shove my inner asshole to the back of my mind.

"He was upset I was able to pay him back and came to enquire how I'd done it. Instead of answering, I vowed that the next time he sets foot on my land, I'll be calling the police to have him arrested. Umberto must have believed me enough to send Cameron instead."

No wonder the asshole shoulder checked me. If I'd known what I know now I would have given him hell for it. "Did he know about the ideas you have for the grove? You said something about a business plan."

"Just the volunteer portion. Initially it was supposed to happen in a few years and be my way for women and underprivileged people to learn about the industry. When he left with those men loyal to him, I sped up the timeline. He doesn't know about my ideas for a scholarship program, which is my ultimate goal."

Giuliana's lips fold into an unhappy line—her eyes shadowed by Umberto's betrayal.

Unable to resist, I rest my hand on top of her tight-fisted grip on the steering wheel so she loosens her hold into something less aggressive. It's whisper soft, the touch so light it tickles my palm.

"Fuck him. I'm here to help. Besides, you've got steel in that spine of yours. No man who stands against you will prosper."

Not even you?

"Are you paraphrasing the bible?"

Shit. Am I? I co-opt so many phrases it's hard to keep track of their origin.

"Possibly. Hard to know since I'm not religious. It's either the bible or Shakespeare. My point stands." And my touch remains.

"Matteo."

I raise my hands in mock surrender, mourning the loss of contact. Giuliana gives me a small smile before shaking her head at me.

"I'm going to do what it takes to make you feel better but I'll try to be on my best behavior. At least for the rest of this mill visit."

Whether she knows I'm lying or not she doesn't say anything. The quiet stretches between us for the rest of the drive —comfortable, like a wood floor warmed by the sun.

The tires rumble down a driveway of hard-packed earth, bookended by a smattering of buildings. The bulk of the operation functions out of the biggest building and we unbuckle and exit as soon as the wheels have stopped turning.

As we walk up to the building—half stone, half industrial metal—it strikes me how old this mill is. The date on the plaque by the door starts with "17" and it's mind blowing something like this has been in one family for so long. Giuliana greets Arturo with cheek kisses, the old man's face folding into soft lines—testament to a lifetime of worries and joy.

I trail them as they catch up in Italian. Arturo looks back to examine me a few times before he launches into his speech and Giuliana translates as we pass at different parts of the mill.

"Arturo uses the cold-pressed method which produces what you call 'virgin olive oil.' The juice is extracted without using heat or chemicals in order to keep the purity of the product and retain more flavor."

Stacked crates line one wall, and a long square arm reaches up from the ground to the top of a large bowl. We're surrounded by stone walls, concrete floors, and at the center of it all is heavy machinery. Through it all the air smells like earth and salt. It's too early in the season for the mill to be operating, but I can imagine the groan of machinery and the din of voices filling the space.

"Because we are so close, our olives are delivered and pressed within a day of the harvest, another requirement for the 'extra virgin' label. Olives are carried up this conveyor belt. Leaves and other debris gathered up during the harvest process are discarded. Once most of it has been separated it goes into the actual mill."

She points at the arm—a little ridged bottom there to push the fruit along, and slats for the leaves to fall through.

"The extraction is done the traditional way. The fruit is ground into paste between these huge granite millstone wheels to press and crush the olives. A scraper moves along the bottom to keep it moving between the wheels of the press." I look up at said wheels peeking out from the top of the giant bowl and I'm struck with a child-like wonder at getting to see how all of this comes about.

Arturo leads us further along the equipment which runs connected from start to finish.

"Once the paste is as smooth as the press can get it, it moves into a kneading machine to separate it out and break the paste into water and oil for the first time."

My arm brushes against Giuliana's as we follow the pipes and something inside me clenches. This room is more factory-like, the modern sneaking in.

"It gets piped onto fiber disks, stacked in layers and piled up, slowly compressed through a hydraulic press over hours until the oil leaks out over the sides and collects into tubs at the bottom. It'll be separated again into unfiltered olive oil, and water."

I'm trying. I'm *really* trying to pay attention to the actual words she's saying. But her words blur in my mind and I can't stop thinking how badly I'd like to taste them on her tongue.

"The unfiltered oil is an opaque murky green, and it gets

stored in these giant stainless-steel tanks until it's ready to be packaged and sent out."

I'm not sure why the stainless steel is surprising to me, perhaps because I thought olive oil and wine might have similar processes. I expected wooden barrels stacked underground.

"*Abundantia* also sells both kinds of oil to cover different spots in the market. Filtered loses some of the taste but it has a much longer shelf life. Unfiltered is the preferred and superior product. Arturo does the filtering through a funnel with cotton wool, dredging the impurities until it looks like the stuff you'd find at the grocery store."

So clinical but she makes it so interesting. I'd never considered the process before—how much work must have gone into a single product.

"Arturo still has a few bottles of last year's harvest. You want to taste the fruits of our labor?" Pride leaks into the words and her expression is open—hopeful. I'd do anything to put a smile on her face. Even if it means baiting her. Even though I'd be breaking my promise.

"Sure thing, sunshine." I can't even get it out without a shit-eating grin and she rolls her eyes.

"I've made my nickname preferences clear, Matteo."

"Ah, but it could be we just haven't found the right one. Is it the English you don't like? Maybe you can teach me a few Italian ones."

I'm rewarded with a scoff and another one of those skin-tingling brushes and she moves around me to exit through the door. Once outside, we walk side-by-side toward a farmhouse, Arturo leading the way. The years cover his body like a thick blanket, back bowed under the weight. How long has he been doing this?

Finally, Giuliana addresses my comment, the air between us supercharged.

"I will do no such thing. Behave, please. I'm trying to teach you the business. You know what's at stake. It's important I get it right."

She's losing steam and I can't keep my hand from brushing against hers, hoping the touch of our fingers might inject some kind of strength or comfort into her. Her pinky twitches against mine and she doesn't pull away.

"You know I can multitask."

We reach our destination and the conversation drops as Arturo explains the layout, Giuliana's mouth closing around unuttered words. Arturo's table is set up with little cups of oil. Some are murkier than others and there's crusty bread set up on little plates beside each one.

I've been to a wine tasting before; this feels familiar.

"We use recioppella as our main cultivar, which is more popular in Calabria but grows well in our region as well. It's an old variety with spicy, bitter notes. When harvested at the right time it has undertones of fresh herbs like basil, sage, and mint."

Shuttered expression back, Giuliana is on task again.

"For curiosity's sake, what happens if they're *not* harvested at the right time?"

"The flavor profile is off. Too soon and it'll be very acidic, too late and the bitterness overwhelms the other tastes.

"You can see the difference between filtered and unfiltered in each variety. The first set is recioppella—our commercial oil from the most populous trees of the grove. The other set is from the small private grove I told you about—peranzana. That one is fruitier, with a fresh and spicy taste."

Swirling the liquid in the cup, I watch it kiss the side of the glass and leave its film.

"Go ahead, you can take a small sip and then drizzle some of it onto the bread."

Giuliana's wide eyes are trained on me as I let the cold oil slide over my tongue. It lights up inside my mouth, smooth and so much more flavorful than I ever expected. The filtered kind is similar, if a little diminished.

Following behind me, Giuliana tastes from the same glass my lips have just touched and I simmer inside. If I kissed her right now, I know exactly what it would taste like. In my distraction I spill some of the oil onto my hand instead of the slice of bread. Shit, gotta focus.

Arturo's watching me, those friendly lines drawn into a look of concentration. Jesus. What is it with this older generation and the staring? Between him and Isabella I'm developing a complex.

Giuliana stops the flow with a napkin before it meanders over my wrist, the heat of her hand scalding through the cloth. Once sufficiently cleaned of oil, I savor the soaked bread, and relish the slight bite at the end.

"It reminds me of artichokes for some reason." I say and Giuliana translates.

Arturo and Giuliana smile, his response sounds pleased though how the fuck would I know when it's in Italian?

"He says you have a good palate and wants to know if you have family in the area. You look familiar to him. I assured him you've never been here before, it's just his old eyes."

They laugh and I join in but it's hollow. Worry creeps up my ribs like a vine. How could I look familiar to him? Do I remind him of someone else or has my father been here before?

Tasting over, Giuliana and Arturo discuss the specifics of the upcoming harvest as we walk back to the little car. It's silent save for their low conversation in Italian. Our feet crunch on the path, birds flitting around and chirping to each other. The trees dance and swish around us from the wind, soothing my nerves enough for me to remember our interrupted conversation. I wait until we're on the way back to the grove before broaching the subject again.

"How bad is it? This volunteer thing can't be more than a temporary stopgap."

Giuliana takes a deep breath, launching into it like she needs to get it out all in one go.

"We're in the red. Those last few years with my dad hurt us and I can't keep running it the way he did before. The bank's given me a lump sum—almost all of it went to Umberto—and the umbrella payment..." A breath sticks in her ribs, shuddering out and I understand the pressure she's under with more clarity.

"If I don't come up with something soon, I'm not sure I'll be able to claw my way out of it. I've been doing some research on other farms and how they've had to pivot when the product alone wasn't enough."

Shifting in my seat to look at her, my stomach drops at her grave expression. Although the words should fill me with joy—this is the kind of stuff Alan wants me to collect, to report on—I feel worried for her sake.

"The volunteer program seemed like a temporary way to hit two birds with one stone. Workers are scarce and a program like this would drum up interest in *Abundantia*. Once we gain traction, I can turn *Abundantia* into a working-vacation destination for tourists. You've seen the old farmhouse. If I could somehow refurbish it into a bed and breakfast, I'd have people paying to stay on the farm—and occasionally helping to lighten the workload."

She lays it out with little excitement and I force myself to keep my hands in my lap—to not reach out and squeeze the top of her knee for reassurance.

"I think it sounds like a great idea! You should do it."

"Matteo, I don't know if you've realized it yet or not, but I have no idea what I'm doing. The night we met I was so desperate to forget all the responsibility waiting for me at home I picked up a total stranger. Do you realize how risky and out of character that was for me?"

Now that she mentions it, taking someone you just met to a secluded spot under a bridge is dodgy as fuck.

"Everyone is counting on me and I don't even know where to start." Giuliana's voice catches and it breaks me. Knowing the woman I met is still there but she's drowning under trying to take care of her family, her workers, and her legacy—it's a punch to the gut.

"You said there are other farms doing the same thing. Why not go check it out and see how they're doing it?"

Flicking away an errant tear, she turns to me again as she considers it.

"At worst it will be an excuse to take a little break from the grove. At best it will give you a way to make *Abundantia* your own. What do you say, sweetheart?"

"I say I'll do it if you stop with the stupid nicknames."

Tension broken, we chuckle and some of the stress melts from her shoulders. A few minutes later we turn off the main road onto the familiar path toward home.

I suck my teeth in mock regret, shaking my head. "No can do. We did things on your terms last time, now it's my turn."

This is a bad idea. This is a colossal, inescapably bad idea. I shouldn't have probed. I shouldn't have encouraged Giuliana, and I sure as shit shouldn't have volunteered to come with her. Because thanks to Isabella needing the Fiat to run errands, here we are again in a painfully familiar situation... Giuliana's nestled between my thighs on the Vespa as we wind through the Italian countryside. But this time I have to pray I don't get too excited by her being pressed against a certain part of me—one that doesn't understand she is OFF LIMITS.

Fighting the urge to wrap one of my arms around her body, I keep my distance as much as possible. Navigation and driving are her focus. My only task is keeping my grip stiff and professional on her waist. Now is not the time to reminisce on how the swell of her breast felt in my palm.

We meander around twisting roads and hills, passing through a few small towns on the way. Far enough for Giuliana to be less recognizable. The drive takes around an hour, and by the time we both shift off of the Vespa and onto solid ground, I have to adjust myself. It doesn't help that my arms are half numb from the bike's vibration combined with me keeping them so rigid. The backpack I've brought along with water, my journal, and our chargers hangs on my back.

The villa rises up in front of where we've stopped in the semi-circle turn-around. It's light brown, almost golden in some parts, and stands tall in front of us. Terracotta tiles adorn the low-pitched roof, and inviting us in is a large, arched entryway leading into a small courtyard.

I'm so caught up in my physical discomfort and trying to distract myself with the scenery I nearly miss Giuliana's unease. She wrings her hands together, keeping her breaths measured and deep.

"You okay?"

Giuliana looks over at me, almost startled to hear me speak, as if she forgot I was here for a moment.

"Uh... this feels kind of wrong. Like *corporate espionage*," she whispers at the end, and I have to fight off a chuckle.

"Trust me, this sort of thing happens all the time. We're not here to do anything but have an experience. An experience which, I might add, is not only public, but advertised. If it happens to be inspiring, then that's a bonus."

Letting out a huge sigh, her face pinches in conflict.

"Matteo... What should I say? If I come across so nervous, they will know I am lying."

"Let me take care of it. No one will expect me to be anything but an American tourist." I give what I hope is a charming grin, trying to bolster my courage even though I know I'm quickly falling down a treacherous slope and every minute with her makes the descent quicker.

"What if they recognize my name? *Abundantia* is a much smaller farm and we aren't really competition... but what if it backfires?"

"What if it works out perfectly? Look, I won't use your name. Just leave it to me. We need to come across as normal as possible."

Our shoes crunch on the gravel walkway. The arch opens up to a beautiful garden of plants lazy with heavy heads of blooms exploding in riotous color. A fountain sits at the center, babbling water soothing to me and I clasp Giuliana's hand in mine before walking toward the open door off to the side.

"What are you—"

"Trust me," is all I say before I plaster a smile on my face and greet the receptionist.

"*Buongiorno. Come posso aiutarla?*"

"Hello, you don't happen to speak English, do you... Francesca?" I ask, reading her nametag. It takes everything in me not to feel like a dick for what I'm about to do, but I have a part to play.

"Yes, of course. How can we help today?"

"I saw online you offer tours of the grove. My girlfriend and I were passing through the area and were hoping to be added to your list."

"Ah, I'm very sorry sir, today's tour is unavailable as the villa is booked for a private event."

Figures. Making decisions on a whim rarely pays off. I'm in the biggest mess of my life because of an impulsive decision to come to Italy and claim an olive grove that technically (partly) belongs to me.

Shit. What the hell do I do now? Gotta come up with something, and quick. They're not going to give two shits about some American and his girlfriend. We'll have to up the stakes. I'm not smart enough to outwit anyone but I can be pretty convincing if I play into the emotional aspect of things.

Here it comes. Another fuck up.

No. This will work. It has to.

Schooling my face into the appropriate disappointment, I give Giuliana a sad look and shrug. Her expression of confusion melts into one of similar sadness and I have to tamp down a smile at her willingness to play along.

"I'm sorry, darling. That's what I get for trying to be spontaneous." I plant a soft kiss against Giuliana's temple, and feel super proud for only spending like two seconds breathing her in.

Yeah, the fucking paragon of restraint.

"Do you have a restroom? I know it's inconvenient but we drove an hour to get here so I'd appreciate it if—" I ask the receptionist and she agrees, gesturing toward a door off to the side of the lobby.

"—thank you, I'll just be a minute. Giuliana, why don't you enjoy the garden?"

She raises her eyebrow at me but nods, leaving without questioning my motives and I know this is my last opportunity.

"Sorry, I didn't want to say anything in front of her." I lean forward over the desk as if getting ready to impart a secret. Francesca comes in closer, curious.

"I feel like a total idiot. I knew I should have made reservations but I just got permission from her father and I didn't want to waste another minute." It's breathless, the fake excitement undercut with sheepishness.

Jesus Christ, you're actually going for it, you crazy son of a bitch.

"What are you saying?" She's invested, I can see it on her face.

"It's our anniversary. I was hoping to propose to her after the tour. Out in the olive grove during sunset—it seemed romantic. We're here on vacation and we leave at the end of the week. It was supposed to be this perfect moment and now it's a total screw up."

Okay, way to lay it on thick. Why don't you conjure a tear or two, to go along with your little sob story. You know Giuliana will never go for it.

Francesca thinks on it for a moment, pulling away to type furiously into the computer.

"Okay, so. We do not have any spots for public tours this weekend, but we do offer an exclusive VIP package."

She turns the screen toward me to show me the digital brochure. Which is in Italian, so my confusion isn't fake.

"It includes a night at the villa, a private tour of the grounds and the process, as well as a tasting. Since it is your engagement, I will also add in a bottle of prosecco and chocolate-covered strawberries. The only trouble is we have sold out of the single rooms because of a wedding tonight. We have one room remaining, but there's two beds you could push together. Would that be okay?"

It's ideal. But she doesn't have to know.

"You're saving my life, Francesca. I don't know how to repay you."

She laughs, turning the screen back. "You can repay me by leaving a large tip."

"It's a deal!"

"I'll get you checked in while you tell Giuliana the good news."

I find her pacing along the flowerbeds, whispering under her breath to herself. When she hears me coming, she turns and starts toward me, words already spilling out of her mouth.

"I knew this was a bad idea. I don't do stuff like this. I don't drive off spontaneously. This is why I plan. This is how I avoid issues."

"Giuliana..."

"And now, we have to go all the way back with nothing to show for it except failure. I feel like such an idiot, I—"

"*Giuliana*," I say again, framing her face with my hands to get her to still and look at me.

"You have a private tour planned for tomorrow, as well as a place to stay the night. It's all taken care of."

"How?" She doesn't pull away from my touch, just stares up at me with those beautiful brown eyes and makes me feel like I've managed a miracle.

"I may have told her a little lie. But don't worry. It's handled."

Her wonder turns to skepticism, her eyes narrowing.

"*Matteo...*"

"Sì, *bella.*"

She huffs at the endearment, stepping away from me and the tightness in my chest gets even worse.

"Multiple nicknames in one day. Your cheeky grin can't be good. What did you do? You know I don't like lying."

"We're just pretending to be here together so they don't suspect anything. We may have to play that up a little but it'll be fine. You get settled in the room. I'm going to run into town for a change of clothes, okay?"

"Are you sure you don't need me to come with you? I'll need clothes as well."

"I—uh—I'll take care of all of it. Just trust me."

Ha! Fucking rich request considering you are actively screwing her over.

But not today. Or tomorrow. Possibly not ever? I'm so torn on this fucking thing. It's my weekend off from trying to steal the grove. Right now, we're exploring her business plan.

My GPS brings me to the closest town, a mere fifteen minutes away. Finding the nearest clothing store, I grab outfits for tomorrow for each of us and some things to serve as pajamas for tonight. I'm guessing at her size—can only hope the clothes will be okay. Since I'm not as well versed in women's clothing when I'm not taking it off, I figure a dress is the best bet. More forgiving if I get the sizing wrong. I can't afford to have her know what an idiot I am, how reckless I was in my deception, and how far I'm going for this ruse.

Not your first rodeo, pal. You're halfway through another con... one you keep trying to pretend isn't happening but she's going to find out at some point and you'll—

SHUT UP.

Clothes and toiletries rung up, some more nicotine patches and gum tucked into the bag, I find what I need next. The jewelry store is nestled between a bakery on one side and a law firm on the other. Kind of fitting.

Lawyer...

Fuck.

I haven't checked in with Alan since that phone call in the grove and I haven't convinced myself to take a real step toward betrayal. The biggest blessing since then is we've gotten rid of the *real* volunteer. Otherwise, it's been long days in the grove learning and long nights in bed yearning. Giuliana's had me all knotted up, twisted until I barely recognize myself anymore. The thought of her is enough to pull my mind from Alan and the lies piling up behind me like a car wreck.

Back to the task at hand. I make my choice within ten minutes, as if I knew the moment I saw it. This time they accept my card—no small purchase limit here. Swiped for an obscene amount of money—the biggest perk to having it, getting what I want when I want. I head back toward the grove before the hour is out. Not bad. Not bad at all.

When I make it back Francesca hands me my own room key and points me toward the room I'll be sharing with Giuliana. She waits inside.

Although "waits" is an understatement. Giuliana paces the thin passage between the two beds, stopping short when she hears the door click with my entrance. I hold up the bag as a peace offering.

"Clothes and some toiletries."

"Where have you *been*? And what have you gotten us into? I can't afford this room! It was supposed to be a lowkey group tour to get a feel for things." The words tumble from her, as if she's been ruminating on them for a while and can't keep them inside anymore.

"Look, I'm sorry. I had to put up a bit of a show for Francesca. I told her I messed up and this was supposed to be a very special outing for us. The tours were all sold out today because of a wedding happening at the villa tonight. She was nice enough to offer a package including the tour, so I booked it." I settle down on my bed, the one closest to the door, and fight the urge to recline. Lying is tiring.

"So, you decided to make me your girlfriend in this little "show" of yours?" She slumps down onto her bed, facing me, knee bouncing in what I assume is irritation.

"It was easier than admitting the alternative: you're technically my boss and we're here to spy on them."

"You said it *wasn't* spying!"

"It's not. I just didn't want to take the chance of having her misunderstand me."

"Instead, you lied to her and we have to spend the time pretending." Giuliana folds her arms across her chest, pushing those plush breasts up and I swallow. Her mouth turns down and her eyebrows pinch into a frown.

"It's *one* day. We'll be gone by tomorrow afternoon. Surely you can manage to endure my company for one day?"

She's done it before and to my recollection she hadn't complained then. Contrarily, Giuliana had made a good show of very much enjoying it. Pulling in a deep breath, air huffing out of her nose as she exhales, some of the tension drains from her body.

"That's not how I mean it. It's just... unprofessional. And I don't like deceit!"

"No one knows but us. You don't even have to talk to anyone about us. It's just some hand holding every now and then, maybe a peck on the cheek. Think you can handle it?"

She nods, her mouth turning up in a reluctant smile when I

reach out my hand. Giuliana slips her palm into mine and I give a little squeeze.

"I should warn you, I may have said it was our anniversary. And I brought you here to surprise you. Just remember to *trust me and go with it.*"

You're the worst, you know that? Asking her to trust you when you haven't decided whether or not you're going to fuck her over... pulling her into another falsehood you know she'd never go along with.

I ignore the inner asshole, though at this point I've got to wonder if he's making too much sense. Giuliana starts to tug her hand away, but I hold on gently.

"Matteo, *sarai la mia morte.*" She rolls her eyes, her shoulders slumping a little.

"I don't know what you said, but I'm going to pretend it was good! For now, let's see what they have for food options because I don't know about you, but all that excitement has me starving."

I rise, bowing to place a kiss on the back of her hand before heading downstairs to bother Francesca again.

This is either going to go *very* well, or Giuliana's going to kill me. Regardless, things have just gotten a lot more interesting.

The lobby, hell the whole villa, is a flurry of activity when I head back downstairs. Wedding prep is in full swing and Francesca looks like she's a mite ticked off. I shoot her a sheepish smile and she holds up her index finger urging me to wait a minute. Leaning against the wall I take in the chaos.

Some are already dressed in their finery—suits, and lightweight dresses fluttering around high heels. Gossamer fabric dances on the light breeze coming through from outside. Behind the double doors of the lobby is a ballroom leading to the grove out back. A wall of French doors has been opened in the ballroom to let the light and air in from the grove side, a gorgeous backdrop to the nuptials.

Someone is putting the finishing touches on an arch in the center, at the end of the aisle. Rows of chairs face the grove, champagne-colored bows tied around them. It's a whirlwind of bridesmaids and well-meaning family members. I haven't been to a wedding since I was a child. Despite being "Italian", my family is small—cut off from the rest—a result of parents who valued societal connections over familial ones. My friends are all still too busy dicking around to settle. Which is a blessing since it would only end in their messy divorces. New York isn't for lovers. Not like Italy. Not like Puglia.

Eventually, Francesca finds time for me and I amble over to her, pulling my thoughts away from the wedding.

"I know you guys are swamped with wedding stuff, but do you know of any delivery services running out here? We're trying to plan for dinner and we're both a little drained after the drive."

No UberEats out in the middle of nowhere farmland. I could drive back into town but then I'd have to admit I forgot about feeding us and I'm a terrible human being.

"Unfortunately, not. We're a little too out of the way. Let me see what I can figure out for you. The chef is catering the menu so I'm not sure if he can fit another two plates, but I can try. I'll be right back."

She walks into the ballroom, her heels clicking against the floor with each purposeful step and I feel a little bad for lying. Francesca is going out of her way to help us because she thinks this is some life-changing event and it deserves to be special. Which I appreciate. But it's also kind of shitty.

Kind of? You know damn well that it's wrong. But when has wrong ever stopped you?

"Shut up," I hiss under my breath and someone nearby speaks.

"Excuse me?" It's a young woman. Blonde hair cascades over her shoulders in bouncy curls with her makeup done, but she's in a set of silk pajamas and a robe.

"Not you, sorry. Talking to myself."

"Well, 'yourself' must be quite an asshole if you talk to him like that." She gives me a wry smile and I can hear the familiar hug of her accent.

"American?" I ask.

"Yeah, you?"

I nod, shrugging as if to say "what can you do?"

"Not too many of us out here in the countryside. At least not any I've encountered."

"You here for the wedding?" I ask.

"Ha, yeah. Yes, I am."

"Wedding party?"

"Yup! You can say that."

"Cool."

It's fucking stunted and I feel awkward as hell. All this does is remind me how little I converse with people back home when I'm sober. And it throws into relief how easy it's been to talk to Giuliana these past few weeks. I've been parched for little bits of her, even mere conversation.

"Hey, you look kind of familiar. Or it could be I've been around Italians all week and you're an outlier, a new face. Where are you from? What's your name?"

Fuck.

Fuck. Okay. Okay. Breathe.

My chest constricts—heart pounding as if I'm running from the red and blue lights of my lies, no getaway car this time. I clench my fists, fingernails digging into the soft flesh of my palms. It will be fine. I just have to wait a few minutes until Francesca gets back and then I can lock myself in the bathroom.

I'm not necessarily a household name. Palmer Enterprises is niche enough. We're not like the Hiltons or the Vanderbilts or other more familiar family names. Still.

"New York. Matt. You?"

"Virginia. Kelsey. What brings you out here?"

God, can I please escape this conversation to go and collect myself? My skin feels like it's ready to peel off, tiny slithers crawling under my flesh and in my veins. Energy builds with nowhere to go. There's no way to ground the lightning driving the thunder of my heartbeat.

"Uh... In the lobby? Waiting to find out if the kitchen can make a plan for dinner. In Italy—"

"He brought his girlfriend here to propose! It's so romantic.

She has no idea. It almost didn't work out because of the wedding today, but he's willing to postpone his proposal plans until tomorrow." Francesca. Sweet savior Francesca.

I turn to give her a relieved smile and the woman in front of me emits a little squeal of excitement.

"Oh my god. Please don't change your plans on my account!"

Her account...

Oh shit. I've been chatting with the bride and making an ass of myself the whole time.

"It's okay. I don't want to overshadow or anything. It can wait. Besides, we'd be in the way."

"Nonsense. I have close to a hundred guests coming, more than half of whom I've only met this week. You'd hardly be in the way. What name is the room under? I'll have Daddy send up a bottle of champagne after to celebrate!"

No. No. This is bad. This is horrendous. Giuliana is going to kill me.

"Palmer," slips out of my parched throat before I can think better of it. It's what's on my credit card. Couldn't be avoided. I'm just glad Giuliana was outside at the time.

Something in her face changes.

"Matt Palmer?"

Sensical thoughts in my brain descend into incoherent internal screaming.

"Uh huh." I squeeze through my rapidly closing throat and her excitement ratchets up a few more degrees.

"Holy shit! What are *you* doing here? You have to come to my wedding! No one is going to believe me when I tell them *Matt Palmer* was at our wedding." It's fired off in quick succession, no time for me to think or process.

"How"—I clear the gravel sitting on my vocal cords—"How do you know who I am?"

"Hottest Bad Boy Bachelors of New York. Buzzfeed did an article! Although you're technically not *a celebrity*. I guess they were counting heirs and heiresses to American fortunes."

My eyebrows knit together, confusion overriding my panic.

"You're kidding me, right?"

Kelsey shakes her head and I half expect her to whip out her phone or some shit to prove it.

"Wait, if you're here to get *engaged*," she whispers the last part, pleased to be in on the secret, "then why are you on the bachelors list?"

"Honestly, I didn't even know the list existed, it's not like they consulted me. I've been here in Italy trying to keep things on the DL."

"Because of the press?"

Because of Alan, and Thomas Palmer, and the ghosts that have chased me halfway around the world. Because I've been trying to find a way to keep my selfish existence and I'm not sure I can. Or if I should.

"Partially. I wanted privacy, and the space to get to know her away from everything back in New York. Away from my name and reputation."

"Wait... does she *know* who you are?"

Jesus Christ. If this woman gets anywhere near Giuliana, I'm done for. Doesn't she have a fucking wedding to get to? I can't say that though, not when both her and Francesca are staring at me like I'm the most compelling piece of gossip they've encountered in weeks.

"Not really. Not in the way you mean. She knows me"—I tap my chest—"but the Palmer stuff... I wanted to make sure she knew the real me first."

It's not a lie. I've been enjoying getting to know Giuliana and her family, and Italy—without the weight of the company and all that comes with it to drag me down.

"Oh my god! This is exactly like *Crazy Rich Asians*. This is unbelievable!" She bounces, like actually fucking bounces up and down in excitement.

"Sure... yeah. Just like *Crazy Rich Asians*. So, I need you to be discreet about this because I don't want to mess it up. She's important."

Both women look up at me with something between crazed enthusiasm and sympathy. They nod though, sincere.

"Thank you. It means a lot to me."

"So, you'll come to the wedding, right? You guys don't have dinner plans anyway. Plus, I'd just *die* to get to see your proposal."

What can I do but nod? It seems like the path of least resistance at this point. Kelsey has an energy I'm scared to cross; especially given she knows who I am. She claps her hands in excitement.

"Do you have the ring?"

I reach into my pocket, offering the box I bought in town for the women to scrutinize and they get close to teary.

"It's so beautiful," Kelsey breathes. "Ceremony starts at six and should finish a little after seven so we can take wedding pictures at sunset. That'll be your best bet! Only a few people from the wedding party will be in the grove and you'll have some privacy."

My panic ramps up, palms clammy around the ring box. Sweat gathers around my temples and forehead.

What the fuck are you doing? Are you really this goddamn stupid? Stop this, you piece of shit. This is too far.

I'm inclined to agree and it's pretty scary when the hateful voice in my head starts to make sense—when it sounds like the voice of reason.

"I... uh. I need to get back upstairs. Giuliana is waiting and I don't want to tip her off."

Kelsey smiles in understanding, tapping the end of her nose —my secret safe with her.

"Of course. I'll see you at the wedding, starts at six! Can't wait!"

Yeah. Yeah.

It's going to be fan-fucking-tastic.

I make it back to the room on shaky legs and if Giuliana notices something is off with me, she doesn't say.

"I have dinner sorted out." Bland. Benign.

Come on, just need to keep my shit together a tiny bit longer.

"Oh, yes?"

"We got invited to the wedding, by the bride herself. She heard me asking Francesca about needing dinner and was nice enough to include us." For the very small price of more secrets and lies.

"I have nothing to wear."

"There's a dress in the bag, I guessed on your size so it might be a little off."

Giuliana reaches into the bag on my bed, untouched. Her phone's plugged in so she was probably dealing with work calls and emails. For a brief moment I panic about the journal, but she shows no indication of having read anything.

The dress she pulls out of the bag is red. Is red a bad wedding color? I don't know, I've heard it somewhere. One of those stupid traditions or old-wives' tales. Bad luck or something? I fucking hope not.

"I'm...uh. I'm going to go shower if that's okay."

"Sure, I'll go after you."

In a different moment my brain might have latched onto that —ran with the idea of her being naked in a space I've just been naked in, and the intimacy it suggests. Instead, I do my best not to stumble into the bathroom and lock the door with shaking fingers. Setting the ring box on the counter of the sink, I tug the clothing from my body—every fiber of fabric rubbing me raw. It's all too much.

My heart gallops, nausea building, roiling. For the first time in a while the urge to vape is overwhelming and I realize how much I relied on it to try and calm my nerves. A fat lot of good patches are doing to help me now. My ribs feel like how I imagine a corset does, pulling tauter and tauter until I can feel my stomach in my chest cavity.

Breathe. Fucking breathe.

Black and white dots dance across my vision. My hand wraps around my phone, turning on the first song I can find to cover the sound. Resting it beside the ring, I close myself into the space and let the panic overtake me.

I manage to turn the faucet, water sputtering on from the showerhead. Cold pelts me as I step into the shower. My shallow breaths morph into gasps I shove my fist against to quiet.

Drowning.

It's been weeks—fucking *weeks* since I've felt like this. It's wretched. Somehow this is worse for having that break and now being shoved back into my skin after freedom. My shoulders hit the small tiles of the shower wall, slick with water, and my knees give in. Sliding down, the wall slows my descent enough to prevent me from straight up falling.

The water's turned, scalding my flesh. It's blistering in its intensity and I know when I step out my skin will be pink. But I don't care. I can't keep going like this. What does it matter? What does the inheritance and the grove and New York matter when it's me that's the problem? No matter where I am or what I call myself, I can't escape it. The least I can do is not pull her down with me.

Tears mix with water as I struggle to breathe air that's too heavy to take in—as I try not to throw up. I lean my head onto my knees and sob. *What the fuck am I even doing at this point? And why does it hurt so much?*

Steam billows throughout the bathroom. My body is sensitive and red by the time I haul myself to my feet and scrub the guilt from my skin. If Giuliana asks why it's taking so long, I'll play into vanity or something. Anything to avoid admitting how fucked up I feel.

Somewhere between the nausea clearing and my chest aching with a full breath, I decide. My life in New York isn't one I've missed so far. The money... fuck, I'll hate going without the money, but it hasn't done shit for the way I'm feeling. What good are riches when I'm on the verge of losing myself? Kelsey and my old life flooding in tipped me over the edge again and I'm not so sure I'll be able to pull myself back next time. The closest I've come to joy is hot days in the sun and Giuliana's warm voice covering me like molten honey as we work side by side. That's got to count for something.

When I emerge—towel slung low on my hips, droplets drying on my chest—she's frowning over her phone screen. I cradle my dirty clothes, phone, and the ring box under one arm. Giuliana glances up, concentration melting into a glazed look to her eyes and her lips part. Her cheeks pinken but she catches herself, gaze dropping back to her phone. So beautiful. Nothing but trouble. Still, it does wonders for my mood knowing I've affected her.

"Your turn." I smile, shaking off the last remnants of my panic and slip the mask back into place.

Giuliana keeps her eyes averted, grabs the dress and rushes into the bathroom. The click of the door is a weight off my chest. I'll need all the courage I can muster to get through this charade, better to gather it while she's not watching. I don a white linen button-up shirt and lightweight slacks. Not necessarily the most formal of attire, but definitely not inappropriate.

Grabbing the journal and a pen from my backpack, I try to purge the last of these ugly feelings before she returns. The box I slipped into my pocket digs into my thigh and reminds me what tonight holds. Probably the last big purchase I'm going to be able to make in a while.

I can't outrun myself. No matter how far I travel, no matter what name I take. I am the same I've always been. Failure clings to my skin like sweat during my panic episodes. There are moments of clarity. Moments of peace where I forget. But the world rushed back in today, reminding me what's at stake. Alan's waiting for me to fail and I'm not sure I shouldn't. My heart isn't in this. The time I've spent with Giuliana and her family have shown me how much I've missed out on. This is their livelihood and decades of their history rest between those rows of olive trees. I don't deserve the grove. Alan's expecting to form me into my father but I'll never be as cutthroat as Thomas or his ruthless friends. And I'll never reach the same heights because of it.

I can't tell Giuliana the truth now. She'll never trust me again. It's been lie after lie. Stacking up like a brick wall between us. Tonight's is a fake proposal one she'd never agree to go along with. Giuliana is too righteous to stoop so low. It's for appearances, to gain insight that she sorely needs. And when we get back to Abundantia, to reality, I will do what I can to help her succeed. The least I can do is make sure my failure means something. She never needs to know that I came here to hurt her, even if it was indirectly. I'll leave with the harvest and go back to my own personal hell and forge something new from the ashes of the life I plan to incinerate.

When the door opens again, Giuliana emerges in red fabric that clings and wraps, hugging her curves and setting my soul on fire. My decision is final—the die cast. My casket is measured and made. I might as well let myself enjoy every shred of what I've been conflicted about allowing.

"Beautiful." It's a rasp of a word, my heart in my throat.

"I didn't bring any makeup, and all I have are the flats I came in." She protests, fluffing her freshly dried hair with her hand.

"*Beautiful,*" I insist and she must see the seriousness counteracting my usual breeziness, because she nods, a blush spreading across her cheeks.

I pack the journal back into the bag, tucking away the lies I'll leave with, and reach out my hand for her to take.

"Matteo..." She gives me a skeptical look, no doubt thinking about keeping things professional.

"Look, it's for show, okay? Why not let yourself forget about work and pressure, and keeping our distance? Have fun. There are two beds in here, no need for us to worry. When we come back tonight, we stick to our sides. I know my place. Out there we have to keep up appearances. So just for tonight, let me dote on you and call you beautiful, and watch that dress twirl while we dance."

"Fine, okay." Her breath leaves her chest in a huff and she slips her hand into mine.

We walk down the stairs and cross the lobby. Every second of her skin touching mine leaves a flutter in my stomach and a giddiness that seems ridiculous.

"Where do we..." she starts, the rows of chairs divided.

"Bride's side, I guess. She's the one who invited us to join."

And I hope to god it doesn't come back to bite me in the ass. Guests file in, chatter lively and eventually so cacophonous I can hardly stand it. I'm ready to cover my ears or leave the room when Giuliana takes my hand from where it rests on my bouncing knee.

She's absorbing the stunning view of the grove up ahead and people watching. But even so she takes the time to squeeze my hand. It's innocuous. It's a familiarity, an intimacy I've never experienced. Although this isn't the messy, gut-churning feeling from earlier, it's still not the unbothered person I present to the world. For her to notice, for her to take the time to soothe...

Fuck.

I focus on that—on the feel of her touch cutting off the rest of the world. I'm so captivated I don't realize the bride's shown up until Giuliana tugs me to my feet. She cranes her neck—closer to the aisle than I am—trying to catch a glimpse of our benevolent bride. My eyes are only on Giuliana. I soak up the smile cutting into her cheeks and her breathless wonder at the ceremony.

There's a mix of Italian and English, so Giuliana gets to enjoy both parts. The crowd laughs at certain points but I barely notice. Giuliana tears up during the ceremony, eyes a sheen of moisture. Looking up at me, she gives me a watery smile. This time it's my turn to squeeze her hand and one of those droplets falls. I steal it with the back of my finger, catching the warm salt on my skin.

The newly-wedded pair share a passionate kiss and the crowd erupts in cheers and laughs. I join in with the clapping and shuffle out with the rest, a cone of rice thrust into my hand to toss at the happy couple as they walk through the wall of windows into the grove. As Kelsey passes us, she gives me a wink and a bright smile and I pray that Giuliana misses it.

It's time. Dusk paints the sky over the sprawling grove, the sun's hazy heat hanging around the horizon like a mirage.

"Hey, let's get some air." Threading my fingers between Giuliana's, I nudge her gently toward the grove.

"I don't think that's a good idea. The bridal party is in the grove." She doesn't pull her hand away but her feet remain glued to the floor.

"It's massive out there. They won't even notice, and this might be the only chance we get to explore without someone watching." It's a lie. Kelsey will be watching. Francesca too. Hell, I have no idea who else might know since Francesca was so free with her information earlier.

"That's a good point. But the second it looks like we might get in the way we are running back here. Is that clear?" Giuliana tries to keep her tone stern and her expression serious. I nod like the boy scout that I definitely am not.

We stroll down the stairs toward the rows of trees—a different cultivar from the one Giuliana's family uses—her hand still in mine despite the fact that no one is around to see. She takes the time to touch the bark, to caress the fruit. It doesn't feel all that different to me but then again, I'm too caught up in the knowledge of what comes next.

Blue summer sky melts into purples and oranges as the sun gives her last hurrah, and I know it's my moment. I stall, Giuliana's step interrupted by my immobility and the connection of our hands. She looks back at me in confusion that only grows when I whisper.

"Okay, so remember when I said there was a surprise?"

"Yes? What did you do?"

"I knew there was no way you'd go along with this and I wanted to make sure you actually *looked* surprised. My mouth got ahead of me when I was spinning my little story to Francesca, and it kind of snowballed from there."

Her brows draw down over those expressive eyes, darkening the spiced rum into something even more dangerous.

"What did you do?"

"You'll see. Try to remember this is for you. I'm doing this to help so please, trust me."

"Matteo?" It's a warning.

"Giuliana, promise me." My heart races, my body itching to run off some of this energy. Nowhere to run now, it's time to face the music.

"Okay, okay. I'll trust you."

I drop her hand and take a step back. It doesn't have to be this extra, it doesn't have to be anything at all. If I hadn't been so fucked with anxiety, I could have told her back in the room and asked her to slip on the ring to cement our charade. But my lies included a grove proposal, and god dammit, I'm going to see it through.

Her beautiful brown eyes stare up at me, lashes impossibly long, the light catching and warming the color to something molten and warm. Skin I long to touch glows in the golden hour around us and I have to swallow twice before I speak—a little louder in case we have an audience, which I suspect we might.

"You are the most beautiful person I've ever known. Not just the way you look but the way you act and are. I see how much you care about your family; about the people you've taken responsibility for who see you as more than just a boss. You've built something amazing."

She starts to interrupt and I'm sure she's going to brush it off so I shake my head and her parted lips close.

"*You* did it. You took what was given and you poured your blood and tears into keeping it alive. And that's how you make me feel. I've never felt as alive as I do with you. Your laugh spreads threads of gold through my whole body. Your lips taste like the sweetest wine. I'm drunk on you, on each drop of your presence. *Lia...*

"Every second of this summer has been the best of my life and I know I'll never forget a moment of it. I'm in awe of you. I don't deserve to even breathe the same air as you. But... we both know I'm a selfish bastard, so."

Sinking onto one knee, I pull out the ring box that thankfully only catches once in my pocket. The lid snaps open, sunset dancing in the cuts and curves of the stone. My muscles shake, my body not realizing that this is fake—this proposal isn't the real deal. I don't even care that I've moved from silly nicknames to rile her onto something that feels very personal—intimate.

"Matteo," she gasps, her breathing getting harsher and I can see something vulnerable settle onto her face.

"*Trust me, for Abundantia's sake,*" I whisper.

"Giuliana Santoro, will you do me the immense honor of agreeing to marry me?"

15

"Matteo de Palma… *che cazzo stai facendo*?" Her voice is a whisper, the meaning clear even if the words are not. Giuliana looks confused and heartbroken.

"You promised to trust me," I remind her, and she takes a deep breath, raising her shaking left hand to her lips. Silence stretches between us and my heart twists in my chest in fear and anticipation.

"Yes." It's a little breathless and it takes me a second to realize she's not just acknowledging what I said. Her hand outstretched and waiting, I fumble with getting the ring out of the box. The velvet square clatters to the ground as I slip the slightly-too-big ring onto her finger.

"You're going to explain everything to me." It's a command, not a request, and all I can do is nod. Stomach knotted into something unrecognizable at the sight of the ring on her finger, I surge to my feet without thinking.

Pulling her into my arms, I spin us both in a circle. Despite the fact that she knows something untoward is happening, Giuliana elicits a squeal of laughter. We slow to a dizzying stop and with her soft body pressed up against my chest I can't hold back. Dipping my head down to kiss her, I lean in to sample the intoxication of her.

"Oh my god! That was so beautiful!" Kelsey and her bridal party emerge from the trees—excited and ecstatic.

Seriously? Two more seconds and we would have been kissing. Talk about shit timing. A bridesmaid shoves two flutes of prosecco toward us and I throw mine back. Giuliana's gaze flits between me and Kelsey—confusion clearing into some kind of understanding. I'll have to explain the miscommunication and my lies. For now, Giuliana's accepted that the proposal is part of what got us here.

"*Grazie*," she says, taking a heavy swig of the shimmering liquid.

Some of the bridal party fawn over the ring. When no one is watching Giuliana worries the white gold band with her thumb. Twisting it to and fro on her finger, the stone catches on the golden hues of the sun's last bit of splendor.

"Thank you for all the fuss, but please, don't stop your photo session on our account. I insist!" I say, hoping they'll catch the hint and let us leave. Threading my hand with Giuliana's, we make a grateful exit.

The ring band is cold where we touch and silence looms between us as we walk back toward the revelry of cocktail hour. Kelsey's spread the good news somehow because wedding guests come over to congratulate us. Thank fuck most of them are Italian. The last thing I need is another person recognizing me.

"I'm so excited we were able to make it happen for you! Your fiancé told me how badly you wanted to see the grove and how he had very special plans for this weekend that couldn't wait." Francesca gushes to Giuliana, my lies unfolding.

I'm on my fourth glass of prosecco—the bubbles doing funny things to my nose—when Giuliana reaches her limit. Tugging me up some side steps to a private balcony, we stand watch over the party. Once we reach the top she drops my hand, her indulgence for my lies at an end.

"Matteo."

"Yes?"

"What did you do?"

Night wraps us in her embrace. The strings of lights illuminating the dance floor below don't reach up to this area. Our balcony is a small alcove overlooking the grounds. Music pulses under my feet. The breeze carries the sound of rambunctious partygoers laughing and dancing. It's the closest I've gotten to the New York vibe since getting here and despite my panic attack earlier I'd been enjoying myself.

Giuliana waits, tension thick between us.

"It got out of hand," I blurt.

She scoffs, the air huffing from her nose emphasizing my massive understatement.

"You've made a liar out of me and I resent that. Forcing my hand like that and pulling me into your pretense... It feels wrong, especially after my father, and Umberto—" she breaks off. I remember what she told me about her father lying about being sick, and hiding the loan. Then there's Umberto and his hidden intentions. The comparison is apt and I feel like hot trash.

But there's no time for me to wallow because she's talking again. "I'm not like them. I don't want to be. So how dare you?" she accuses before hissing, "*Engaged*?"

"Francesca said the villa was closed because of a wedding. It got stuck in my head and an engagement was the only thing I could think of to keep us here despite the private event. Francesca got super excited about it and I got sucked in. When I went down to ask about dinner the bride was there. Francesca filled her in on my fake plans, only she didn't *know* they were fake." I lean against the stone terrace, my back turned to the party below.

"But a ring? One that looks and feels very real?" She has her hand between us, examining the proof of my harebrained scheme, and all I can think is how well the ring suits her.

"When I went to town."

"For God's sake. What were you thinking? Where did you even get the money for this? Why didn't you *tell* me?"

"I'm not here because I'm hurting for money. This plan was stupid and impulsive but I wanted to take care of this for you, to save the situation. I'm not used to being the one to step in and fix things. Back home I'm a fucking joke but here…"

I don't finish the sentence—I can't. Because I'm a joke here, too.

"It got out of hand. As soon as the words left my mouth, I knew they were a mistake. I know you're too honorable to go along with the lies. But I stuck my foot in it. It felt like you depended on me to make this work and then Francesca and Kelsey expected this wonderful proposal—rightfully because that's what I sold them—and I panicked."

"It *was* wonderful, but you can't go around *proposing to your boss*." It's hard to make out her expression in the dark but there's sadness there, regret.

Maybe that's just me.

"Yeah well, maybe I kind of fucking hate the fact that you're my boss." I need to leave before I say too much.

Rushing past her, my arm brushes against hers as I start down the stairs.

"*Teo*, you can't say something like that and leave." Her voice follows me down the steps.

Slightly wobbling, I stick my hand out and trace my palm against stone walls as I stumble down each step. Prosecco on an empty stomach was such a rookie move. When did my feet get so heavy? Halfway down my brain catches up. Her nickname for me pierces the haze.

Twisting to face her, I drink in her expression—the concern and vulnerability there.

I open my mouth to ask her to say it again so I can watch the word leave her lips. But as usual *drunken mistake* is an ethos I live up to.

My shoes slip against the floor as I'm sucked backwards, the earth calling me down. Giuliana's expression shifts to one of fear, that hand with the ring outstretched toward me but it's too late. Gravity wins.

A sick thud, a faint scream, and then darkness settles around me like an old friend.

Ice is painful when you think about it. It pierces. I've heard freezing to death is a peaceful experience, but that's a fucking lie. The back of my head is wet and freezing. I blink up into the light of a chandelier and the second sensation I'm aware of is Giuliana's shaking hands surveying my body.

"*Teo*... Please. Wake up." Her voice sounds different than I've heard it before, shaky and scared.

"*Lia*," I groan, pain filtering in through the haze. And then her hand cups my cheek, the warm pad of her thumb stroking to soothe.

"Francesca went to find help. One of the guests is a doctor. For now, I just need you to stay awake, okay?" Her voice is gentle, kind and caring as it wraps around me. I want nothing more than to have her keep talking while I slip back under.

"I'll try. I'm assuming I fell down the rest of the stairs?"
Fucking idiot.

"Yes, but it doesn't look like anything is broken. I'm more concerned about your head."

Her words filter through and I realize the wet cold is an ice pack against the back of my skull.

"Ow... Could have been worse."

"How?"

"Could have been *all* the stairs," I joke, and she gives a little laugh and a shake of her head that tells me she thinks I'm totally ridiculous. But beneath it there's a softness and I wonder if I heard her call me "Teo" or if it was my own deluded fantasy from my drunkenness and the bump on my head. I'll likely never know. Even if she did slip and give me a nickname, Giuliana will probably want to pretend it never happened.

Francesca, and a small group of people filter into the bottom of the stairway. The supposed doctor kneels beside me, a phone flashlight shone into my eyes. He asks me to follow the movement of his finger and then probes around the giant goose egg on the back of my skull.

He presses against parts of my body to assess my pain and within a few minutes he's deemed me okay to try and sit up.

"There's no bleeding, no broken bones. You might have some muscle soreness, especially on your back, and your head is definitely going to hurt for a while. It doesn't appear too serious but given that you've been drinking and we can't rule out a concussion, you'll have to be observed tonight."

"No, no hospitals." The last thing I need is to have to deal with that on top of everything else.

"The hospital is quite far and we've all been drinking. It might be best to stay here if you have someone to look after you tonight."

I've never had anyone to care for me overnight, not unless you count the nannies my parents paid for. My mom was a hotshot model, my dad a mogul. Neither had time for a sick or scared child. Before I can protest, admit that I don't have a person, Giuliana speaks up.

"He's my fiancé, I'll take care of him tonight. You just tell me what I need to do."

Her statement does something funny to my insides, leaving them warm and gooey. Despite the fact that I should decline—should definitely not infringe on her whole evening when I know she's mad at me—I don't.

"First thing is getting some food and water in him. Then you'll have to try and keep him awake for a bit. After that he can sleep for short periods of time but you'll have to wake him up sporadically to check for any issues. If he starts throwing up at any point, especially if there's clear liquid or blood coming from his nose, you call for an ambulance *immediately*."

It does me no good to remind them that I might throw up anyway because I've been drinking. We'll cross that bridge when we get to it.

"I'll send some food up to the room," Francesca promises.

The doctor helps me to my feet and I only flounder a little before I'm able to right myself. Giuliana wraps her arm around my waist, propping herself under my arm to help with my balance. Once I find my feet her touch is gone.

When we walk up the stairs to our room this time there is no hand holding, no pretend affection. I change into pajamas in the bathroom and Giuliana does the same when I'm done.

Shortly after, Francesca sends a tray of food up for each of us and I might die from how good it smells. Italy never ceases to astound me with its beauty and its *food*. The antipasto is a plate with summer melon wrapped in prosciutto and burrata cheese adorning it. The taste dances on my tongue like I'm the rat in that scene from *Ratatouille*. By the time I get through the primo piatto of pasta orecchiette, I feel halfway human. The pasta are these tiny bowls perfect for holding the delicious tomato-based sauce.

Giuliana makes me drink water and I hate to admit it's definitely helping with the swooshy feeling. The meal is quiet except for the clank of cutlery against plates, and when we're done eating, she carries the trays down without a word. When she gets back, Giuliana gives me some Tylenol she obtained downstairs. I throw it back and chase it with a heavy swig of water.

Tucking myself into bed, I stifle a groan. Pain sinks into my muscles and the buzz of alcohol fades. All I want is to escape into sleep. What a fucking mess of a day.

"Are you hurt anywhere else?" Giuliana asks from the doorway, her hand poised over the light switch.

"I'll be fine. It's not my first drunken tumble and it probably won't be the last."

Her lips thin into an unhappy line and she gives a terse nod before turning off the lights. Sheets and blankets swish on her side of the room as she slips into her own bed. The darkness is too intimate and although we're not sharing a bed I hear her breathing—every shuffle against the covers. It's obvious that she's uncomfortable, if her tossing and turning is any indication.

"Giuliana..."

"You can't say stuff like that and then fall down a flight of stairs." Her voice is tight. The words are sharp as if she's throwing them in my direction like daggers.

"It was only *half* a flight of stairs."

She huffs.

"But, I'm sorry. I'm sorry I dragged you into this and forced a lie between us. I didn't tell you because I knew you'd come up with a better excuse—one where I wouldn't get to enjoy the little bit of time I got with you. Even if it was only pretending."

Silence stretches for too long and I wonder if she's gone to sleep.

"It's not... I—" She struggles before sighing. "I'm not keeping my distance for nothing or because I'm being difficult. My livelihood depends on this. As much as I want this to be real... as much as I want *you*, I can't afford it right now."

It shoots through me like electricity and she's the live wire. Although I understand she's letting me down easy and reiterating again why this can't work, all my stupid brain focuses on is she wants this.

She wants me.

"All I was trying to do was help, as misguided as it was. *Abundantia* is lucky to have you and I'm not going to stand in the way of that." In more ways than one. "How can I help? What do you need?"

Fabric rustles against fabric again and she turns to face me.

"I have all these ideas and I'm terrified to implement them. Convincing my Nonna of the volunteer program was difficult and that's the tamest idea of all of them. Part of me thinks she'd rather I just let the grove go. She doesn't even know why we're here. When I called her earlier, I told her you wanted to go sightseeing and I felt it was my duty as your host."

I chuckle at knowing no matter how old we are we still lie to our parents like we're teenagers. Although Giuliana still has to live with her elder, so I can't complain.

"I know about the B&B idea since that's why we're here but what else? What is your big dream for the farm?"

"Obviously I want the farm to succeed but more than that..." She takes a deep, steadying breath. "*I* want to succeed. The grove was never supposed to be mine. It was meant for the son my father never had and although he tried to pretend otherwise, we both knew it. I mentioned a few of the workers quit after he died and I took over. They left *me*. It wasn't just Umberto's influence." My stomach sinks as I mull it over. I wish I could take away the hurt in her voice.

The covers are cool against my skin and the mattress dips

around my body, cradling my sore muscles. I open my mouth to speak, to apologize but she barrels on before I can.

"I tended to him for years—running the grove and trying to care for Chiara. That's why Nonna moved back in with us. She has a house in Gravina that she lived in before—the one where we—anyway, she ran a shop where she sold the olive oil we made, among other things. When my father got too sick to work, she gave it all up."

I never considered what that might have looked like, what sacrifices the family had to make to keep their world spinning right side up. Just what did Giuliana have to sacrifice?

"And you? What did you have to give up?"

The air buzzes around us. It's as if I can feel her considering whether or not she should say. She keeps quiet and I probe her again, a soft plea wrapped around her name. One breath passes. Two. Until she finally speaks.

"Time. Relationships. University. I was supposed to go to study agriculture. I *love* the land. It's all I've ever wanted and I thought if I could prove myself... If I could show I'm as worthy as any of the men in that course I could earn their respect. But then Papa got sick, and I inherited it by default. When I stepped up and started running the farm myself, Umberto resented me for it. Our relationship shriveled and now only those who stayed respect me. I live with knowing I was a disappointment to my father until the end."

Her words clang around my mind, echoes of those I've had in the past when it came to myself and my father.

"I understand." Now it's my turn to sigh and gather my courage.

"My father died last year and he was this bigshot business-man. The expectation is that I'm supposed to take over the company. He pushed me toward a business degree, I got a writing degree instead. He ignored me to focus on work and everything I've done my whole adult life has been to spite him. My existence was nothing but a source of shame to my father when he was alive and I have little to show for myself now."

My heart constricts. My ribcage is too large for the tiny stone of pain I've repressed and compacted all year.

"I came here to prove I was worthy of something, capable of more. But he's not around to see it and I'm not sure he'd care or approve."

"What a mess, huh? The pair of us."

We both chuckle, pain lancing through the mirth. God, if I could only be beside her right now so I could pull her into my arms. As soon as we leave here it'll be back to business.

"Tell me more about your dream for the grove. You've mentioned it but I love hearing how excited you get about it."

"You know a lot of it already. A teaching program, a kick-starter for small female-owned farms and businesses." She says it so quietly I can barely hear it but when I do it makes sense. Giuliana wants to provide what she was deprived of: resources, respect, and a chance to forge something independent of the men who came before.

"Female farming girlboss." It sounds stupid as soon as I say it but she laughs, a light bell-like sound. The way it makes me feel curls around my stomach like a snake—traitorous and too slippery to catch.

"It won't bring in much money. That's why I'm trying to find a way to make the grove a success first. No point in me attempting to teach people when I can't even do it myself, but that would be the goal. To provide an opportunity for people like me and young girls like Chiara. Not that I think she has an interest but I want to give her the option."

"It makes sense, and I think it's a wonderful idea. You could change someone's life with a program like that. I'll do anything in my power to help you see it through, I promise."

"It's not your problem, Matteo. You're only here for another month or so at the most. There's no obligation or pressure."

She doesn't need you. You have nothing of merit to provide. You'll only get in the way.

I shove it all aside. This isn't the time.

"Maybe I want there to be. Maybe if I had my way I'd stay. But I understand and I won't push. Please know I'm here for you, okay? No strings. Just a friend who cares."

"I appreciate it, and what you tried to do tonight, as idiotic as it was. You have a kind heart and I'm glad to call you a friend."

I let the words wash over me. It's the closest I'll get to feeling good about myself and feeling okay about my lie. Body aching in more ways than one, at this point even holding her hand in the dark would be exquisite. But we've made it clear we're just friends. I'm kicking myself for not kissing her quick enough this evening. Fucking Kelsey.

There might never be a chance again. One month and I lose it all. I have one month to help her get stuff set up before Alan or Umberto step in. I can only hope it will be enough. Sleep swallows me and pulls me another day closer to my life as I know it changing forever.

16

Why does the bed always feel best when I have to leave it? Giuliana's hands shook me awake multiple times last night but our brief conversations never strayed back to that vulnerable place. Now, I'm left with the fuzzy tired feeling of interrupted sleep and the dread that returning to reality brings.

We don our clothes from the night before. A headache splits my skull from the fall and not a hangover for once. The ring still rests around Giuliana's finger and something fizzes inside of me to know she's slept with it on. We pack our stuff into my backpack and tidy the room, ready for checkout by ten. No words are exchanged except for a soft good morning and stolen glances.

Francesca greets us both with a smile and congratulations before setting us up for the tour. The space has been transformed back to normal, wedding tables and chairs a hazy memory from last night. The ballroom is now a sitting room with little groupings of armchairs and end tables. It feels kind of like a hotel lobby—a place to enjoy a coffee as you stare out at the grove.

It's luck, or serendipity, that the owner decides to do the tour for us.

"We really don't want to put you out!" Giuliana insists but the older man shrugs us off.

His black hair is shot through with silver at the temples—distinguished; exactly the kind of man you'd picture owning a grove or a vineyard, capable and smooth. When we shake hands, calluses brush against my palm and I know he's more than just a paper-pusher. Like Giuliana, he's involved. He works hard.

The grove is bathed in warm midmorning sunshine, and I wish we were lounging by a pool or something. When all this is over and I get back to New York—whatever I get back to—I really need to take some time to just be. I've been running from myself for so long I don't know how to exist in a space for the sake of it. It might be time to figure it out soon.

The owner—Claudio—tells us about how the grove was passed down from generation to generation, son to son. His story is similar to Giuliana's—this is still a family business, one that pivoted when times got harder. The villa has been expanded on and upgraded through the years and about five years ago he made the choice to open it up as a boutique hotel and wedding venue to supplement their income.

"Well, it's beautiful and you've done a fantastic job!"

"It wasn't easy. It still isn't, but seeing people enjoy the home I grew up in and the land that's part of my blood is all worth it." Claudio's pride is evident and the way he talks about it sounds so much like Giuliana that I can't help but smile.

We walk some more of the grove and stop near the house to try the olive oils and vinegars they've produced. Bread and oil. So simple, yet the livelihood of so many people—the legacy they get to leave.

Giuliana thanks him for his time, another genuine handshake shared between us and Claudio, and then it's time to head back to *Abundantia* and the work awaiting us there. When we greet Francesca, she slips us a business card to consider the hotel for the wedding or even a honeymoon location and I chuckle. Ballsy. Kind. She's been lovely throughout this experience.

Giuliana and I settle onto the Vespa and the wheels crunch

over gravel as we head back to the main road. The drive takes less time than it did before, or I'm just so reluctant for it to end I wish time would stand still. Pulling up to the house, we stand on shaky legs. Giuliana considers me for a moment, something akin to regret on her face.

"Matteo," she says on a sigh and I know it's back to business. "I know."

Tugging the ring from her finger, Giuliana places it in my palm and curls my fingers shut around it. The stone cuts into my flesh and I tighten my grip, hoping it'll break skin.

Giuliana looks like she wants to say more but then Patrizia comes rushing out the front door, a slew of frantic words barraging us. Wasting no time, Giuliana heads into the house and throws over her shoulder like an afterthought, "Something important has come up. Why don't you take some time off for the weekend and we'll start back up on Monday, okay?"

Not waiting for my response, she disappears inside. The walk to my room is slower, reluctant. The backpack slips from my shoulder onto the floor. I drop my phone onto the bed and then proceed to fall face first onto the mattress. I unleash a burning scream of frustration into the covers before I collect myself. Unzipping my backpack, I reach inside for the ring box. I tuck the ring inside and throw the box and my journal back into the desk drawer, hidden. Out of sight.

The following morning, I change into my grove clothes and head down toward the old farmhouse. Giuliana never said whether she intended to convert either the main house or this older building into the B&B, but it'll need to be inspected and cleaned out.

The grove is quieter than I've ever experienced with most employees away for the weekend or their midday rests—something I wish was a staple in the US because disappearing to eat and relax in the middle of the day would be amazing. Mostly, my father never even took a lunch break.

The untamed brush near the house almost swallows the path. I'll have to tackle that soon to get wheelbarrows and stuff through here. There's a broken window on the lower level but the walls are still in good shape. No cracks that I can see. Part of the facade is covered in beautiful creeping greenery. The door needs a new coat of paint. It hangs lazily off the hinges when I push my way inside and I add new mounting to my growing mental list. Screws pull away from the doorframe and the wood drags along the stone floors. I have to prop it up just to swing it all the way open.

I'm not sure what I was expecting but it wasn't furniture. Not much, like the main house, but there's a small console near the door and I can picture old envelopes of mail tossed there along with house and car keys.

The narrow foyer leads into a heavy staircase against the wall and beyond that an open door to the kitchen. The settee in the living area hasn't fared well. Feathers and padding are scattered around the floor along with leaves and dust. Some animal made its home in the cushions at one point since this place was abandoned. This is the room with the broken window and it shows.

To the left is a dining room and a sturdy wooden table scarred with age and years of disuse. Four chairs sit around it and I'm unsure if the set is incomplete or if it's only supposed to be four.

My feet pull me up the stairs and I'm helpless but to follow the whim of my body. I can picture what this place must have looked like when it was loved and cared for. Did Giuliana ever live here? Or did they move into the big house before she was born? The ghosts of laughter—of lives—seem like they're embedded in the walls.

History. All I feel in Italy is a history I've never had the luxury to have. Thomas and Genevieve Palmer changed residences as soon as they stopped feeling en mode. Only the best, only the newest, to distract from the restlessness of their lives. No wonder I'm so unsettled and unable to stand still.

Did my father walk these floors? Did he know the family living here or was he a silent partner? Just what was his involvement because I really can't picture it? I can't marry the images in my mind of the aloof man I knew and the type of person who would've helped this grove.

Upstairs is emptier. The bedrooms are naught but bed frames and furniture too heavy to move out, or too old-fashioned to be considered worth it. The bathrooms are revolting. Thick rings line the insides of toilets with no water in them. Sinks and tubs are yellow with age, and the musty smell of stagnant water permeates the space.

It's going to be hard work. It's going to take a while. If I throw enough time and money into this, I could potentially have it ready for her by the end of the month. Before I get cut off.

Hiding it from Giuliana—or potentially asking her to leave it up to me—is going to be near-impossible. But this is my chance to make amends, to fix what she doesn't realize is broken, and prove I can do something on my own.

It's not running a grove. It's not a business takeover. Fixing the old farmhouse is not what Alan or my father had in mind when they told me to make something of myself. But it's an opportunity I'm grabbing with both hands. Firstly, I'm going to need to clean—clear out the brush and the rooms, then I can tackle the walls and the floors.

I trek back to the big house and encounter Chiara, the young girl leaving the kitchen with red sauce on the side of her mouth and the unbridled energy of someone who's been made to sit still for too long.

"*Buongiorno*, Matteo."

"*Buongiorno*, Chiara. Is Nonna nearby?" Isabella is the only one I can think to ask who might keep this secret for me, at least for today.

Chiara gestures with her thumb to the kitchen. "Do you need me to come with you?"

"Yes, please."

Both of us file into the room where a plate waits. I'm not sure who it's for but Isabella makes me sit with a wave of her hand and an insistent "*mangiare*" which again isn't hard to decipher with context clues.

"It's called '*melanzane ripiene*' and they're stuffed eggplants," Chiara informs me. "I, uh... Giuliana told me to keep myself busy so I thought I might do some yard work?" I explain between mouthfuls. "Do you have any gardening equipment, gloves and the like to protect my hands?"

Best she believes it's for vanity—me not wanting to rip up my soft palms (although I already have some calluses from helping on the grove).

Isabella gives me that look again, the one where she makes it very clear she's aware of my bullshit, but for whatever reason she lets it slide. She makes Chiara promise to take me out to the shed for anything I need and I finish my delicious meal.

"Nonna says I have to show you the tools and stuff. It's dark in the shed but you can look inside. I'll just wait with you." It's cheeky and I kind of love that Chiara is making the limits of her help very clear.

"*Grazie*, Isabella... Chiara. Seriously, you've both been a big help."

Chiara translates and I get a wry smile from the old woman,

her response relayed through her granddaughter as we head back out for my secret mission.

"She says don't mess it up. And also, you can call her Nonna."

"*Grazie, Nonna.*"

Isabella gives me a little 'humph' of agreement before shooing us out again and telling us dinner is at seven. With that I'm left to my own devices (dangerous) and at the mercy of a seven-year-old who will be far too curious for her own good (terrifying). All I have to console me is the hope this will be enough. What I'm able to give Giuliana is at least a small gesture of apology and support.

Digging around the shed, I grab shears, heavy-duty gloves, and a rake for outside. For inside, I find a large push broom, a bucket, and several old rags.

"Chiara... can you keep this secret for me?" I ask as we carry the items up the hill toward the old house.

"Giuliana says secrets are bad." Fuck. Of course, she does. She's trying to set a good example for the kid and as usual I'm asserting my bad influence.

"Okay. Not a secret then. A surprise."

Chiara nods, a giant smile lighting up her face, missing teeth and all.

We crest the little hill and the house is in view, every dilapidated inch.

"I want to help Giuliana, surprise her by cleaning up the old house. I don't want her to know yet because she'll want to help and she's already so busy with the grove."

The little girl looks down and gives a solemn nod.

"Nonna says she looks old and worn down. All she does is frown and worry, and she'll never find a man to love her because her face is always miserable and crinkled like an old prune."

I laugh at that, fully in disagreement with her looking old

and worn, or like an old prune but I don't fight it. To Chiara, Nonna's word is law. Who am I to argue with the old lady?

"Exactly, so I want to help her with this so she has one less thing to worry about. Can you keep it between us so she doesn't have to take time on this as well? Will you help me?"

"Yes."

"Good. Can you come fetch me around six so I have time to clean up before dinner? Can't have her figuring it out on day one, yeah?"

She laughs and gives me a thumbs up. "I'll bring you some water, Teo!"

So excited, so happy to be involved. Hearing the nickname jolts me and I wonder why she's decided to use it. Has Giuliana called me that in private?

I try not to let it get to me. It could just be a common thing, a colloquialism. I've never had a nickname before—not when I basically go by one on a daily basis. But "Teo" is so much *more* than Matt. It feels special. It's Giuliana's voice wrapped around the word like a secret she's kept to herself all this time.

I swallow the unexpected emotion sitting on my throat and give her my thanks. Watching her disappear back into the grove, I'm left with a feeling of "what now"? Where do I even start?

Grabbing the thing closest to me—shears—I hack into the overgrown foliage covering the path. Sweat gathers along my temples, droplets snaking down my neck. By the time I'm done, a pile of growth sits beside the front door and my shirt is plastered to my back. Chiara rushes over with a few bottles of water and skids to a stop outside the door, looking over at the large pile of greenery.

"*Wow.* I've never really been here to the old house but this is a lot. Are you going to fix it?"

"Yeah, that's the plan. I'm going to clean it out this weekend and then I'll see what else needs to get done after that."

"Do you need help?" Sweet, searching. Like she's afraid I might say no and send her away.

"That would be wonderful, thank you."

Her smile is back and she enters with wide eyes, taking in her family's history and the living that happened here, the same way I did before. Kinship lances through me. This little girl and I have a lot in common, I think. She's never known this part of her history, just bits and pieces from other people since her parents passed. But these walls—this story isn't one she's been told.

I shake myself from my introspection, from my stupid thoughts. Next, I'll have to drag all the furniture on the main level into one room until I can decide what to keep and chuck. I wipe the back of my forearm against my forehead, clearing off some of the sweat dripping into my eyes and look around the rooms.

Are you sure you can do this? You've never done anything like this in your whole life. Do you really want to fuck around with Giuliana's history?

The voice is right, but at least this time I have more than "shut up" to offer in response. Because I know I can do this. I have no other option. This isn't for me and that's what will keep me going. At worst she can throw me out. She's bound to do so anyway when she discovers why I'm here. At best I can help her set up the future she wants to build. Either way, there's no time to fuck around arguing with myself. I need to conserve my energy for what matters.

"Let's do this!" I say as I step inside.

It's going to be a long day, so we better get started. It's time to save *Abundantia*.

It's surprisingly easy to keep Giuliana in the dark, especially when I find out she's not even *at* the grove. She's in Gravina to finalize the list of locals coming to help out with the harvest. And buy a ton of food to feed us all. Last minute preparations. And something else. No one has mentioned what, but tension ripples through them and I can't escape feeling like something happened while we were away. It's hard to gauge when my information comes from a seven-year-old translating what Isabella deigns to share.

Did Giuliana really have to leave this early or is she hiding from what happened between us? Is she running the way I did?

Chiara joins me after breakfast, careful not to divulge anything to Nonna. But Isabella takes in the rips on my hands, the scratches along my arms and legs. When she asked about it Chiara primly responded that it was a surprise for Giuliana and we weren't going to say a word.

Isabella gives a rare, genuine smile, and a little nod to me as if to say thanks for taking Chiara along with me on this fool's errand. Chiara spends the majority of the morning with me, dragging what she can into the living room. We empty out kitchen cupboards and scuttle away when we hear scratching sounds that *have* to be a mouse. By early afternoon Chiara loses interest in the "renovation" project and I'm left to my own devices. It's hard not to panic at the scope of what I'm attempting.

Matt Palmer has never had to clean a damn thing his whole life, so I have no idea why my Italian alter ego, Matteo de Palma, decided to overhaul an old farmhouse. Heat bakes into the stone building. Lack of ventilation has sweat pouring off of my body and I have to shuck my shirt, pants slung low on my hips. I crack open the intact windows to let some of the pent-up dust escape.

Has no one been in here for the last decade?

I lean into the push broom, gathering years of dirt and grove earth that's blown into the house into a neat brown pile. Dust leaves the back of my throat scratchy, my sinuses heavy with the proof of neglect here. By the time afternoon rears its head I'm on the even-hotter second floor trying to figure out how the hell I'm going to organize all of this stuff.

There's no plan, no foresight. As usual I've jumped into something heedless of the work, ignoring the fact that I have no idea what I'm doing. Just like when I came here, and every second since. I collect broken pieces of glass and ceramic from windows and tiles, dropping them into a bucket I found under the kitchen sink with a clink.

Where the hell am I going to put all the furniture? Do I keep it? Toss it? I can't talk to Isabella about this (and not just because of the language barrier) because I'm not sure if Giuliana has mentioned the B&B aspect of things. I don't want to cause a fight between them if I can help it. For now, I'll try my best to clean it all up and I'll go from there.

My bones ache by the end of the day. Dragging heavy wood furniture does have consequences, it seems. A layer of grime lines my skin. It settles in the cracks on my hands and the furrows in my forehead where I've wiped sweat away too many times.

God, I need a shower. And a meal. And twelve hours of sleep.

Slinking back into the big house, I leave my gross shoes by the front door, shirt draped over my forearm. Smells drift down the hall from the kitchen and my stomach gurgles in response. Although I'd prefer to soak in a tub for at least an hour, I content myself with a quick shower—punishingly hot and fucking amazing. I watch brown slough off my body and swirl down the drain, proof of a hard day's work.

Tomorrow I'll start the washing portion of the day—counters, windows, floors. I can't wait to see things gleam. It might be stupid to be this excited for hard work, but I am. The chipped paint will have to be redone; windows replaced.

Isabella and Chiara are chatting in the kitchen when I join them. Giuliana is still nowhere to be seen and when I ask, Isabella is surprisingly tight-lipped about it.

"Nonna says she'll be gone for a few days, taking care of business. She'll be back eventually. No big deal," Chiara informs me, shrugging before digging back into her meal with gusto. Somehow, I don't buy it. What happened to send her away? Why was Patrizia so worried when we got back?

I dig into the meal—body tired and stomach desperate after a day of physical labor. I'll feel it tomorrow. I'm not unfit, but my muscles have never been used for this kind of work. I've exercised bits of myself I didn't even realize existed. Conversation flows mostly between Chiara and myself. She takes time to talk to Isabella too, however that conversation does not get translated for me.

I might have to convince Chiara to teach me some Italian. Not so that I can snoop, of course, but so I can be more helpful.

Yeah, right.

It's mild, barely a negative thought, but I'm surprised my brain still has the energy to want to fuck with me. I'll have to speak to someone about this, a professional or something. There can't be a coincidence that it started last year and has only gotten worse since. I can't outrun myself, that much is clear.

I keep the thought, ruminating on it through dinner until I collapse onto the bed and pass out within a few minutes.

I thought I was being resourceful, using YouTube to learn how to turn the water on at the mains. Brown liquid pours from creaking kitchen taps, spurting to a stop before exploding back out and onto me.

So resourceful. Super glad you decided to get this disgusting water all over yourself. Might as well take a bath in tetanus.

It can't be that bad, surely? The brown has to be dirt and maybe a little rust? Nothing dangerous, I hope.

Eventually I've gone around the farmhouse, opening each tap and running it until the sputtering water turns from a gross russet to mostly clear, if a little beige. Only then do I fill the bucket with water and soap. Warm water would be better, but beggars can't be choosers, especially when this is supposed to be a secret project.

Chiara checks in with me a few times to bring me some bottled water and a sandwich around lunch time. Since the majority of my work includes cleaning, she makes herself pretty scarce.

With each dip of a rag into the water—every bucket replaced once the water is gray with filth—things start to take shape.

The kitchen has beautiful handmade tile on the backsplash and floor. Although there are no appliances, just cupboards and the heavy farmhouse sink, it feels homier. The bathroom is a harder endeavor. I'll need something stronger than dish soap to tackle the years of water rings and yellowing ceramic. I'll bother

Isabella for some bleach or something later. I have no idea how long Giuliana will be away and I want to get as much done as I can.

I haul my tired body upstairs, eager to see the transformation there before the sun sets and visibility is too poor to work in. Repeating my process from downstairs, I drag furniture out of the way to sweep and wipe and wash. The bedframes stand like skeletons of a past life—ghosts of comfort and home.

In the second bedroom I move a desk away from the wall to sweep when I hear a clatter inside the wood. Most, if not everything, has been cleared out. What could possibly still be in here?

Tugging open a deep drawer, pens and pencils roll with the motion. There's a paperweight and some notepads. Nothing out of the ordinary. I'll need to bring a tote or something to put this stuff into. There's no point tossing it out if it can be repurposed somewhere else. Pulling the desk further away from the wall I feel part of the wood move under my hands.

A small compartment under the lip.

It slides out easily enough now that I know it's there. Inside I find yellowing paperwork, some of it brittle with age. It's in Italian, of course. Should I even be surprised at this point? Drawings and plans. It takes me a second to realize it's a rough mockup of the grove and some of these notes have to do with the business. Gathering it up, I tap the papers against the surface of the desk to straighten them out. The pile hits the wood with two soft thwacks and then something smaller flits out of the plans before I can straighten the stack again.

It floats to the ground like a leaf from a tree, swaying side to side for a second before it meets gravity and wood. My dirty fingertips pick up the square, one side smooth to the touch.

Fuck.

Staring up at me are faces, familiar and uncanny at the same time. Giuliana and Chiara's features are echoed on the man in the center, and beside him a woman I don't recognize. On the other side, with an arm thrown around the shoulders of Lorenzo Santoro is a face I've grown to despise. It's a kick to the gut to realize without the years and polish he looks just like me.

Time and money had hardened Tommaso's look into something distant and cold. Here, his hair is longer and curly like my own, haloed around his head. His cheeks stretch into a gigawatt smile, dimples carved deeply. Gone is the slicked back, short hair. Lost is the tailored suit and the scowl. It's like looking into a mirror to the past and I stumble back, sliding down the wall to slump on the floor.

My hands shake, the photograph blurring as the past catches up to me. Finally.

I turn the picture over—a single line in pencil. It's the same handwriting as on the contract, that flowy script of my father's signature continued here.

La mia famiglia
1989, Abundantia

I don't need Italian lessons to translate this. Not when his eyes sparkle with a joy I've never seen and affection jumps out of the image like a striking snake. This man is not my father. But I wish I'd met this man, at least once.

There will be no more cleaning tonight, no renovation or organizing. I've left this alone for too long and it can't wait anymore. My mind is made up on what I'm doing with the grove now but I still need to know what happened back then. How could everything have gone so wrong?

One person might be able to shed some light on the situation.

And she's in the big house right now.

She knows.

She's known this whole time. There's no way she could have looked at my face, seen *me*, and not also seen my father at the same time.

It's time to talk to Isabella. It's time for the truth.

I storm up to the house, my breath a caged, wild thing in my chest. The photograph shakes in my trembling grip and I almost start patting my pockets for my vape before I remember that it's been ages at this point since I've been able to use it.

I'm not sure what I expect to happen. I can only assume that my shit's about to be blown wide open, but I can't wait anymore. Running isn't an option at this point. I've avoided my father long enough. There's no rationality here, no more hiding. Giuliana might not know who I am and what me being here means, but I'm betting Isabella is more informed than she's been letting on.

The sun hangs lower, not quite sunset, and I could've gotten at least another hour in before the sky changed colors. Storming in through the front door, I don't bother with my shoes. I don't even check if she's even in the kitchen before I burst in.

Isabella looks up startled when I intrude, an explosion of ingredients on the countertop in front of her.

"Matteo!" she scolds, her hand against her heart as if to still the sudden ferocity of its beating.

"Isabella, we need to talk."

She must see something on my face—must know that what I have clutched in my hand is important.

"*Si*. Go shower. Then we talk."

My rage and confusion drain away when she speaks to me. In English.

"You speak *English*?" It sounds stupid but I'm being torn in so many different directions.

"Of course. Who do you think helps Chiara with her schoolwork?"

"I just assumed that Giuliana... and you... *why didn't you say anything?*"

"Giuliana is busy working. I look after them both," she says with a gravity I know I don't understand. I've never had to care for another person and see to their wellbeing on a daily basis. I know without her saying it that it's more than "looking after." It's feeding and clothing, and crying and worrying. It's midnights and early mornings, scabbed knees and rumbling tummies, and heartbreak.

"And also, maybe I don't like to talk to you. I speak Italian so you leave me in peace. Shower. You stink." She chases me out with a wave and I set the paperwork on the table we've eaten all our meals on, before escaping to my room.

The spray is scalding but it washes rust and dust from my skin. After a few minutes of scrubbing, I'm grounded again.

You knew this was going to happen, sooner or later.

Yeah, but I'd hoped for later. Much later. So much later I'd be gone and I wouldn't have to face Giuliana and my lies.

I pull on a pair of loose shorts and a t-shirt, my bare feet cool against the stone floors. They slap as I jog down the stairs, eager to get into this conversation.

The countertop is littered with flour, olive oil, tomatoes and fresh herbs, among other ingredients. On the stove something else bubbles away. Isabella glances up from what she's doing and we both look over at the stack of papers. The plans wait and hidden between yellowing sheets—the photograph.

"You know. You know who I am."

Her lips thin into a line, her face pulling down into unhappy wrinkles.

"It wasn't difficult to recognize you. You walk around with his name and his face. No measure of time is enough to erase him from this land and its memory."

"What happened? I... I came here—"

Isabella huffs a sigh, wiping her forehead with the back of her hand. She looks tired, weary in a way I haven't noticed. Is the stress of the harvest getting to her too? Where has Giuliana been and has Isabella had to pick up the slack in her absence?

"I know why you came. You lied. You are not the volunteer Giuliana was expecting."

She lets the words hang there for a second and when I don't deny it, she quirks a brow and carries on.

"I kept waiting for you to tell the truth, to open yourself up to us but it seems you never planned to. My granddaughter is working her hands to the bone and trying to run from her heart, and you stand here and lie to me. Be honest, Lorenzo is dead and now you came to *take*." She spits the last word like a curse and I lift my hand to stop her, to calm her like I would a wild animal.

"No."

She scoffs, sucking her teeth at me with a dismissive gesture thrown in for good measure.

"Maybe at first. But not now. I didn't know what I was going to find. I didn't even know it was an olive grove. My father's lawyer told me it was some kind of farm and I needed to come here and—"

"And *take*," she reiterates, and I nod.

"But I met her in Gravina and I didn't know who she was— only that she knocked me right off my feet and onto my ass."

My statement is met with a dry chuckle and Isabella sprinkles flour on the counter as I talk.

"I'm giving it to her. All of it. It's not mine and it's never been mine. The land belongs to her. It's in her blood."

Isabella sighs. Another pot beside her boils, steam swirling and her exhalation interrupts the cloud of heat. "Even if you tried to take it, she won't let you. I would leave, and go back to Gravina and my shop if we lost the grove. But Giuliana... *testarda*. Stubborn." She emphasizes it with a flick of her wrist.

"I'm *not* taking it. That might have been the plan at first but I know her." I care about her. "I can't hurt her like that."

"So, you hurt her with lies instead?"

"It's too late for that. It was never going to end happily for me. She doesn't need to know. I'll leave after the harvest and the grove will belong to her. I'll be nothing more than a summer distraction."

"*Idiota.*"

"Yeah, what else is new? But I also came here for answers." I head over to the table and rummage through the sheets of paper to grab the photograph again. It shakes in my grasp as I walk it over to Isabella, to show her what I've found.

She wipes her hands on the apron tied around her waist, flour sticking to the fabric in stripes. Taking the photo from me her face changes incrementally, softening, fingertips caressing Lorenzo's face. She does the same thing I did, turning it over to read the inscription on the back.

"I know nothing of my father's life before he came to New York. He all but erased himself. Changed his name. It was as if Tommaso de Palma was a demon he had to exorcize. Why? Why did he leave? He looks so happy in that picture."

It takes her a second to turn her focus from the photograph of her deceased son to my questions.

"They did everything together. High school friends. Your father grew up in a lonely home in Gravina. Your nonno was often away on business and Tommaso had no siblings. Lorenzo struggled at school, better with his hands than with the books. They balanced each other. Tommaso helped Lorenzo with studying and Lorenzo brought him to my shop after school. During holidays he came here to the grove."

I imagine my father, or more accurately myself at that age, trying to figure life out on my own. Isabella turns the heat off of one of the pots on the stove, the roiling water stilling after a minute or so.

"When my husband died a few years after they graduated, Lorenzo had to take over. He struggled. Tommaso stepped in, offered him a loan but Lorenzo refused. Tommaso called it an investment instead. They lived at the old farmhouse. They worked the land. It took a long time for the yield to come but they were so happy when it did."

"And then what happened?"

She hands me the photo, turning away to pull a few potatoes out of a now-cooling pot with a pair of tongs. It feels so strange to me that we're doing this here. My past is being unfurled before me in a cozy Italian kitchen. Chiara's little ears are probably nearby and about to be my undoing.

"Where's Chiara?"

Isabella laughs, a harsh sound. "She is helping Patrizia with a litter of kittens they found near the farmhouse. Don't worry. Your secrets stay in this room."

"I know I don't deserve that, but thank you anyway."

Isabella shrugs as if to say it's a stupid choice but it's mine to make.

"What happened to them?" I repeat.

Isabella points at the photograph, to the woman's face.

"Young love. Stupidity." The words are filled with venom and I take a closer look at her face. I find none of Giuliana in her.

"Not their mother?"

"No, thank God." She says it with such vehemence I wonder if there's more to it. What did the unraveling of these friendships and relationships look like on this side of the world?

"So, she came between them?"

Isabella nods and opens her mouth, no doubt to spew some more angry words, but the front door slams shut in the distance. Isabella's words are a low rush when she speaks.

"Now you know. No good looking too long at the past. My concern is now. With my granddaughter. What is going on with you and Giuliana?" Isabella hits me with that stare—the one I know she's perfected over years of being a mom and grandmother.

"She wants to keep things professional, and it's for the best."

"But?"

I suck in the aromatic air, my heart constricting in my chest.

"She's... devastating. There's no way I'm going to walk out of here and be okay." It feels good to be able to talk about it—to say the words out loud. I'm not going to go so far as to drop the BIG word, but this is accurate enough.

"Then fix it. Make it work." Clipped, brokering no argument.

"I can't, not while I hold the grove hostage. I need to find a lawyer so I can sign it over officially."

Isabella nods, tapping her finger to her chest as if she's ready to hook me up with someone, when we hear a voice break through our conversation.

"*Sono tornata!*" Giuliana shouts from down the hall and my stomach drops. I grab the papers, gathering them into a pile again and clutching them to my chest.

"Give them to me." Isabella hisses under her breath, hand outstretched. I hesitate for a second but if she's going to out me it'll happen with or without these papers. "I'll bring them to you later, with some more information. For now, you stay. Fix."

"Isabella, please don't leave me with her. I don't know what to do with all this mess inside me," I plead, dumbly.

She ignores me. The papers are tucked under her arm as she walks toward her granddaughter, and I wait for my world to collapse. No arguing with her, and my respect for her only grows. She's raised these girls and kept everything together despite loss and grief beyond my comprehension.

Wouldn't it be nice to have grown up with someone like her around to care?

It's not as mean as usual, more like a longing that we both share and I can't help but agree. A grandmother would have been nice; a sister and a stable home where you could rely on everyone, even nicer.

Giuliana enters the kitchen, blinking when she sees me standing there near the ingredients.

"Nonna said..." she trails off, confused at my presence before she collects herself. "Nonna asked me to finish making the focaccia."

I look down at the counter, at the flour and potato and various other ingredients and my confusion grows. "As far as I know focaccia is a bread, so where does the potato come in?"

"It's specific to the region. The potato makes the bread softer."

"Do you mind if I watch?" So I can spend time with you. So I can experience a bit of the culture I never got to enjoy.

Giuliana looks reluctant but shrugs. Coming up to the counter, she adds flour and yeast, swirling them together with her fingers. Once sufficiently combined she pushes the potatoes through some kind of press to deposit them out as potato bits. Better to incorporate, I suppose?

"How does this work? I've never seen bread made before."

"Focaccia Pugliese is different from other kinds. We add potato which changes the consistency and gives it a more robust taste. First, I'll make a little flour volcano and I'll slowly add the other ingredients until it's a dough. Then comes kneading and finally resting so it can proof. Only after all that can we put it in the oven. It's a labor of love and worth the wait."

My stupid heart wants me to contribute to the conversation —feel it flow between us—but the extent of my cooking knowledge is that episode of Schitt's Creek where they're arguing about what it means to "fold in the cheese." What *does* it mean to fold in the cheese?

Giuliana adds the potato and then the rest of the ingredients. Her hands work the dough until it's incorporated enough to move around the work station. Sprinkling some more flour on the worktop, the dough ball glistens from the water and olive oil on its surface.

The silence should be awkward—hell, I'm standing watching her knead dough—mere feet between us. But it's the most delicious feeling being this close.

"About the other night—" she starts.

"I'm sorry. I put you in an uncomfortable position and it wasn't right. I should have consulted you on all of it. Getting caught up in stuff is a bad habit of mine, but it's not an excuse."

Her hands still, and she looks up at me. Her eyes are naked, her mouth soft, and I wish I could close the distance between us. I'd kill to kiss away the uncertainty I see there—the conflict of the chasm between us.

"Where did you go?"

"Umberto. He called Arturo and tried to move our harvest date. Thankfully Arturo had the foresight to call the grove to confirm before he did. It could have been a disaster."

Fatigue sits in the hollows under her eyes and I want nothing more than to take all this away.

"I'm getting so sick of that motherfucker."

"*Matteo!*" she admonishes, her hands gripping the dough.

"I mean it. Something's got to be done."

Giuliana nods. "I've been in contact with Arturo. Between him and Nonna, I think we have a plan. There's still some finalizing to do, so I'll be in and out before the harvest. Hopefully we can pull it all together without any further sabotage from his end."

"Oh, he has no idea what's coming. Umberto will rue the day he tried to mess with the Santoro women."

Some of the stress melts from her shoulders at my joke and Giuliana manages a half smile. God, she's stunning.

"The grove feels so empty when you're not here." It's impossible to miss the longing in my tone. I know I've said too much but I can't care anymore. We're on borrowed time.

Heat fills her cheeks at my statement, her gaze filling with emotion before she looks away. Giuliana refocuses her efforts on the focaccia dough with renewed vigor. Saying that was stupid but I have nothing left to lose. I'm hyper aware of our breathing and the little hitch in hers before she speaks again.

"Matteo, we're so close to the harvest. I don't want to mess this up."

"I know how important *Abundantia* is to you. I'm not going to jeopardize that."

Giuliana's voice is soft when she responds. "I'm not talking about the grove."

"Lia?" Stepping up to her back, I close the distance between us—catching her between my body and the counter. We don't touch, but I can feel the body heat coming off of her and bask in the faint scent of her skin. My lungs stretch with the desperate breath I take, hoping to imprint it onto my memory. It's sunlight and earth soaked in the first raindrops of the season, clean linen and the tiniest hint of something floral. Giuliana smells like summer and everything I've been missing my whole life.

"Please. We're friends. Everything is muddy enough as it is." She punches into the dough as if it's personally offended her. Hell, she's probably picturing my face.

Her hair is tied up into a messy bun. A few errant strands

escape their confines and I caress the back of her neck with my thumb, unable to keep my distance anymore. She halts, her breath catching in her throat, and her body leaning back into mine.

"Teo..." It's choked, the words a mere wisp and I know that she feels the same way I do. The nickname was real. I didn't imagine it that night. The implication of it spreads through me with unbearable heat. My name is on her lips and my limbs are molten honey at the sound of it. Giuliana is similarly affected. Her body melting into mine tells the truth even as she tries to deny it. Why won't she just let herself have this?

I lean into her to whisper back, to exorcize some of the yearning threatening to drag me under. "I can't stop thinking about you. You haunt me. The feel of your skin, the sound of your moans. I remember it all and it's torture."

Her hands grip the countertop. The curve of her back presses against my chest and I feel like I'm going to burst out of my skin, as if this emotion is too much to physically contain.

"Tell me you think about it, too. Put me out of my misery."

I hear the hitch of her inhalation—the shudder as it leaves her lungs and her body eases against me. Wrapping my arm around her, I pull her tighter to me. Splaying my hand across her soft stomach, every hot curve of her is pressed against my body. My lips find that spot beneath her ear, along the side of her neck—the one I know will raise goosebumps on her skin.

Giuliana whimpers. Her hand raises up to grip my hair, arching her neck to fall into the sensation.

"*Tell me.*" Please. I can't be alone in this. I can't stand it.

"You're being cruel," she says. It's bordering on a sob—an angry huff—and a malicious part of me delights in knowing I affect her as much as she does me. Her hand drops from my hair, clutching the countertop again.

"You're the one driving me to madness. Watching you every day. Seeing the sunlight catch on your hair. Hearing your laugh, watching it flow through your body. Your hands teaching mine, showing me the care you coax into something from nothing. So close and not close enough."

My hands stroke down the outsides of her arms, prying her grip from the counter and threading our fingers together. I work our hands into the dough, feeling it give beneath us, and her body moves against mine as we do.

Heat rises within my core and I know it'll go unanswered, unsatisfied. But this is more than I hoped for and more than she should allow. It'll only wreck us more when I leave.

"Matteo, we can't."

"We won't. Let's just have this moment, no further."

I can tell she's thinking about it—considering the ramifications of letting down her guard and crossing this line, even if it's just a tiptoe.

"I miss you."

It's an admission I hadn't planned to make, one that isn't very sensical considering I'm closer to her now than I've been in weeks. But it holds true. I want so much more than this. I want it all.

Giuliana nods. There's no more talking. She can't say it —can't give in to this—no matter how much we both might want it. We stand like that, getting the dough ready. Working it, rolling it, our bodies undulate in their own kind of dance that serves only to seduce, never satisfy. I'm acutely aware of our bodies touching. It's impossible to tell how long we've been here but the sun dips toward the horizon and Giuliana turns the *pasta e fagioli* on the stove to a bare simmer.

I stand, shadowing her, caught in her gravity as we pretend time doesn't exist. She works the dough into a longer, rectangular shape and places it into a pan. Spreading the pan with olive oil that I'd die to lick off her fingers but don't.

"When it's done resting, I'll chop the tomatoes, sprinkle them over the surface, and crack salt over the top. For now, we give it a few hours to rest." Her voice is husky, overly loud after our weighted silence.

Giuliana shows me how springy the dough is, both of us creating divots on the top that are supposed to add to the texture. I don't step out of her orbit until she has to cover it and put it aside to rest, and it astounds me how far a few steps take me. We won't have a moment like this again, not so close to harvest. Not with everything riding on this succeeding.

I'll finish up the renovation (as much of it as I can) and get the papers signed over to her. No one, least of all me, will take this from her—from her family. And I'll tuck these moments away for when my mind threatens to drown me in hate. I'll know what I had here, what I chose to protect, and it will be enough.

"It'll take a while, likely overnight before we will bake it. There's nothing else to be done now."

Just like that the spell is broken. Giuliana wraps her arms around her abdomen, as if to shield herself from something— from me. I nod and turn away before I do something else we'll regret, like sampling her lips and losing myself.

The sunset paints the sky like a bruise, purple and red that melt into flame.

I stand there until my body feels like a stone and the cool breeze clears my mind. In the distance Isabella calls for Chiara to come back to the house. They must be getting ready for dinner, the soup somehow not appetizing after all that.

Chiara's little legs come bounding up the hill, and she pauses to look at me while catching her breath. She smiles up at me and I know she's about to launch into a breathless ramble about the kittens. But she stops, looking at me, puzzled. Isabella calls out for her again and she shrugs, rushing toward the house.

Chiara looks over her shoulder as she goes, giggling, the words almost lost in her haste. "Matteo... why do you have flour in your hair?"

My slip—my selfish indulgence—has the benefit of extra space between me and Giuliana. Since the night we spent in the same room—that night and every one that followed—I've dreamed of her. Tangled limbs and sweet kisses, that elusive idea of my nickname on her lips, all of it haunts me. I wake up aching and hard, and angry at how ridiculous it is. After our night in the kitchen, it took a cool shower to even touch the fire she'd ignited, but even that wasn't enough, and I lost myself in my hand with her name on my tongue.

I've never been this caught up in a woman before. Maybe for a night or two but this—repeated torture in the form of dreams —is new. And it just makes me crave her. The closer I want to get, the further she pulls away. Or at least that's how it feels.

Logically, I know she's dealing with preparation and the proverbial hanging sword that is Umberto. It's on her to oversee the details that will make for a successful and efficient season, which means testing out the weird raking tools for shaking olives from their branches.

Inspections are underway on the nets to catch the fruit, and the rows I've gotten so used to walking will soon be covered by a sea of synthetic material. More and more people show up to the grove and I have no idea what to expect. We've spent so much time on what goes into making a good product and the result of all this work, but the big day is upon us and I'm wholly unprepared.

So, I do what I do best and procrastinate. Giuliana lets me. The distance between us is a canyon of words unsaid and yearning unsatisfied.

Isabella and I have a tentative truce, even though we both know I'll be causing Giuliana at least a small amount of hurt in the next few weeks. My deadline from Alan is fast approaching and I need Isabella's help ASAP if I'm going to be able to protect the grove before I lose everything.

We pile into the little Fiat, super close to the ground and tighter than I'd prefer. Isabella does her mirror checks, leans her arm across the back of my seat, and proceeds to reverse out of the alcove the car's been kept in. Her spin to straight jolts my stomach and I'm a little glad we skipped breakfast this morning because from the look of things she's a reckless driver.

You don't have room to complain considering the menace you are on your Vespa.

Fair. Fair.

The drive into Gravina rushes by, although that could have something to do with me spending every second staring out of the window with longing. I didn't have time to drink it in when I first left for the grove a little over two months ago, but as a passenger I'm gifted with beautiful countryside zipping by. It helps that Giuliana isn't here to distract my gaze.

Gravina looks like part of the landscape. Its buildings have sprung up and multiplied on top of each other into a small sprawl down the hill. The streets I'd searched before don't feel as novel now, but their beauty isn't diminished at all. Cobblestones and brick and asphalt all meld together as the old and the new give way to each other.

The lawyer we've come to is in the new part of the city and

Isabella maneuvers into a tight parking spot in a way that would make anyone from the DMV weep with joy. I follow her like a duckling into the office building, glass doors closing behind us and a sleek secretary greeting us with a bright smile.

We're shuffled into a private room, an empty chair at the desk across from us. I want to ask her how she found us an appointment so quickly, or how we're going to pull this off, but questions are wasted on Isabella. Her determination is something I won't challenge or question—not if I want to avoid getting chewed out.

The lawyer doesn't keep us waiting long. The first thing I note is how he looks nothing like Alan. His face shows the proof of living and all the emotions that come with it. Lines fan out from the corners of his eyes—years of smiling and squinting into the sun. A few deep-carved lines run across his forehead in a physical show of rumination and worry. Dark hair interwoven with silvery strands is coiffed away from his face and so thick I'm sure Alan would sell a kidney for that kind of volume.

We rise to greet him—me with a handshake, Isabella with some cheek kisses and she ends up patting the side of his face with affection.

"*È bello rivederti, Isabella,*" he says to Nonna and she gives what I'm pretty sure is a *giggle*? I didn't even know she could do anything other than sarcastic snorts and huffs of humor.

"*Anche per me.*" She gestures to me before speaking again. "*Questo è Matteo. Lui è Americano.*"

"Ah."

I know what that "ah" means. I've heard it multiple times since arriving here. "*Ah, I have to switch to English.*" or "*Ah, he can't understand us.*"

"It's a pleasure to meet you, Matteo. I'm Andrea. What can we help with today?"

I pull my passport and the contract out from the folder Isabella so graciously provided, one containing the plans and other business-related documents I found in the old farmhouse. Andrea accepts the mess I've tried to smooth out—corners still curling and creases I've worried my hands over to try and flatten.

"I came into a stake on some land. Since I have no interest in upholding the original agreement my father made by claiming a non-return on the investment, I'd like to relinquish it all to the current co-owner, Giuliana Santoro."

The words take a weight off my chest, one I hadn't even realized was choking me. Isabella rests her hand on my bouncing knee, so much like her granddaughter had at that wedding. Though hers is dappled with freckles and age spots—papery skin with veins like tributaries branching up her fingers.

Andrea takes his time scrutinizing the contract and pauses on the last page, much like I had, his fingertips tracing over a different signature. He takes a deep breath before he turns his attention to us again.

"So, you're Tommaso's boy?" It drives a sharp pang through my body, radiating out from my chest.

It's different. Other. It doesn't rankle the way the question usually does—the one I'm used to. Someone muttering "Oh, you're Palmer's kid" followed by a disappointed once-over. This is wistful. I nod, unable to muster much else around the weird lump in my throat.

"My father helped them negotiate this contract. I knew Tommaso as a boy. I'm sorry to hear he passed on."

There it is again—a weird swirl in my gut like I'm about to dissolve under too much pressure. Maybe it's because he didn't phrase it as being sorry for "my loss" since all that usually does is prompt my inner asshole.

Can't lose what you never had.

No, this phrasing emphasized Tommaso no longer walked

among us. Not just gone from Italy but the world. There's more than a hole. The absence is absolute this time.

Get it together. You never gave much of a fuck before. There are more important matters to deal with.

"It would be simple enough to arrange a new contract, one where you state you're relinquishing your father's claim and the caveats around the investment."

"It's time-sensitive." I know it's rude to push it, but I have no idea what Alan will do or how things are going to look now. I have to make this work before I lose agency.

Andrea lifts his brows, those forehead lines moving in question.

"My father left very specific instructions in his will when he died. If I don't prove I have what it takes to run the company by the anniversary of his death, I lose the right to my inheritance. The grove was my test—one I failed since I have no intention of jeopardizing Giuliana or her family. It's imperative I get this sorted before the deadline so the Santoros don't lose *Abundantia* to Palmer Enterprises."

Isabella gasps but I avoid her gaze, even though I can feel it burning a hole into the side of my face.

Andrea sees something in my expression, or his connection to my father is enough to sway him, because he nods.

"Give me a few days and I'll have a new one ready to sign."

Standing, I thrust my hand out to shake his again, and take my leave before the emotions inside my chest have a chance to leak out.

One part of me hates how rude and brusque I've been. The other predominantly stupid side that runs most of my life is done, already focused on the next thing. Now I'm in town it's the perfect time to find some stuff for the farmhouse. I can take time to see a doctor.

I can't keep pretending my years of fucking around have no

consequences. It's better to find out now. If I'm starting out on a new leaf, I'd rather know where I'm at to plan accordingly. Sticking my head in the sand has gotten me nothing but anxiety.

"Matteo," Isabella says somewhere behind me. A second, more insistent and intimidating one following.

"*Matteo de Palma.*"

Stopping on the sidewalk, I turn to face the short old lady scowling up at me.

"What?"

Rolling her eyes, Isabella waves her hand at me in frustration. "Don't '*what*' me. You didn't tell me what would happen if you let go of *Abundantia.*"

"Because it doesn't matter." Not when the alternative is them losing their home—their history and lifeblood.

"Of course, it matters. Just because you made mistakes and lied to my granddaughter and our family doesn't mean you should suffer."

"Wow, way to guilt trip me while giving me grace."

"I'm Catholic. Guilt comes free with the rosary beads."

"What's more important is making sure you are taken care of. There's no way to know what my father's right-hand-man will do when I don't meet the terms of the inheritance. All I can do is my best to protect you." I give her what I hope is a reassuring smile.

"Now, I'm sure you've figured out I'm fixing up the old farmhouse for Giuliana. Would you help me find what I need?"

Having someone to translate would be extremely useful.

"Furniture might be difficult depending on what is in stock," she says, "but we can get paint and more cleaning supplies— some decor."

"I'm reusing as much of the furniture as possible and polishing or sanding what I can to spruce it up. We'll need mattresses and pillows." I tick off a few things in my mental checklist and Isabella and her little legs keep up with me easily once we head out to find items at various stores.

Her suggestions are super helpful, especially when we go to the hardware store—things like primer and a long roller being better than paint brushes for wall painting. All stuff a regular person would have known.

But you've been stuck in a glass cage for years, every whim catered to. Useless.

Not anymore. That's not who I am anymore. This renovation is for Giuliana's future but it's also something I can do to prove myself—to show I'm better than I was. Not to Alan. Not to Giuliana since she never even knew me before. No, this is for me.

Between tins of paint and a wall of swatches, I breach the silence.

"Giuliana mentioned Umberto tried to mess with the harvest date and you had a plan to take care of it, but didn't say any more."

Isabella's hands ball into fists at her side, strong from years of work. "That man... so greedy and so good at pretending. Lorenzo didn't see it and Giuliana found out too late. I was so focused on caring for Lorenzo and Chiara, I missed it."

"It's not your fault. Men like him—like *me*—we keep our cards close to the vest."

Scoffing, the rage melts from her body. "Matteo, you are nothing like him."

The words soothe something in me I didn't know was smarting until now. And then the comfort is promptly dashed by Isabella's sharp tongue.

"Even if you didn't look like your father, I saw you from a mile away. You've watched Giuliana like a lovesick calf for months and there's not a mean bone in your body. If you really wanted to take the grove you could have done it from New York with one phone call to the lawyer and an expensive investigation."

Words of defense spring to my lips but she's not wrong. Alan ordered me to lie low and stake my claim. I could have done it from my loft with a few emails or calls and stayed under the radar. Binge-watching old TV shows and weeks of takeout delivery would have kept me busy for the rest of the time.

"I think you came here to learn about the past, about your father. Mostly, I think you came here to learn about yourself."

Her words ripple through me, the pebble of truth far-reaching inside my chest. So, I deflect. "*I* think you're far too wise for your own good and you believe it gives you permission to say and do whatever you want."

"Audacity comes with age, not wisdom. I know plenty of old people who say whatever stupid thing springs to mind."

Laughing, the tension and tightness around my ribs ease.

"So, this plan for Umberto—the one you cooked up with Arturo..."

A hot blush spreads up Isabella's cheeks and she wrings her hands together. Does she have a *crush* on the old man? I didn't see any proof of a wife when we went to the mill but then again, I was preoccupied in Giuliana's presence.

"I don't want to jeopardize anything. I'll be doing some work on the plan while we're in Gravina today and Arturo is doing what he can from his end. We should know within the next few days if it worked."

The blush blazes deeper when she says his name, but her lips tuck into a staunch line and I know this conversation is over. We pack our finds into the Fiat with each new purchase until we can fit no more. Isabella heads out for her secret plan and I walk over to the local clinic for tests.

Digging my fingernails into the flesh of my palm, I distract myself from the bite of the needle. Blood pools into little vials and the tie around my bicep cuts into my skin. It strikes me as I stare down at the crook of my elbow that I've never been this tanned. My hair has gotten much longer—a mess of curls—and my stubble is more of a short beard since I haven't been shaving daily.

Matt was considered lazy, sure, but Matteo is the first time I've actually felt like I look laid-back. The anxiety and that fucking voice in my mind may not be much improved, but there is something to be said for the peace that comes with doing the right thing.

The nurse sticks a band-aid to my arm where a droplet of blood pools on my skin. Labeling each sample, she informs me I'll be notified in a few days when the results come back. Even if nothing happens between me and Giuliana, the information is useful. I can protect myself and others better if I know what's going on in the body I've neglected and abused for far too long.

Isabella is at the same cafe I left her at and we head back to *Abundantia* as soon as she's wrapped up her conversation. Walking the cobblestones to the car, I take in Gravina for what might be one of the last times. After I sign the contract, there'll be no reason to come back. Barring the need for more supplies, I'll be leaving *Abundantia* straight for the closest international airport after the harvest. Two weeks.

Two weeks to pull together Giuliana's idea and help show her there are people who believe in what she's doing here.

Once we make it back through the curving countryside, Isabella drops me off as close to the farmhouse as she can and I unload my haul. Step one is washing the walls and laying down some tarp to paint them. Next will be sanding and treating the furniture I can salvage. Lastly, I'll clean and polish the brass bed frames, fixtures, and faucets until they gleam. I'll order mattresses online and pray they can deliver out here, but I've got bedsheets and blankets, and decorative pillows sorted.

I work until after the light has leached from the room, darkness making progress impossible. A lantern might be needed soon if I'm going to pull this off. Chiara brings some of her kittens by to play but I'm not much company when drenched in sweat and struggling.

After the third F-bomb I gently asked her to leave, if only to save my own skin. The last thing I need is Isabella on my case because the little girl is cussing up a storm. By the time I've walked back to the big house, crickets and starlight leading the way, the family has already eaten. Isabella's left something in the fridge for me but for all intents and purposes I'm alone.

Sitting in the kitchen, moonlight filters into the room and lends some illumination. I could turn on the light, but I won't be here long enough to justify it. Instead, I let the evening settle around me—darkness and quiet. Peace.

The hallway upstairs is quiet when I head to bed. Chiara and Isabella are already asleep. But there's a crack of light under Giuliana's door—a slice of gold calling to me so strongly I have to turn away to avoid it. I shut myself in my room and attempt to clear my mind and scrub away the lingering dirt from my day's work in the shower.

When that doesn't work to still my thoughts, I pull out my journal—stroking my fingertips over the blank lined page after my previous entry. My writing degree was intended to be spiteful, a way to get back at my dad for expecting me to get my MBA to take over the company. I never expected writing would end up helping me deal with myself and my feelings. My pen scratches against the paper, words indented onto the page.

I did it. I went to a lawyer today and gave up my portion of the grove. I don't want to take Abundantia away from them for the sake of my father's money I don't want to be that man. Thomas made his own mistakes, ones I'm only just starting to unravel. He missed out on this, lost his best friend, and left his home behind. Even if Thomas turned out to be a total asshole, I'm hoping Tommaso left for the right reasons. The same way I plan to.

It's too late for me and Giuliana. Too many lies stand between us, so no matter how much I feel for her and how desperate I am to stay, I lost whatever place I might have had by her side. It would have been so much simpler if I'd come out and admitted who I was when I first got here. But I wouldn't have gotten all this time with her if she knew my initial intentions. I fear I'll never have the chance to tell her, to show her, before I need to leave. Whether she finds out about me or not, it's not fair to stick around past the harvest.

I'm going to miss this so much.
Not just Giuliana but everything. Waking up to birdsong, breathing in air that tastes like sunlight baking into the earth. Isabella pretending not to speak English to mess with me. Chiara chasing after us with whatever story she has to tell that day.
And everything I could have had with Giuliana if I'd been a better man.
That's what hurts the most. I've finally found something that makes the pain and doubt worth it. The one who makes me want to be a better person and who I'll risk everything for. And when I leave, I'll carry this love home with me like a souvenir of hurt.

Because I do love Giuliana. So, she comes first. Everything else is just background noise. I have to make this worth it for her. I have to finish the farmhouse before the harvest and then somehow, I have to find the strength to let go of everything I've ached for my whole life.

I slap the journal shut, shoving it in the desk drawer. It was supposed to be a way to calm my feelings, not ramp them up to an unbearable level. All that's left is to gather the courage needed to ruin my whole life. *Lovely.*

It took Andrea longer than I'd have liked, but he managed the new contract in time. I channel all my frustration and anxiety into the farmhouse and by the end of the week it actually looks like *something*. The walls are a fresh soft blue in the main living areas and gentle sage in the bedrooms. Wood floors gleam despite being pocked and scarred from many years of use.

Isabella even got someone to fix the broken front window. Mattress delivery was as covert as I could manage it. I even bamboozled a couch into the deal which now sits in the living area with decorative throw pillows finishing the look. Chiara ran interference by bringing the kittens into Giuliana's office while the van kicked dust up along the drive. There's been this unspoken pact between all of us. And now we have something to show for it.

I need to head into town to sign the contract but this evening I'll finally show Giuliana what I've been up to. A week until harvest is cutting it close but I've managed it, with help of course. It really does take a village and I'll be sorry to leave this one.

The clinic called with my results so I head there first—relieved when I get a clean bill of health and for the first time in my life, I don't take it for granted. I actually care about the fact that I'm not physically rotting from the inside after using my body as an escape. The vaping's been hard to kick but ultimately, it's for the best. New leaf Matteo won't be stumbling around clubs trying to crawl out of his skin. No, I'll be slowing down, I think.

I can't flee what I'm feeling, and in trying, I've made mess after mess. It's clean-up time.

My Vespa vibrates down the road in Gravina. By the time I make it to the lawyer's office my hair is damp with sweat from the helmet. The curls cool against my neck with the breeze winding down the street. Hanging the helmet from the handlebar, I prop up the bike in plain sight from the office window.

The secretary waves me through as soon as I step inside and Andrea has the new contract ready—tucked in my folder atop my passport and the old agreement that led me here.

"I'm sorry it's taken so long. Since you're a citizen but not a resident here, it complicated matters. But it's all taken care of. I need a few signatures from you and then you should be good to go!" Andrea pushes the stack of papers toward me and my signature slashes above the line, Matteo de Palma now for real, not just in the pages of my passport.

He flips each fresh leaf of paper and explains the sections to me before I sign. I appreciate it. He's probably covering his ass but it's nice to know he's forthcoming.

"I do have a question before we finish up here. Giuliana's talking about adding a B&B on the grove in addition to her volunteer program. Does she need any extra permissions to do that, since the land is probably only sectioned for farming?"

"Ah *agriturismo*, it's a good idea! In the villa?"

"The old farmhouse," I say, and his brows raise in surprise.

"That surprises me, but it makes sense and gives the guests some privacy."

My curiosity gets the better of me and I ask before I can think it through. "Why is that a surprise?"

The house is sitting there, decaying. Why wouldn't it be the immediate thought?

"After the accident I didn't think her family wanted anything to do with the farmhouse, but now that Lorenzo is dead, I suppose it doesn't make much of a difference."

"Accident?"

He smacks his forehead. "You look so much like your father I forget you're not from here. After Aria's death, Lorenzo had the big house built and your father left the country. There were some rumors because he left so quickly, but it was just a tragic accident. The incident drove them apart though, and Lorenzo never spoke of your father again."

"She *died*?" The word "rumors" ricochets inside my head and a chill snakes up my spine. Isabella left out some important information.

"Yes, but like I said, it was just an accident and it's in the past. With regards to Giuliana needing permission, I can give you a list of things she needs to register it as an *agriturismo*."

While he jots down bulleted steps on a lined page for me, I flick my last signature onto the final page. I'm left with this weird bittersweet twist in my chest. I want to find out more about my father and his time here, but part of me never wants to think about him ever again. Regardless, I need to focus on the present. I've let go of my part in Palmer Enterprises and what my father left for me when he died. All that matters now is the legacy I'm determined to protect: Giuliana's.

"Can you do me another favor? Can you email and fax this contract over to this person?" I slide Alan's business card over to Andrea and thank him for his help. He makes a copy of the new contract and when I head back to *Abundantia* it's with a brittle determination to see it through.

I seek Giuliana out, Andrea's note about the B&B in my back pocket and the contract safely delivered to Isabella. She's promised to keep it to herself until I'm gone and I can only hope she'll stick to that.

Staring out at the grove, Giuliana sits in her office with her head resting in her hand. She must be so exhausted. Startling when she sees me, her fatigue gives way to a carefully blank expression.

"Something wrong?"

"No, I just wanted to check in with you. It's been a couple of days." Since that day in the kitchen where we played with fire and the smoke still cloys the back of my throat with emotion I can't put a name to.

"Running things alone is harder than I anticipated. Even though he was too sick to do the work, my father was there to give me advice last year. Umberto was here to help with the heavy lifting."

"Is the issue with him resolved?" I've been so busy with the farmhouse I forgot to pester Isabella with more questions.

"It seems like it. Between Nonna's network from her old shop in Gravina, and Arturo's mill connections with all the groves in the area... they did a fantastic job of getting him blacklisted. No one in this industry will touch him with a ten-foot pole now. His reputation is ruined."

"Wow, remind me not to get on their bad sides. Again. Your nonna only just started speaking to me in English. The last thing I need is for her to ice me out again."

Her tired expression shifts into a tiny smile and I tuck it away like a little charm—mine to keep.

"She made me promise not to tell you. Our bet was whether the volunteer would leave within the first month. If you proved yourself by then she'd cut the act. I told her that first night not to underestimate you."

"So *that's* what the bet was all about. I've been wondering.

What did you win for being right?" I smirk and raise an eyebrow.

Giuliana huffs out a little laugh that turns somber. "My prize was a volunteer who stuck around. Which, I'm sorry. I know I should be doing better with the program but stuff is getting away from me and..."

And I keep pushing the limits—testing the line that stands between us.

"I understand. I..."

Thoughts of what I *should* say dance around my mind: I'm leaving. I don't want to go. I've never felt like this before. But I settle for something tamer, more neutral.

"I have a surprise for you."

Reluctance twists her features. Her mouth—that gorgeous fucking mouth—ready to shoot me down without even knowing my intention. Given how my previous surprise went, I can't blame her.

"For *Abundantia,*" I clarify, emphasizing it isn't personal. It's not intimate like the last time I caught her off guard and ended up coercing her into a fake engagement.

It's all I have to say because she rises. Pushing her chair into the hollow of the desk, she dusts her hands down the wrinkles that have gathered on her outfit from hours of working at the desk.

We make it most of the way down the path, toward the brambles that are no longer there. And then she hangs back, her eyes large in question. I don't know if she knows the history of this place, the lives that blazed and faded here. My father and hers, and the stain of broken hearts and severed ties.

Turning, I reach out my hand for her to take and she stares at it with hesitation—as if this choice takes a toll I can't understand. But I do. I know. Slipping her hand into my palm, I thread my work-roughened fingers between hers. Calluses to match. Her eyes are large as she takes in the neatly cleared path—the gravel that's been tamed into an actual strip leading to the house.

And up ahead... light invites us in.

Gold from the lanterns beside the front door pools on the ground, refracting against the cut glass covers and overflowing. The warm glow illuminates creeping vines on the facade of the house, lending to that rustic feel. The sanded and newly-painted front door beckons and I urge her forward to do the honors, dropping the bliss of her hand in favor of watching her soak it all in. Sheer curtains impede the view but give enough of a tease that we can tell the interior is not the way it was left.

Her hand rests on the knob, her breath shuddering out as she looks back at me with fear in her eyes.

"I wanted to thank you. Being here with you... working alongside you this summer, I finally understood what's been holding me back. You gave me the opportunity to delve into my roots and experience a joy I can't begin to put words to. The least I could do was give you a tiny leg up for you to chase your dreams." I try to keep my voice steady. I keep my heart shoved down and away from my throat lest the words shake and the emotion churning in me leak out.

"Teo..." Her eyes shine, tears and disbelief.

"I didn't have time to do it up the way I wanted but I did the best that I could. I've been thinking about this since the moment you mentioned it and after our trip... I needed to show you it's possible. I believe in this, and you." This time I do get a little choked up and she gives me a watery smile before pushing the door open and stepping inside.

Gone is the debris, the bird's nest by the window, and the dust that cloyed the air so badly I wanted to choke. Grime and years have been erased and in their place is why I've scoured Pinterest for hours.

Italian Farmhouse Aesthetic. It'd taken too long for me to realize I had to add the fucking word "aesthetic" to the search or I'd just keep getting products to buy. But it worked. New and old merge into a warm, welcoming space. A large rug covers the worst of the scuffs on the floor.

The plush couch I'd snuck in under her nose is the perfect place to curl up with a drink in hand. There's no television, but you don't need one when the windows open to glimpses of the grove.

Her hand at her throat, breath coming in little gasps, Giuliana walks the space. Fingertips brushing against the smooth new paint, her other hand roams free. Ending on the edge of the dining table that's been given some extra love to make it shine.

She doesn't say a word as she absorbs it all, wandering into the bathroom to admire the new shower curtain and sparkling surfaces. Giuliana touches and takes in the hallway walls and inhales as if new paint is her favorite smell in the world. When she looks back at where I wait in the threshold her eyes rise above the lintel and the emotion shimmering there tips over, overwhelmed.

Above the doorway hangs her past and mine. That old and weathered sign is the focal point, letting you know exactly where you are and where you're headed when you step foot outside of this house.

Abundantia. Abundance.

She's shown me a life of abundance where before there was only emptiness and dissatisfaction.

"It was a bitch to try and sneak it out of your office. I had to do it under cover of darkness and try not to wake the whole house."

A sob catches in her throat and she clutches at the banister behind her, easing herself down to sit on one of the stairs.

"Hey now, you haven't even seen the bedrooms yet. I had to ask Nonna how to make a bed properly with hotel corners. I've never seen anyone so precise over a rectangle of fabric." The joke fizzles, the edge of her mouth barely lifting as she's swept away in something I can't begin to guess at.

Crossing the invisible line between us, I walk toward her with sure steps and cup her cheek, wiping away a trail that's burned down her skin.

"Lia?"

I have so many questions in that one syllable. *Are you angry with me? Did I ruin this, too? Will you look at this place and see what I intended: gratitude and heart-rending love? Or will your tears turn to stones of hatred when you find out all I've done?*

"It's too much."

"It's *not enough*." Whispering into the crown of her head, I plant a forbidden kiss there, lingering only a moment before I wrench myself away and give her the space she deserves.

"Now come, there's more to see."

More I want to give you; more I want to say. Every brush stroke is a love letter. These rooms are my apology. They're the only thing I have when my words fail me and the truth has turned to ash on my tongue too many times.

This time she slips her hand into mine without me needing to ask or even blinking, and I lead her up the staircase to where her guests will be staying. *Will* be, not might be, because there's no doubt in my mind she's going to make it a success.

Her hand strokes over the cool brass of the bed frame and the texture of the quilt folded at the end of the bed. Giuliana drinks it in like she's been denied a taste for far too long and I realize what I'm seeing. Ambition met, desires within reach. This is a small mark she can leave that's hers. This will help her take that coveted step closer to making this grove all her own.

And my heart aches with pride at knowing I've played a

small part in it. It's been worth it. She's worth it all. One of Chiara's kittens finds its way to us, winding between Giuliana's legs, desperate for some attention. But she has eyes only for one thing and her mind speeds ahead, even after we leave.

"This is going to be so perfect. You've done such a good job. I doubt there will be much else we need but we could potentially start getting people in after the harvest!"

I manage a soft hum in agreement, trying to relish it while I can. Reaching into my back pocket I hand her the checklist.

"This is what you'll need to make sure everything is above board, but yeah, it should be fairly close. You've got this."

She presses the scrap of paper to her chest before folding it and tucking it into her own pocket.

"I can't believe you did this, Teo. I'll never be able to thank you. This could make such a big difference to the grove's success. We'll have volunteers to learn the trade and I'll be able to use the money from the B&B to supplement teaching women in the area. It's going to be wonderful!"

"There's no need for thanks. I was glad to get to do this, to contribute a small bit to what I know is going to be a massive success. It was a team effort anyway. Isabella was a godsend with helping me source this stuff. I was just the muscle."

Giuliana gifts me a smile that will keep me going through the lonely nights to come. If I ever question whether this was the right thing, that bright smile and those warm eyes will be the answer.

We walk back to the big house with her chatter filling my mind, the hand not currently within my grasp gesticulating as she speaks grand plans and dreams into the evening air. Night wraps us in a shroud of darkness—in a place where secrets are whispered between friends and wishes thrive. Where the sky listens and maybe, hopefully, grants them.

We part at the hallway between our rooms, a pause in the

movement. Our hands outstretched for a moment to make the contact last as long as possible, she heads her way and I head mine. Our bedrooms are so close and too far. Pausing in her doorway, Giuliana looks back to where she's left me and nods her head once more in thanks. And then she's gone, reality clicking between us like the latch of her door.

I flop onto my bed, staring up at the black ceiling feeling both overjoyed and grieving. I'm out of time. Next week it's the harvest and then...

The maw of the unknown gapes wide open, threatening to swallow me whole.

And then we go back to that nothingness where I hate you and you hate me and no one is around to notice the war we wage within. The voice in my head is almost poetic, almost sorry that it hurts me so much.

A light hits the ceiling, a square cutting through the black. It's not my door opening, not as I hoped. It's the vibrating phone on my bedside table, Alan's name flashing across the screen. It's time to face the music.

A heartbeat passes—two—before I press the button and hold the screen against my ear.

And wait.

"What the fuck is the meaning of this?" Alan hisses, sounding incredibly far away. A lifetime away.

"I take it you got my fax?" Turning on the flippant attitude he expects, I can't let him know there's weakness here. I can't give him anything he might try to exploit. Better he believes in my failure and ineptitude, than tender-heartedness... sentimentality.

"Matt, don't play with me." It's little more than a growl and I understand for the first time how he could be intimidating. When you're not looking at his ridiculous face, the flint in his voice is clear.

"I thought that you'd be happy."

He scoffs, "And I thought you might actually have it in you."

His words don't hurt because I *did*. I had it in me to do the right thing, something beyond his scope of understanding. All I can do is deflect and hope it was enough. *Abundantia* is out of his grasp, even though I'm about to lose everything to him and the company, at least he can't take this.

"Well, seems we're both wrong. So, cut to the fucking chase already." Tell me my punishment and let me drown in it.

"Come back. The anniversary of your father's death is tomorrow. You have to come here, now."

To formally relinquish my claim.

"That's not going to work for me." I can't leave until the harvest, until I've seen this through and helped them as much as I can.

"I don't give a *shit* what does and doesn't work for you. You haul your ass back here, now."

"What does it matter, Alan? I'm losing everything anyway, what's a few more days? I told you I intended to stay until I've helped with the harvest and I plan to."

There's a loaded pause. I may have made a mistake somehow in saying that.

"You care enough to help but not enough to claim it?" The suspicion there confirms my fuck up and I swallow to keep the tremor from my voice as I respond.

"Farming's not for me. I'm not cut out for a life of physical labor. But there's going to be a massive party and I've been so busy trying to adhere to my father's expectations I haven't had any time to play."

Don't let him know. Don't let him realize. Andrea has the new contract but I don't know how long it takes legal stuff to settle. If there's even a chance Alan will want to use this to screw me over even more, I don't want to risk it. Better he not know how important it is to me so he can't use it against me later and hurt them in the process.

"I tried to be a good guy but you and I both know that's not who I am. So, I intend to actually *enjoy* some of Italy before I come back to nothing. Surely, you can grant me some clemency to do that. I get pretty cranky when I haven't gotten laid."

I can hear Alan trying to slow his breath. He's always hated how little respect I show him and it gets under his skin for some reason.

"You're a piece of shit, Matt. We'll be glad to be rid of you."

"Yeah, like you were glad to be rid of my father. I heard you at the funeral, Alan. I heard you tell my mother you'd make sure she didn't see another cent of his money. You said the best thing my father had ever done was trust you to take care of his affairs so his bitch of an ex wouldn't have any power."

It's my breath I hear now, angry and rapid, and filled with a darkness—an oil slick that's finally been let to settle on the surface.

"You really think I'm so stupid to think this doesn't all work out so well for you? I also heard you later, with one of the board members. Bragging about how you'd both become some of the richest men in New York and all it took was for my sad sack of a father to keel over. Good riddance to the fucker that had just set you all up for life. I heard it all."

I don't know what I expect—don't know if my words have done a damn thing but I'm glad they're out there and freed from my memory.

"Now I get to be rid of you as well. You drag your ass here or I'll come get you myself. There are papers to sign. You made this choice, now I need your name on that dotted line saying you understand exactly what you've done."

He doesn't even try to deny it. Doesn't show a shred of remorse. No wonder my dad died—surrounded by such corrosive people, sinking to their level. He was culpable as well, but it cost him his life.

Part of me wishes I'd met the terms of my father's will so I can make sure Alan burns, even if it means taking him down with me.

She's worth it.

And the flames that licked inside me, fueled by my rage, cool.

"No need, spare yourself the trip. I'm not changing my mind and I'll be there soon. You're getting what you want, no point in tantrums. Let me have my last hurrah and then all of it is yours."

I wait, wanting nothing more than to press my thumb to that red button and say to hell with him. But I need to know Giuliana is safe—*Abundantia* is safe.

"Fine. After the harvest then."

He doesn't wait for a response, wanting the last word. Alan hangs up before I can take a breath. It's a reminder that he holds the power now. I'm on borrowed time and playing a game I'm wholly unprepared for just for the sake of selfishness. It's partly the promise I made—the volunteer bargain that wasn't even my own. Mostly it's because I don't want to go yet and leave them behind—leave *her* behind.

The harvest will come in a couple of days. Everything is done. The players are in motion. All I can do now is hold on to this thread of happiness for as long as possible.

My fists ache where they've been bundled throughout that conversation. My phone is surprisingly intact despite my death grip on it. Rage that had been banked flares back to life and I need to do something other than lie here and dwell.

Bare feet padding across the floor to the kitchen, the cool stone is a familiar friend by now. I tug the fridge open. Jars and condiments clink in the door with the motion, waking one of the kittens curled up in a little bed by the back door. It stretches and a tiny pink tongue peeks out with its giant yawn. The kitten makes its way over to me and I give it a little scratch behind the ear before returning to the task at hand.

The cool light from inside the fridge wraps me in its luminosity and I stare at the contents like some miracle is going to expose itself to me. Opting for a carton of juice that's close to finished, I don't even bother with a glass, tipping the lip to my mouth and drinking deep.

"You showed it to her."

Isabella's voice scares the shit out of me and I choke on the final swig. The liquid lodges in my throat as I sputter through my shock and the kitten skitters back to its bed.

"She wants to make this place her own, to make it a success. I wanted to help, even if it is only in this small way," I say once I've regained the use of my vocal cords, the hacking cough still straining my throat.

"What you've done is no small thing. If she knew…"

"But she won't. Because you're not going to tell her. And I'm not going to tell her." Selfish 'til the end and not wanting to taint our time together with the black smudge of my betrayal.

"And you're leaving." A statement, not a question. As usual she's far too shrewd for my good. "When?"

"After the harvest. I promised to help and I'll keep that promise. The man in charge of the business expects me back to sign the paperwork. He wanted me there tomorrow on the anniversary but —" I shrug, gesturing at the space around us and all that awaits.

"The anniversary?" Isabella asks and for the first time since his death it actually feels real to say it. He's gone. For real.

"My father's death. I had one year to prove myself."

She sighs, and I wish I could do the same. If I could just suck in enough air and release all my feelings out along with the exhale my life would be so much simpler.

"I'm sorry, Matteo. I know it doesn't change anything with the man in charge but you did prove yourself. To me and Giuliana, and every person that relies on *Abundantia* to live and thrive. You made a difference here."

All I can do is nod, emotion choking any words from escaping.

"Will you say goodbye before you go?" Isabella asks.

I can't help but wonder if she means to Giuliana or to her. To her and Chiara and all the people here who have wormed their way into my chest, diving into the decay.

"I—" don't know if I can promise that but I can't finish the sentence.

"Get some sleep, we have a long week ahead of us." Dismissing me without another word, Isabella turns away and back down the corridor.

Harvest is coming and the air is heavy with ripe fruit and my regret.

ime, like reality, is cruel and comes swiftly. The harvest arrives in a few breaths and I soak it all in. Soak her in. God, she's beautiful. Giuliana moves with a grace that comes with familiarity and confidence. This is where she belongs and that refrain echoes over and over as I watch her work through the culmination of all our effort. The farm workers have stashed away their baskets for the day, their haul ready to be sorted and shipped to the mill for processing, but still she carries on.

Although, "workaholic" isn't what I see when I watch her. I know what that looks like, having lived with that my whole childhood. Giuliana *cares*. She keeps going to honor her father. Her hands are calloused, same as her employees. Even now, she has a smudge of dirt on her forehead where she tried to wipe sweat away and only succeeded in getting dust tacked onto her face.

The early evening light reflects in her brilliant eyes as she prattles on and I take a long, heady breath. The first cold fingers of autumn tint the air. The breeze is thick with the smell of the earth we've walked all over for the last two days. Olive fruit that hasn't made the cut litters the bases of the trees and the distant sounds of revelry pierce the night.

Nonna helped by delegating in the kitchen today— smacking more than a few hands when their culinary skills weren't up to snuff or they tried to sneak food too early. I think I even heard an English cussword thrown in once or twice and it warms the fucked-up cockles of my traitorous heart.

Chiara chased down the rows, chattering with everyone as we worked—a flash of tanned skin and bare feet in my periphery. Too excited to be still but too fickle to be a real nuisance—she hung around me and Giuliana the most.

Italy... *Abundantia* specifically has grown on me, to the point where I'm surprised I'm not covered in vines already, like the old farmhouse is.

And Giuliana...

She's a punch to the gut every time I look at her.

Feeling my gaze, she looks up at me. She's noticed my attention is only partly focused on what she's saying as we walk, carrying the last few things we need for the party.

"It's been a long day. I'm boring you." Giuliana shrugs like it doesn't bother her. But I've been watching her for weeks, scavenging for the parts of her that she doesn't like to share.

"Not at all, I'm just tired."

"You don't have to lie to spare my feelings."

Oh, but darling I do and I have no other choice.

"It's not a lie. It's the furthest thing. You light up when you talk about this and I can see how much it means to you. I've watched you work yourself into exhaustion and then get back up the next morning as if it was nothing. You are astounding." I want to say so much more.

But the words don't come.

Won't come.

Not when I know how cruel it would be to cut the wound even deeper. She will never forgive me. Giuliana lives her life without guile—genuine. I've lied to her for weeks for my own gain. Best I tuck tail and leave, slink back to New York and nurse my wounds in private. Even though I've surrendered my delusions of grandeur into her perfect, work-hardened hands it doesn't matter.

Giuliana doesn't need to know I'm devastated, ruined completely, with every moment in her presence.

I don't realize that we've trekked up the hill to the massive old tree that started it all until Giuliana comes to a stop. Pressing her palm against the bark, she strokes her thumb over it with reverence.

"I'm so tired." Her voice breaks, shoulders rounding in as if finally bowing under an invisible weight.

"Lia—"

"I love this. I do. How could I not?" She interrupts, gesturing around us to the grove stretching out below.

"My father put everything he had into this: blood, sweat, tears. Cliche, but true. And he didn't want to leave it to me, but he wanted to keep it in the family. I was the last resort, and then he was dying, so I became the only option."

The light fades from her eyes.

Setting down the basket in my grip, I step up toward her and cup her shoulders in my hands.

Stop. Don't do this. Don't touch her. You're leaving.

You're leaving.

It's a warning for once, not a beratement—one I should heed.

The pink sunset glistens in the tears on her lashes and I can do nothing but lose myself in her pain. I have grief, sure. But mostly I have anger.

Giuliana carries so much more.

"I loved him, *so* much!" she bites out, wiping her tears away in frustration. "He was all I had after my mother died and all I ever wanted was to make him proud."

My hand lifts of its own volition, stealing the tears from her cheeks.

"He's proud, *cara*, you know he is."

She snot-laughs at my attempt at the Italian endearment, though I know I'm getting better at rolling my r's. Still, it has the desired effect. It breaks through the sadness that pulls at her features and makes my heart ache.

"You and your damn nicknames." Shaking her head, Giuliana doesn't wait for my response before carrying on.

"This first harvest without him went beautifully, and it feels wrong." Her voice is small, even quieter once she tucks her face into the crook of my neck. Gripping my shirt in her hands, she whispers. "I miss him."

Cradling the back of her head with my hand, I hold Giuliana while she sobs out her grief. The day blazing to an end around us sets her rich brown hair alight with gold. When her sobs calm to little hitches in her breathing she finally looks up at me.

"I'm sorry," we both say, followed by a chuckle.

"What are you sorry for?"

"I wish I could take away some of the pain. I wish things were different."

Because she's hurting. Though mostly I don't, because if any of this was different, I never would have met her.

She gives me a rueful smile, because we both know that no matter how much we want something, it doesn't change the way things are. It doesn't lessen our grief, and it doesn't excuse my deception. With that thought I step away, trying to put distance between us again and respect the space she wants. Despite my numerous indiscretions the past few weeks, the least I can do is try to preserve the professional relationship she insisted on.

"Matteo?"

"Yes."

"The harvest is over." It means something.

I know it means something. But I can't put my finger on it

when she's lit up by the magic hour and all I can think about is how I long to kiss away the taste of salt on her lips.

"Yes?"

Stepping closer, her vulnerability from earlier bleeds into something else—something raw.

"The harvest is over and so you don't have to be here anymore."

Of course. Of course, she's sending me away.

Just as well. It could have been so much worse.

At least this way we will part on good terms and I won't have to pretend anymore. I can wallow in my feelings back in the States. I almost thought "back home" but that's not true anymore. Giuliana showed me that home is more than a place, it's people. And reality can only be postponed for so long.

"I—I'll be packed and ready to go first thing in the morning."

Anxiety ramps up my heartbeat at the prospect of our parting, but I'm out of time.

"No." Firm.

"No?" I ask, confused, frustrated. Just let me go, damn it.

"I'm not telling you to leave, I'm telling you there is no longer an obligation to stay."

She's so close I can reach out and touch her.

"Well, what the hell is the difference?"

"Matteo, why must you be so difficult about this? Are you really going to make me spell it out for you?" Part of me wants her to, because I'm not sure where she's going with this and I'm scared to hope.

The other part just wants to be a little shit.

"We both know you're the smart one, so if you wouldn't mind..."

"As of the last olive pulled from those trees, you are no longer my employee, volunteer... whatever. And that means—"

This is real. That means...

"—we finally get to do this," I finish, surging toward her and gathering her up into my kiss.

Giuliana's hands are in my hair, tugging me down toward her and threading between the strands as if she doesn't want to let go.

It's exquisite. It's agony. It's such an enormously fucking bad idea and I don't care at all. Because I've waited weeks for this moment. Every ache-filled day watching her from afar, all those little brushes of skin driving me to a frenzy. Each night burning for her and unable to drag her over the edge with me as I touched myself. They bleed into this kiss and she moans against my lips.

Forcing myself to pull away, I try to do the right thing.

"Are you sure about this? Summer is over. I don't want you to regret it again."

I don't want you to regret me.

"What?"

Her beautiful face folds into concerned lines and knitted brows, her mouth pulling down at the corners.

"Why would you think that?"

"Because of what happened last time. I know you regret our night in Gravina," I say. Her reaction that first day made it abundantly clear.

"Matteo, I was terrified. What happened that night in town shook me, and you left me. I know we didn't make any promises but when I woke alone, I thought you were the one who regretted it. So, when I saw you here and I realized that you came for the grove, not for me... I was embarrassed. Besides, I had to maintain some semblance of professionalism."

"I—I didn't know until I got here. You scared me too. You frightened the life out of me and I ran away like a coward. I figured that if working here with you was the only way I was going to get to be around you, then I'd be okay with it being strictly professional. You drew the line in the sand, I was just respecting that—most of the time."

"God, we're idiots." Her mirthless chuckle kicks up something inside me—a dark curl of desire I've tried to keep smothered for her sake.

"Giuliana, you have to know that I've wanted you, this whole time. I've worked alongside you. I've yearned for you, *every day.*"

Our foreheads resting on each other, we spill our secrets onto the earth we've worked together all summer.

"I longed to walk down that hall and open the door. I wanted to go to you so many times." Her words settle deep within the burning hunger of my need for her.

"I dreamed about you," I rasp. "Thought about you and that night in Gravina so many times. That night at the villa, I drowned in every breath you took on the other side of the room. I would have crawled to you if you'd asked."

It didn't matter that I'd been concussed, I'd have done it. The space between us disappears. Holding her face in my hands, I tease the pad of my thumb along her bottom lip.

"*God*, I've ached for you." My confession is whispered against the seam of her lips, waiting.

This time she comes to me, rising just high enough onto her toes for our mouths to meet. It's as if we've both been parched, left out in the sun without relief and this kiss is a thunderstorm. Giuliana fills my lungs with her scent of sweet blossoms, summer, and the earth. Hands roaming over my body, it's as if she's been just as starved of my touch as I've been of hers, and is eager to reacquaint herself with my planes and angles.

I respond to her kiss in kind, my fingertips trailing along the sun-heated skin of her arms and neck, down her back. I try to content myself with the parts I can reach but it's not enough. Kissing her will not be enough.

She seems to agree, pulling away from me, panting. Giuliana wastes no time going over to the discarded basket and pulls out the oversized picnic blanket rolled up there, the one intended for the celebration. It will no doubt see a more decadent feast here than over at the big house.

Blanket grasped at the corners, shaken out and laid carefully in place, Giuliana shucks her shoes. Following closely with her breezy overalls, then her thin t-shirt and underwear, and through it all I stare in awe.

Night approaches fast, but the silhouette of her naked body against the scorched sky will follow me into my dreams—branded onto my memory.

"Your turn," she says, standing there in all her glory, a goddess to be worshiped.

And worship I will.

Ridding myself of my clothing, I'm strangely liberated. We're out in the open but far enough from the party, in the opposite direction of the celebration. This moment exists only for us.

It's primal, intrinsic. Standing beside the old tree I can almost believe we've been swept to a time long past. Planted in a moment where we weren't rivals, and there are no secrets... and we're untouched by the history between us.

We meet on the blanket, tangled limbs and heated mouths. Sampling and testing, we enjoy what we've been denied for so long. I trace my fingertips over every lush curve and dip of her body, relishing the feel of goosebumps raising on her skin. Her nipples harden from my touch and the cool breeze that night ushers in.

Intertwined, I clutch her to me and taste her like this will be the last time, because it may well be. Cupping her generous breasts in my hands I kiss down the side of her neck, over her chest and flick my tongue over one of her nipples. Giuliana moans and it's like daylight through my veins. Marking my way down her body, worshipping as I said I would, I try to express the depth of my feeling for her through every touch of my mouth to her body.

Caught between her thick thighs, I sample her and the sound of her cursing my name will haunt my dreams for many nights to come. Her hands clutch at my hair, scrunching the curls in her fingers as I push her closer to the edge. Pants and hitches, moans and curses, I drive Giuliana to her first peak with pleasure. I will give her this. Tonight is hers.

She tugs me up by the hair and I crawl up over her body, helpless. And when she reaches down to touch my hardness I hiss in a breath, cursing myself for not thinking to slip a condom into my pocket. But we've been a little preoccupied with the renovation and the harvest, and the fact that I never imagined I'd be blessed with this again. So, when she urges me onto my back and moves to straddle me, I still her by gripping her hips.

"No condom," I manage between gritted teeth, wanting nothing more than for her to move down a few inches and envelop me.

"I'm safe."

"I got tested and I'm safe too, but…"

"I'm on birth control."

It's all she needs to say. Skating my hands up to rest against her ribcage, I cup one of her perfect breasts in my palm, tweaking my thumb over her nipple.

Settling herself against me, Giuliana gasps at the contact. She sinks inch by fucking painstaking inch and I swear my chest is going to burst. Her heat grips me and it's too much and not enough to slake my thirst. I will never drink my fill of her.

Tracing my touch up the ridges of her back, I stroke her hair, tucking a strand behind her ear so that I can trail my fingertips over that devastating face. Expressive eyes, filled with more than I can fathom, stare down at me and we breathe it in. Summer's final breaths, the sunset, the rich smell of earth, and something that is wholly her.

Tilting her hips, Giuliana tests the friction, and I suck in a desperate breath. There's no going back from this. There will never be any going back. She's changed me.

Giuliana's stuck her calloused little hand into my chest and rearranged it all so slightly I hardly noticed until it was too late. It's like the way you learn to navigate your space—to the point where you can walk it in the dark—but then the couch gets moved two inches and suddenly you're lost and aching from an unexpected collision. I reach out for her to steady myself. To guide myself home.

Because that's what she is to me. Her skin is soft under my hands and I drown in her quiet gasps as we move together. I lose myself in the best thing I've ever savored, the essence of life and love and happiness.

Even if there's never a single moment with her again it will have been worth it.

For once I agree with the voice in my head. In the years to come this will be the memory I cling to. The last light of the day kisses the edges of her hair and brandishes her skin in a warm glow.

Giuliana angles her hips to take me deeper and thought flees my mind, replaced with a keen ache in my chest with the knowledge that this is goodbye. Then I'm lost in the uncoiling low in my abdomen and the exquisite pleasure we take in each other.

Settling her onto her back, I lean over her to stare down at the little freckles on the tip of her nose and her kiss-swollen lips that would tempt a dead man back to life. She's already done that—pulled me from my half-existence into her brilliant daylight. Giuliana is stronger than any spirit I've imbibed, softer than any goodnight.

Surging within her, I relish the feel of her legs wrapped

around me to keep me close. Grunts and whines are swallowed in kisses I wish would never end. Cries increase in intensity as she gets closer, her body undulating beneath me.

"Tell me what you need, beautiful. Tell me how to take you there," I whisper into her hair before burning a trail of kisses down her neck.

"Don't stop, Teo. Don't stop, please. Just keep touching me. Never stop touching me."

Fuck, I wish I could. I wish I could praise her beneath the stars every night, bathe in her divinity until she burns me alive with her light.

"Anything for you. *Anything.*"

Even though it means letting go.

I'm not sure if she can sense the desperation rising in me but she meets me thrust for thrust, our bodies entwined and breaths mingling. Giuliana falls apart beneath me with a primal cry loosed into the night. Following soon after, I breathe her in, shaking with fear and love and need.

This will never be enough. But I wouldn't trade it. Not for all the money or land in the world.

"I miss you." It comes out broken, already aching for her. *I'll miss you.*

"I'm right here," she soothes, pushing my curls away from my face, so much longer than I've ever let them grow.

"Yes," I say, at a loss, unable to express how no amount of time with her will ever suffice. It doesn't matter that I'm still inside of her, with my essence buried within her body, and the beat of her heart thrumming against my skin. I will never get enough of her.

"We should probably head back before Chiara or Nonna come looking," she giggles, tickling my cheek.

"Heaven forbid," I choke out, pulling away with reluctance.

Morning will come, and with it, finality. I can't lie to her anymore and there's nowhere to hide. Giuliana's made it clear how she feels about liars and deception. She won't forgive me. But I know it's what I need to do. I don't deserve forgiveness anyway.

We dress in silence. Twining our hands together, we head down the hill to the brightly-lit party. Every step brings us closer to laughter and music, string lights and family. Before we climb the stairs up to the house, I lift her hand to my lips and press a kiss to the back. I stroke my thumb over it as if I can imprint it there out of wishful thinking alone.

"Can we keep this as our own, for tonight? I don't want to let go of the haze... the moonlight on your skin." It's a plea, a way to delay the inevitable.

Isabella will know though. I can only hope she'll comfort whatever hurt I leave behind, coax anger to replace it. Better she hates me. Better that than her pain.

"Of course, but one day soon I'm going to walk down the hall and finally knock, and you're going to answer."

I chuckle through the lump in my throat at the picture, the impossibility.

"Deal."

She walks up ahead of me and I give her a few minutes head start, to douse suspicion of course. Not because I'm breathless at the feel of my heart breaking.

Harvest is over and I'm out of time. At least I have the small comfort of knowing Giuliana and her family are safe. The grove is protected and there's hope for its future. I shouldn't have given in to my feelings last night. I'm sorry and not sorry enough. It'll only hurt us more now that I'm leaving, but I've always had a bit of a problem with letting go of my vices. She's like a drug, in my bloodstream and on my mind, every second of every day.

I love her. I've finally fallen and I understand. You want them to be happy above all else. Their needs supersede your own. And Giuliana doesn't need me. No matter how desperately I need and want and love her. She's better off.

It's time to say goodbye.

I look back at the semi-packed bag on my bed, the lid flipped up, the last three months of my life strewn across the covers of my crudely made bed. How has it only been three months? How can one summer feel like a lifetime and a breath all at once? Cruel and beautiful, it's been a season of firsts and lasts.

I toss my journal into the desk drawer and rise. It's time. I need to get this out between us so I have the courage to actually pack my things and leave. My feet drag me toward her office despite my heart's reluctance. Giuliana's bent over the desk, typing like she's on some kind of deadline and I have to clear my throat for her to notice I'm there.

Looking up, that glazed look of concentration softens into an easy smile. The intimacy of her gaze leaves my stomach lurching. I can't do this. I can't do this. How can I leave her?

The words don't exist. I can't pull them from the mess of my mind, even the voice that's been my constant companion is silent.

I open my mouth to try, gaping, a stutter of a sound squeezed from my throat. I want to say so many things—tell her my feelings, drop to my knees and thank her for our night under the stars. In an ideal world I would be doing that right now. But this world is far from ideal and there's no way to turn back time.

I'm saved for a moment by my phone buzzing insistently in my pocket. If it's Alan I'm going to toss it across the room.

"Sorry, one sec," I say as I pull it out and press the end call button, not even bothering to check who's calling.

"Take your time."

"It's done, I just needed to turn that off." Letting out a deep breath, I steel myself.

"Hi," she says, that same gentle look from last night on her face and it trips me.

"Hi," I murmur back, lost in my feelings for her.

This time her phone and mine blow up at the same time. Hitting the end call buttons simultaneously, we scoff at the coincidence. Maybe the universe is trying to give me a sign, though I doubt karma is kind to people like me. The powers that be want to drag this out to fully enjoy watching me squirm.

My phone rings again, hers following soon after, and this time we pay attention. This time I press the green button and lift the screen to my ear. She does the same.

"Bro, what the fuck? You disappear for the summer without a word, ignore my texts, and now your face is all over my feed. Is it true?"

I pull back to double check the name—Brandon. I'm sucked back to that sweltering night in New York before I left to come here. The drinking, the desperate feeling clawing up my chest. My hands gripping the guard rails on the balcony and wishing they were just a *little* shorter so I could—

"What are you talking about?"

"Hold on, I'm sending you the link now."

This can't be good. Whatever this is cannot be good.

Giuliana is listening intently to whoever is speaking on her phone call, rapid Italian filling the silence as I wait for Brandon's message. And realize I have about fifteen others. Not counting app notifications I've had turned off for weeks. A link pops up into the chat.

Matrimony Matt.
Palmer heir's secret proposal in Italy.

Oh no.

Oh no.

No. No. No

Fuck.

"Listen, I need to go."

"But! You didn't answer me, is it—" Hanging up before he can finish speaking, I click the link to motherfucking Buzzfeed.

My stomach drops, settling low with the lead balloon of dread accompanying the words on the screen.

Mind spinning, I scroll through the pictures, not even bothering to read the text. My mostly harmless Instagram pictures are splashed across the beginning of the "article." But then, nights of inebriation and fucking around, drunken red irises from the flash's glare. The photo of me wrapped around the Senator's daughter resurfaces again.

And under that, toward the bottom, is a gallery of pain.

Me on one knee with olive trees framing our bodies, and Giuliana staring at me in shock and awe. Her hand outstretched. My face lit up with a joy I've never seen in the mirror or in those intoxicated photographs. Our bodies in motion as I spin her around and then that moment with my hand cupping her cheek, where I thought I might lean down to kiss her. My heart in my eyes.

I'm going to be sick.

Looking up from my phone to face her, her cheeks are ashen as she scrolls through her own phone.

"Matt Palmer?" she asks and the panic rises in my body. I can't speak. Can't answer. Can't focus on anything but the frantic need to run. "Matt Palmer, not Matteo de Palma?"

There's something dark in her tone and she rises from her desk.

I want to say something—offer to explain—but there's no good way out of this.

Taking a step toward me, Giuliana reads off the screen. "The heir to illustrious Palmer Enterprises, last seen at a party for his birthday with his tongue halfway down political princess Cassidy Bridges's throat, has apparently given up his wicked ways."

Another step and I feel like a rabbit caught in a snare, Giuliana the hunter.

"Matt Palmer, everyone's favorite playboy, has lost his heart after a hot and heavy Italian summer. The lucky lady is known only as 'Giuliana.' Will this be another stint on the long list of Palmer's antics or is this the real deal?"

A final step and she's right in front of me, staring up at me with fire in her eyes. It doesn't matter anymore that I'd hoped to leave on good terms, with only some aches but good memories of our time together.

"Sources present at the proposal describe the couple being very much in love. Buzzfeed has reached out to Palmer for comment but has received none."

I slip my phone back into my pocket and gaze down at her, helpless.

"Who are you?"

I don't even know anymore.

"Both. I'm both. Matteo is my birth name. Matt is the name that worked best for my father's rise in society."

"Did you know about the photos, the article?" It's a broken whisper. Anger fading for a moment, her hurt peeks through.

"*No*. I had no idea they were even taking pictures. But the bride knew who I was. I should have expected this, anticipated it. I'm sorry. I'm so sorry." For more than just this.

"You should have told the truth about who you are! You should have said something before now. How can I trust whatever this is between us? Has it been a lie the entire time?" Her voice rises and there's nothing I can do but take it. I deserve it.

Poking a finger into my chest, her voice shakes with emotion. "I am not some mindless, one-night fuck on a laundry list of your indiscretions. I thought we were friends. I thought I could trust you. This would never have happened if I'd known you—"

"He told you?" Isabella asks from the doorway, drawn by the sound of Giuliana's raised voice.

She whirls around to face her grandmother and I breathe for

what feels like the first time since Giuliana pinned me with that gaze.

"You... knew?"

"Of course, he looks just like his father. It wasn't hard to guess. But I'm glad it's out in the open now. You know the truth about the arrangement between Lorenzo and Tommaso, and Matteo making it right. I'm just glad he told you before he left." Isabella nods at me in what I assume is some kind of pride, giving me kudos for doing the right thing, when I absolutely have not.

"What arrangement? Making *what* right?"

I watch like a ghost outside of my body as my life implodes right before my eyes.

Isabella clicks her tongue and says, "He gave up *Abundantia* for you. Your fathers had a contract, if the grove wasn't successful Tommaso was going to take it all. Matteo might have started out trying to do that but he signed it over to you. It's all in your name, every inch of it. We never have to worry about someone coming to take it ever again."

Giuliana turns to me again, achingly slow. Chest rising and falling with angry breaths, her whole body trembles. Unshed tears gather in her eyes.

"Lia..." I finally find my voice.

"Get out." Grave. Final.

"Lia, please." Give me a chance to tell you everything. Give me the chance I lost and desperately want back.

"*Get. Out.*" So quiet, seething rage contained by the barest veil of control. "Leave just like you planned to do. I never want to lay eyes on you ever again. Get your shit and get the hell away from me."

My feet obey her command, my body bowing under the pressure of the hate in her voice. There's talking behind me, Giuliana and Isabella discussing the depth of my deception.

It's strange, I think as I shove things into my bag. I'd have expected to be a total mess right now—panicking, shaking. My breath should be clawing up my throat. But there's no cold sweat, no racing heart. I tuck away the last of the things on the bed and sling my backpack on my shoulder. The wheels of the bag click over the stone floors on the way to the front and Chiara finds me in the hallway, feet from the door.

Stopping, she takes in the bag in my hand, and asks, "Where are you going?"

"Back. I'm going back to New York."

"But..." She looks so much like her sister, her eyes staring up at me conflicted and confused. There are a few different arguments and I don't want to delve into the cause of that "but."

"Giuliana and Nonna are fighting," is what she settles on.

"I know."

She tugs at my shirt as I turn to leave.

"I hate when they fight." She's stalling and I hate how much it pierces me to see. It may not have seemed like much but all the hours she spent telling me about everything her curious mind could grasp and talk through made the time fixing up the farmhouse less lonely.

I'm going to miss her and I'm sorry to be another person leaving her.

"I do too. I'm sorry."

"I don't want you to go." Soft, devastating.

Letting go of my bag, I drop down so I'm closer to her level, and stare her straight in the eye.

"I know. I don't want to go either but I have to. Take care of your sister, okay? I'm trusting you to do that."

She nods, solemn, and throws her arms around my neck. I squeeze her for a second, this little sister I never really got the chance to have.

"*Stammi bene*, Chiara."

Dropping her hold on me, Chiara's face is so full of sadness I can't stand it anymore. It's time to go.

Somehow, I keep it together. I strap the bag to the back of the Vespa and tear down the dirt road. My phone gives me directions through my headphones and Puglia blurs past me as I drive, no thoughts, no feelings. Nothing for hours.

I leave the Vespa outside the airport, free for whoever wants to take it, and I don't even spare a moment for the memory of Giuliana and that bike. With a flight booked I sit in the airport lounge with a drink I know will only be the first of many. Time ticks by. My phone vibrates in my pocket until I turn it off.

They call my gate and I make it to my seat. First class this time. For what may very well be the last. I order another drink and am barely aware of the burn of it down my gullet. Hours fade away between little bottles of liquor and the flickering screen of a movie I don't even watch.

It's not until the wheels touch down in New York, my body lurching with the rough landing, that I realize why I'm so calm. It's not because I'm drunk off my ass. I've been there plenty and still struggled. Now, my chest and mind are empty, no space for guilt or self-hatred or love. Just a disgusting apathy like the beige walls of the waiting room of a doctor's office. It's a vacuum of space, years-old magazines on the corner table and a water cooler that's near-empty with no cups to go along with it.

I'm not in my body. It's not mine anymore. My heart beats, my lungs stretch with breaths in and out. I step between a crush of people and turn my phone back on, pressing the only number I can think of and it rings twice before a voice answers.

"Hey mom, can you come pick me up? I'm at JFK, international arrivals, terminal 4."

"Of course. I'll send my driver right away. Just hold on." Her voice is pitched at the edges, like she's worried. Did I say it wrong? Or was it just the fact that I never pick up let alone call.

Hearing from me at all constitutes an emergency. She hangs up soon after and I wait again, the passage of time something I've come to accept as inevitable but barely feel at all. This will be my life from now on. Every tick of a watch.

I don't care anymore. Not when it means I'll never see her again, not when all they are is one click closer to being done with it.

There's no panic, no anxiety, no tears. My body holds no anger.

I slide into the backseat of the town car my mom sent for me and watch again as New York moves by me in stops and starts. Blaring horns and police sirens. The shadows of buildings defying gravity block out the sun and I rest my head against the back of the seat, shutting my eyes.

It's all gone and there's no room for anything else. Not with the giant maw of darkness that's opened up inside of me. It swallows me whole, deafens me, and silences all my worries and thoughts. Loss. There's no point in any other emotion when loss this profound has taken residence in my body and I know now why that voice inside has stilled.

I have a new companion—one I've evaded for a year and finally caught up with. A new "friend."

Grief.

"You have to talk to me at some point. Alan keeps calling." Staring out at the city and seeing none of it, my mother's voice breaks through the near-meditative trance I've been sitting in. "He knows you're back and he's insisting you come to the office."

Nothing new. Alan's always insisting on something. I remember our bargain and the promise I made to come hand it all over to him, but I can't get my body to move. It's so heavy. The fog of being back here the last few days feels like cinder blocks dragging me down feet first.

"Matt... talk to me. I've never seen you like this. What happened in Italy?"

She sits beside me on the couch and rests her hand on my knee, long, manicured nails against the simple fabric of my pants. Genevieve Palmer has always been so elegant. I look at her then, taking in the fine lines beside her mouth and eyes, the start of age that she's fought so hard to combat. Her blue eyes were ones I'd wished for as a kid.

My brown hair and eyes always seemed so dull, especially with a mother like her. Blazing blue, like a flame so hot it's cold. Her hair gleams chestnut, thick and straight, not a gray in sight with volume that landed her plenty of hair commercials. I know a lot of it comes from salons but still, I've never looked much like my mother. Thomas Palmer put his stamp on me and there was little leeway for anyone else's genes.

Floor to ceiling windows stretch throughout her living room, the corner delineating two opposing views. Central Park is on one side, the impossible reach of Manhattan's skyscrapers on the other. Halfway between the ground and the clouds, we sit suspended. Am I the only one that doesn't like being this high up? Everyone around me seems to relish being part of the sky and all I want is to sink my hands into the earth again.

"It's been days. If you won't talk to me then at least..." She takes a deep breath, handing me a business card.

"I made an appointment for you to see someone. I'll keep Alan off your back for as long as I can but, Matt... it can't go on like this."

My mother rises from her perch on the sofa, the warmth of her hand gone.

"Your appointment is in an hour. The driver knows and will be waiting for you downstairs. Please go."

I say nothing.

"Matt," she urges, her voice stronger than I've heard it before. She never was one to raise her voice, to discipline. The moments I had with her growing up were always too distant for that. It's enough for me to drag my gaze to meet hers. My eyes feel like sandpaper, every blink painful. When's the last time I took a shower?

"Promise me."

There's no denying her, not when she's agreed to let me live here after the loft's taken away. That's the answer I gave her. Not the fact that I have nowhere else to go and I haven't had the courage to go back to my loft where I'll be truly alone.

"I promise," I say and it feels weird, the words clumsy and thick coming out of my mouth. Days without speaking will do that. Fuck, I should brush my teeth.

"I'll see you tonight for dinner." Gathering her stuff into a small purse, she slings the strap over her shoulder and puts on a pair of sunglasses that probably cost more than the fucking Vespa. She's trying. Now it's my turn.

I drag my body through a shower and clothe myself in the first things I can find that make sense, and sit in the silence of the apartment. Spoon clinking against a bowl of cereal, I force myself to breathe as deeply as I can. The bran feels like chewing sticks but my stomach is glad for the sustenance. My mother's pulled me from my little cotton wool haze and now I'm noticing just how fucked the last few days have been—how deep I've sunk into myself. It's been almost a week since I drove the dirt road away from *Abundantia* and I haven't heard a word from any of them.

My phone has been a minefield of "friends" I haven't spoken to in months, who never check in, never ask, suddenly giving a fuck. It's also Alan and his threats. A few places have reached out for comment but hopefully this thing will fade with the next big story.

Still, nothing from them. Not sure why I expected anything else, but hope is hard to squash.

The car ride is short and the therapist's office not what I expected. Instead of a sleek medical-looking building, it's a townhome; a brownstone, aged by time and the weather. The driver finds somewhere to park and it dawns on me that he's going to have to sit and wait for me.

I've never thought about it before, the people tangential to my life that I've ignored, barely noticed.

"What's your name?" I ask.

Glancing up from the newspaper he's unfolded in front of the steering wheel, he makes eye contact with me in the rearview mirror. "Clyde. Clyde Adams."

"Thank you for driving me, Clyde. Appreciate it."

His eyebrows twitch once, like he needs a second to absorb what I've said.

"No problem, Mr. Palmer. I'll be out here if you need anything."

I walk on leaden legs up the steps, read the little sign asking me to ring the doorbell for entry, and wait. So much of my life is going to feel like waiting now. Just passing time until it stops meaning anything.

"Hi, how can we help you?" comes through the electronic doorbell.

"Matte—uh, Matt Palmer, I have an appointment."

A few moments later a young woman opens the door for me, gesturing that I follow her inside and toward an office near the back garden. Inside what looks more like a study than an office is a bowed head with long, salt-and-pepper hair, engrossed in writing notes.

"Mr. Palmer to see you," my escort says from the doorway before walking away and the therapist nods for me to join her in the room.

"Shut the door behind you and come take a seat, Mr. Palmer."

"Please, don't call me that, my first name's fine."

"Okay then, Matt. I'm Dr. Pritchard. What brings you in today?"

"My mom made me an appointment?" I phrase it as a joke, the question going up at the end and even I can tell the facade is wearing thin.

"Be that as it may, you still showed up and she was concerned enough to make an appointment for you. Is there anything specific you'd like to bring up or would you prefer we go over some of your history first?"

"I guess I've been a little 'off' lately." I stare down at my hands in my lap, fingers tightly-laced, skin white where it's being squeezed. "I lost someone I was close to and I've been having a hard time with it, I suppose."

You're having a fucking ball. *What did you expect when you fucked everything up? Did you really think she'd forgive you for lying to her* over *and* over?"

"Ah. Yes, I'd heard about your father's passing. My condolences."

Jerked from reminiscing about Giuliana, I look up at her, confused for a second. "No. No, that's not what this is about!" It's stronger than I intend, almost offended.

Dr. Pritchard tilts her head as she assesses me, and I'm reminded of Isabella's fathomless gaze. It's a look that says she sees so much more than just what's presented on the surface.

"Isn't it? Tell me then."

And so, I launch into it as briefly as I can: the contract, the trip, the lies compounding and growing—snowballing until it swept away the life I want more than anything else.

"Why do you think you kept the secret from her? It sounds like there might be something else there, not just you avoiding getting caught."

"At first it was me being stubborn, selfish, but then I didn't want to lose her. And once I was caught up in it all I didn't want to let them down."

"Them?"

"Giuliana and her family."

"Did you ever feel like you were letting your family in New York down?"

"Growing up or with the company and the grove? Because I know I've been failing them for years. Some of it willful, some of it was me chafing at their expectations."

"You say you *know*. Did they ever tell you that? What makes you feel like that?"

How the hell did we get so off track? We're just supposed to be talking about my fuck-up with Giuliana. I'm going through a breakup here and it's tearing me apart. Clearly now's not the time to bring up the man who ruined my life with his anticipations and demands. I almost want to interrupt her and tell her that, refuse to answer, but the truth is easier. I'm too tired to fight.

"My father expected me to take over the business. Had a whole clause written into his will to disown me if I didn't make a success of myself."

"Have you seen this clause? That sounds very extreme."

"No... uh, my *mentor* Alan—his right-hand-man, told me about it while I was in Italy. I haven't been to see him yet given my—mood. But from what he said either I take over the grove and prove I have what it takes to run the company, or I lose my inheritance."

"So, you lost both the grove and your inheritance? And the connection you'd made with this family."

"Yeah, hence why my mom made the appointment for me. Needless to say, I've been a little numb—very little pep in my step these days."

"Were you close with your father?"

"No. He was busy with work and growing his empire."

"Do you think you resent the business for taking him away from you?"

"Probably."

"When you were a kid or now, in death?"

Fuck. I've never connected the two but that makes sense.

"Both?"

"Do you resent your father for not being there for you, not taking the time to get to know you and what you wanted?"

"Yeah. We've never been on the best terms, which is why I'm not surprised by the move he pulled. Keeping it a secret was a shitty thing to do, though."

"Matt, I don't want to agitate you when you clearly want nothing to do with your father's business but I do suggest you look into that clause on the will. Take it to a lawyer, get a second opinion. Is there a reason you're taking Alan's word as law when you haven't even laid eyes on it?"

"I mean, it sounded like something my dad would do. He'd been pestering me for years, why not try to force my hand?"

Her questions are a barrage, forcing me to think on things I've never even considered. Given how I've trudged through the last few days this conversation feels like a tennis match, balls volleyed back and forth. As soon as I answer she serves me another question I'd rather avoid. Picking at the chair I'm sitting on, I try to ground myself in the physical space. Her office. I'm in her office and I've got to focus on that.

"Matt, how could he have known when he was going to die? Without the heart attack he might have had another twenty years and died an old man, a grandfather even? Do you believe he thought you'd have nothing to show for yourself your *whole life*?"

The words sink into the abyss of my chest like stones clattering over themselves and tumbling to the bottom. I mull it over and consider what my father may have thought of me.

"Yeah, I did. I do. But how can I reconcile that man with the man who helped Giuliana's father? *That* person left them alone despite having sunk money into a business venture. He paid for my writing degree, even though it wasn't in the field he would have preferred. There are these glimpses of a man I didn't know —someone I wish I had gotten to before he died. But it's too late now. I know I disappointed him but I'm not sure if that's all he saw me as."

Don't try to kid yourself, you've always been a disappointment.

"What's going on? You just tensed up and you seem to be preoccupied about something. Tell me."

"I... uh, I have this voice inside me that talks to me?"

It sounds fucking ridiculous. Who doesn't have an internal voice? People talk to themselves all the time. Right?

Wrong. It's deluded. You're walking around with a pocket asshole in your mind and you spend so much time telling me to shut up you don't even wonder why I'm here in the first place. Your brain is fucked, dude.

"And what does this voice say?"

Go on. Tell her how messed up you are.

"Nothing good. Most of it is pretty fucking shitty actually. It just pops up and I've kind of gotten used to it. I call it my companion because it won't go away. It's mean."

"Mean to you?"

"Yeah."

"How long has it been around?"

Casting my mind back, I try to pinpoint it but it's hard to sift through weeks of internal abuse. It popped up during the funeral, after I heard Alan call my dad a good riddance. The voice agreed.

"Maybe a year?"

"And is it just the voice? What does it tell you?"

Here we go. I'm about to get shrunk.

"Mostly hateful stuff toward myself. Negative. That I'm a worthless sack of shit and nothing I do means anything. The occasional feeling that it might be better if I wasn't around. There's been some physical stuff as well."

"Like?" She drags it out, clearly onto the fact that I'm trying to procrastinate this entire conversation or avoid it entirely if I can.

"Trouble breathing, shakiness, heart racing, dizziness, kind of your general panic. I ended up doing a lot of drinking and vaping to deal with it. Worked sometimes." I shrug, trying to play it off.

"Same length of time?" Looking up from my fisted hands, I

notice she's writing on her notepad, scribbling as I speak. *Great.* That can only be a good sign.

"Yes, I guess."

"And are you still smoking and drinking to help with dulling the voice and the feelings?"

The question is innocuous but it shines a light on how ineffective my coping strategies were. The vaping and drinking and partying did absolutely fuck all to help me. If anything, it added a level of physical pain and anxiety that made it easier to ignore the emotional side of things. But once those things were gone, I still struggled.

"No. Not for a little while now. At least not consistently."

Dr. Pritchard jots it down and it feels strange to see someone take stock of my life like that. Little scratches on a paper attest to how fucked up I might or might not be.

"Anything significant happen about a year ago?" It's a leading question. I've seen enough courtroom dramas to know this is a trap. There's no way. It can't be connected.

"Uh... my father passed away."

Pritchard stops writing, looks at me—sees me. I'm bouncing my leg, hands balled up. I feel like a caged animal, under scrutiny in a zoo. The enclosure is too small and keeps getting smaller the longer I sit here under her eye. Dr. Pritchard pushes her glasses up the bridge of her nose and takes a deep breath before talking.

"Grief is a funny thing."

"What are you talking about?"

"May I be frank with you? And possibly unprofessional? Because I don't know if you're going to come back."

"Sure, doc. Go ahead." Lay it all out for me.

"You've grown up in an environment of neglect and abandonment that you've blamed on yourself your whole life because none of the adults took accountability. When your father died it was just another kind of abandonment, but this time you weren't to blame and you didn't have the tools to deal with a grief you didn't want to feel. Mourning someone who hurt you felt like a betrayal to yourself. He didn't deserve your grief and you couldn't control that feeling, so you shoved it down and what came back up was different—pointed inward."

Swallowing hard, my Adam's apple bobs in my throat, impossibly thick.

"That cycle of internal blame is hard to break. So, when something profound came in to disrupt the only constant feeling in your life, you may have felt out of control. Hence the panic, hence the voice trying to blame and shame you at every turn. You've been trying to regain an environment you're familiar with even though it's a harmful one."

Out of control is a pretty apt descriptor for how I've been feeling, especially when my body betrays me.

"You could have come clean in Italy and told the truth. But you wanted to avoid failure—avoid feeling like you were a disappointment and it was all your fault. You didn't want to be left again. So, you lied. And as those relationships grew you kept lying, even though you knew it could only end badly. Because that's the default: badly. You're in this pattern of self-destruction and blame because that's your comfort zone."

Pritchard pauses, watching me, waiting for the words to sink in. It takes my mind a minute to catch up and process what she's listing out. It resonates. Hard. I've never thought about it this way or known how to talk about it. Now she's cataloging my whole life in such clear terms I feel stupid for not realizing it sooner.

"I just want to fix it. I want to go back and change everything and never be in this place. Because it fucking sucks. My whole life feels alien to me. I don't know where I fit anymore. I wanted Italy. I wanted Giuliana and stability and family and joy. I'd never had that—never even realized how badly I needed it until I found it there."

Pushing a box of tissues toward me, she nods and I realize I must be crying. My face is wet. When did that happen?

"And I can't. I can't do any of those things." The words are shaky, broken up by little catches from my crying.

"Now you're dealing with your grief, for real. Not pretending it doesn't exist. You've allowed yourself to feel for them, to care and love, and grieving that kind of loss is hard. The feelings you ignored around your father are coming back up and it's compounding. It's going to take time."

I sniff, wipe the hot salt from my cheeks. "What can I do? I can't change the situation but what can I do about the mess inside of me? I don't want to be like this. I'm so tired of feeling like this. I hate my brain and it hates me, and that can't be what the rest of my life is going to be like, right?"

"You can come here and put in the work by sorting through your feelings and finding *healthy* coping mechanisms. You mentioned a writing degree. You could try and journal to untangle some of what you're feeling, and face it. Fear and avoidance aren't a good combination when it comes to healing."

I could try and journal.

Journal.

My journal. Fuck. It's in that desk drawer, in Italy.

Pritchard's still talking though so I force myself to tune back in despite the flare of dread shooting through my body at the thought.

"You chose to help that family, despite what was on the line for you. Knowing it would have made you look like a 'failure' according to your father's supposed clause, you did it anyway. You're already trying to break the cycle and become the person I think you want to be deep down."

I can do nothing but nod.

"So, homework for next week. Ask to see that will and the clause, get a second opinion. You don't need to punish yourself for doing the right thing, even if you went about it the wrong way. And maybe try to write a little, get it out of your head. Okay?"

"Okay." I can do that. I *should* do that. Even if I get nothing from the will, at least I can say I tried and fought.

"Next week, same time then."

Rising from my seat, I push out of the chair and try to ignore the scrape of it against the wooden flooring.

"See you, Dr. Pritchard."

"Robin. You can call me Robin. Take care of yourself, Matt."

My mind races, trying to think of where to start to settle back into a body that's been working against me for a while now. First in panic and now in apathy. I pause in the doorway—my hand wrapped around the knob and turn back. "I'd prefer Matteo actually."

She gives me a smile and a nod. "Take care, Matteo."

Robin's given me a purpose, at least a short term one. There's so much to sort through, so many questions I need to ask myself. Firstly, why I haven't mourned my dad and how that's been affecting me.

So, I'll start there, with him. With the will and my part in it.

Settling into the town car, Clyde heads us back to the apartment. If there's anyone with experience in dealing with Alan and going up against my father where the law is concerned, it'll be my mom.

I wait until at least four bites into dinner to bring it up to my mother. At least that way there's a small portion of food to combat the inevitable burn of stomach acid.

"So, I don't know if it's true or not but Alan told me if I didn't take over the grove, I lose the business and my inheritance as well. He's been harassing me to come into the office and sign it all over. Needless to say, I'm not jumping for joy at the prospect, even though I don't want to run Palmer Enterprises. But it was a dick move on his part."

"Matt, I wish you'd told me Alan's been threatening you!"

"I was preoccupied with other stuff, sorry." I try to sound contrite but it's hard to feel much more than apathy giving way to anger. How could I have been so stupid, with Giuliana and with Alan?

"I saw." She scoffs, pointing at the messages lighting up my phone screen throughout the meal. No more vibrations or chimes, it's been soundless beacons hounding me for almost a week now. "Are you going to tell me, or do I take Buzzfeed's word for it?"

"I heard it actually got picked up by People, so even non-internet people will be aware of it soon."

Genevieve Palmer levels me with a look, one saying I won't enjoy this path if I continue down it, so I sigh and come clean.

"It's not what it looks like. I was trying to help Giuliana spy on a business model and got carried away. They didn't have any tours left—I told the receptionist I was bummed because I planned to propose... and then all of a sudden, I had a ring, and the staff and other guests were in on it. Giuliana didn't know. Her shock is real."

Chest aching with the massive breath I try to suck in, my lungs stretch within my ribcage.

"It bit me in the ass. I had no idea someone was taking those pictures, and even less of an inkling they'd leak them. I've lived in this world, she hasn't. I should have known better."

Our cutlery scrapes on our plates, tiny parcels delivered into waiting mouths. It's nowhere near Nonna's cooking, a little too bland for my preference. Steamed asparagus, poached white fish, no crispy skin to speak of. There's a hint of lemon and pepper—a saving grace—but I'd sell my left kidney for the pizza I had in Naples, or the focaccia Giuliana and I made that day in the kitchen. I'd *have* to sell my kidney, considering I'm supposedly broke now.

"How is Giuliana handling all this?" my mom asks. "I can't imagine it's been much easier for her."

"I have no idea. After the pictures were leaked, she was pretty upset. That only got worse when she found out I'd lied to her about why I was in Italy and then kept lying throughout the summer. She said she never wanted to see me again, so I went. I haven't heard anything since."

"You need to make this right. That poor girl."

Tension grows between us. Agitation spreads through me with each bite of food I'd rather not eat, stuck in a conversation I'd rather not be having.

"I don't know how, not when she won't talk to me. I already gave up my inheritance for her, I don't know what else I could offer that would make it right."

Please drop it, Mom. I'm so tired.

"Have you tried?"

"I don't deserve to talk to her after I caused nothing but mess. No way am I going to insert myself there again when all I've done is hurt them. She made it clear she wanted me gone, and it didn't seem like a temporary thing."

It sounds noble, maybe I even mean it a little. But I think back to my session with Pritchard and the fear of failure—the abandonment and rejection piece rears its head.

"Then fix it without talking to her. The least you can do is reach out to the press and deny it, get them off your backs. It's been days and it's still going strong. I don't think it'll blow over this time, kiddo."

I want this to feel normal. The conversation flowing—the intimacy of us sitting down to eat a meal together—shouldn't pinch. But then I'd have to ignore the view of the city and the couch that costs more than a car, and the sleek bar top we're eating at in lieu of the well-used wooden table from *Abundantia*. I want to tell her all about it and share the sweet moments with Chiara where I barely got a word in. I'd love to laugh over the long-game Isabella played in pretending not to understand me. It's my *mom*. But we've never been close like that, and I don't know how to bridge that gap.

"We may not talk all the time, but I love you. I care about how you're doing and I'm here, okay?" Her manicured hand rests on top of mine, calming me where I've got my fork in a death grip.

"I love you too, Mom. I appreciate that. Enough about me though, how've you been?"

Her smile grows, eyes soft and I see some of those wrinkles she tries so hard to hide. My mother rarely smiles with her whole face. It's a pleasant change.

"I've started working on a shoe collection. I'm not doing much runway or editorial anymore. Older models aren't in demand. *But* I've spent more than half my life in a pair of high heels so I'm working with some designers on a line to go along with next year's New York Fashion Week."

The excitement beams off of her and it fills my chest with an ember, a spark of something good.

"Yeah? That's so exciting. I'm happy for you!" And I mean it, she's managed to thrive in an environment that's rough on women and come out on the other side, still enthusiastic.

Smiling at each other, I want to bottle this moment, save it and send it back in time. Toss it into the Hudson or the East River and watch it bob along until an eleven-year-old me found it. I wish I could tell younger me that my parents loved me in their own way. It's not my fault it wasn't enough.

My parents loved each other at some point too, but by the time I was old enough to know what relationships were, there was a coldness. The ice grew and cracked until separate sheets floated, pulling us further away from each other. Now there's dry land and my mom's on it, solid and strong. It's time to ask for help.

"What can we do about Alan? My therapist thinks it sounds a little shady, especially since I haven't even seen the clause or the will itself."

"Your therapist? You'll go back?"

Can't she stick to the topic? It's hard enough asking for help, derailing my request does nothing.

"Yes, next week. But seriously. I need your help."

"I'll reach out to someone on the board tomorrow to get a feel for the environment there, make it sound like it's about me. We'll get my lawyer lined up and I'll ask Alan for a copy. If he refuses to provide one, we can have Charlie send discovery demands and claim we plan to dispute it."

Relief washes through me, sudden and overwhelming. It's been just me for so long. I've never had someone to rely on, even with Giuliana I kept so much to myself. It's time I let someone in.

"You can tell him I'm drying out somewhere; he'll believe it."

"Matt... I'm not going to badmouth you, even if it's to lie. You're better than that and I won't give him the satisfaction."

My throat constricts with emotion, with this sense of family I found and lost and have somehow tentatively found again with my mom this time. How much of the distance between us is because of my father and his looming shadow? Gathering the courage, I ask her about him, even though bringing him up might hurt her.

"Hey, do you know why Dad left Italy? I've been trying to piece it together and I keep getting these bits from different people but nothing makes sense."

Isabella spoke about him with love—for the most part—and the inscription on the photograph told its own story. Andrea dropped that piece of information about Aria's death and I have no idea how to unpack that. Everything my father said about Italy in the press made it sound like something he'd rather forget. His name change spoke to that.

Sighing, my mother tenses and I know this is a mistake. The words are out, though. All I can do is hope she doesn't brush it aside.

"There was a woman, Aria, I think it was. It's been so long. Thomas and I met shortly after he got here. He was clawing his way up the corporate ladder trying to fill a hole in his heart and I was getting my start in New York's modeling scene. Both alone. Both hungry for success and fame, and everything that made us hate each other later on."

Staring out at the city, her eyes are glassy with the past. I wait, body poised—drawn back and taut like a bowstring.

"I only asked him about it once, after we were engaged. Thomas told me that he'd betrayed his best friend and he couldn't stand to face him. They had feelings for the same woman, but she was closer with his friend. One drunken night Thomas came onto her and they shared a kiss. Aria pulled away shortly after, explaining her feelings weren't as strong as his, but his friend…"

"Lorenzo," I supply, giving her a piece she doesn't have.

"Lorenzo saw them and left, very upset. Aria wanted to go after him and she fought with Thomas, urging him to give her his car keys. Since they'd been drinking and she was so upset, he tried to stop her. When she insisted, he begged to go along with her, but she refused."

My mother's breath shudders out of her chest now. The past glistening between us, I can picture it somehow. Casting my mind's eye, I see the living room how they'd left it, and the gravel road twisting up through the grove.

"Your father stayed behind and finished off the bottle. He woke up to his best friend in the hospital and the woman he believed he loved dead. Apparently, she'd caught up with Lorenzo and tried to get him to stop, but lost control of the car."

Oh god. The photograph flashes in my mind, their broad smiles so clear in my memory. I can only imagine how ugly it must have gotten between them after.

"The rift couldn't be repaired. Lorenzo blamed your father, Thomas blamed himself. He couldn't stay, not with things the way they were after what he'd done. It was one of his biggest regrets. Lorenzo accused Thomas of being selfish, greedy. Always wanting what wasn't rightfully his."

All words I can see myself using against my father. But now I know he's suffered loss—know he walked away from the only family he had because of the shame he felt. I'm about to be sick. Guilt drove him away the same way it did me. He wanted more than he should've. So have I.

Abundantia wasn't rightfully mine. In trying to get both the grove and Giuliana, my greed tore it all away from me. And that rift can't be repaired either.

"Are you okay?" my mother asks, probably because she's watching me have some kind of fucked up epiphany.

"Yeah, uh... I think I might be relating to Dad for the first time and it feels like an out-of-body experience." I try to laugh it off but my heart aches with something I don't know how to put a name to.

With every year passing, my father seemed like more and more of a stranger. The distance grew until he began to feel less like a person to me. Thomas Palmer became a figurehead in my mind—a name, a bogeyman. Something to be defied and hated, and feared.

But maybe. Maybe he was just a man. Like me.

Flawed, fucked up. Incapable of loving in the right way— drowning. I wish I could face him now to ask him the questions I've finally found the words for. If I only had a few more minutes with him—to rail at him and forgive him... To look him in the eye as a man and not the lonely little boy with a stone in his chest.

Like it or not, Thomas Palmer had an immense effect on me and my life. His choices echo through mine and I walk a similar path he did. I want to tell him that I'll fix it. I'll do better. I'll heal what both of us have hurt. But I can't.

And somehow it cracks me wide open. That... missed opportunity to know him, and for him to know the man I'm becoming.

I taste salt at the back of my throat, on the corners of my lips. Air won't pass through my nose and I'm gasping, little catches in my breathing through my tears. My mother, bless her, hesitates for only a moment before wrapping me up in a hug.

"I never cried. I never cried at the funeral." I sob into her shoulder. "I never said goodbye because I was too pissed."

Shushing me, she runs a gentle hand over my curls but it's

like bloodletting. The poison I've kept inside of me for so long is finally seeping out.

"Alan said he was glad to be rid of Dad, and I hated him for it. I hated myself even more for thinking the same thing. I'm so sorry." I don't know who I'm apologizing to, whether it's her or Dad or me.

It's sure as fuck not Alan but I can't even spare another thought for him under the torrent of this grief and guilt that I've carried with me all year. Anger, black ichor, leaches out and my body releases it through every sob and tear. My mother holds me through it all, rocking me against her shoulder.

I'm all stages of myself at once. I'm the petulant child, the rebellious teenager, the broken angry man. Every part of me clings to her as my repressed pain pushes toward the surface. My father wasn't perfect, and I'm not either. But I can let him go now, after almost thirty years I finally have a grip on the man I wish I'd gotten to know.

I grieve for the untouchable Thomas Palmer and the unfamiliar Tommaso de Palma, and by the time my tears have dried he's not a stranger anymore. He'll be a part of me forever and the best way I can honor him—both the good and bad parts—is to learn from his mistakes.

"Thank you, Mom. I'm sorry for all of this, but I'm so glad I have you." Pulling away from her, her eyes are red-rimmed too, and the tip of her nose pink.

She plants a kiss on my forehead and although there's no medical reason why it should, it makes the pounding in my head just a little less painful.

"I love you, and he did too. Even though he didn't know how to show it. Even though he did it wrong."

"I know. I know that now."

"We're going to figure this out, I promise." My mother's smile is kind, tired but full of reassurance. Choosing to believe that despite how drained I feel now, I nod.

I close myself off in the guest room. The space is dark except for the city lights beyond. This world is familiar but so different now that I'm the one changed. New York never fit properly, and now I doubt it ever will. Italy gave me a peace and happiness I'd never imagined for myself.

The least I can do is try to return some of that peace and happiness to Giuliana.

Opening my laptop, I pull up a blank document and get started. It's time to set things straight and to fix what I can, for myself and for Giuliana. For our fathers and the past that sits between all of us like an open wound.

alling in all the personal favors I can, I pull from every single reserve I have. I draft and redraft until it's somewhere between an article and an essay. It'll never be an adequate apology but it's something. Finally, I have a chance to put my writing degree to use.

My mother's attempt at contacting a few board members proves enlightening. Apparently, the board wasn't notified of my little jaunt to Italy, business running the same as usual, and the members were under no expectation being CEO was contingent on taking over the grove. Alan proves as difficult the next day with my mother as he does with me; first screening her calls and then having his secretary give my mom half-answers and platitudes.

By the time Alan sends along a scrap of the will, it's been redacted to hide company information (something I doubt he has the power to do), but he cites "removal from my position" as his reason. Only the page relevant to my part in the clause is readable. Mom's already dropped it off with her lawyer, Charlie, and he's filing a motion of discovery, as well as a contest to the will. The will is old—older than we expected—which was a surprise.

When Charlie pushed for access to the will he hit a wall. Even though it's supposed to be public record and probate was filed (whatever the fuck that is), it's been filed under seal. The sensitivity of the will and my father's considerable influence are the excuse but my mother and I both agree: this is suspicious. If Alan truly won—if he gets everything regardless—then why is he even bothering to pester me? Why is the will hidden from us?

So, we gear up to fight. I never thought I'd be doing this when I was ready to walk away from it all. But the thought of Alan getting it pisses me off to no end. I don't want to win. I just want Alan to lose.

I keep away from the process, preferring to leave it in my mother and the lawyer's capable hands, because I have a bigger mess to contend with.

Starting with this essay. Pulling it up, I paste the preliminary link into the email. It'll go live tomorrow but Giuliana deserves a heads up, since I couldn't give her that last time.

My Italian Summer of Renaissance and Regrets
My reputation precedes me. It affords me a certain amount of privilege and notoriety. I've made many missteps in my colorful life as one of New York's corporate progenies. The opportunity to fade into being a stranger on an olive grove in Puglia, Italy proved too good to resist. This is my recounting of a summer of change and one giant mistake. Strap in for lies and fake proposals and very, very real love. The 'Palmer Playboy' (as I've been dubbed) falls, then crashes and burns.

I scroll through the introduction. The editors still have one more pass before it goes live. It's not great but it'll get the point across. For now, I need to get some of this out. I don't suppose she'll even open it but hopefully it'll get some of the press off our backs.

Most have heard the PR story of my father's start in New York, but his life in Italy has been somewhat of a mystery to me—or was until I ventured back to where he grew up. Grieving my father since his death a year ago hasn't been easy but getting to know the man he was in his youth put a lot of things into perspective. The biggest takeaway has been how lies and scheming don't have a happy ending. In trying to follow in my father's footsteps— to assert myself in business in Italy—I've lost the only person I've ever really loved. And I'd do it again. I'd lose her again if it means protecting her and her family from men like me and my father: people who focus on legalities over legacy, financial gain over family.

Alan is going to have a motherfucking field day with this. I wonder if we'll drop in points again, like when some of my escapades made the papers the last time I was in New York.

If you've managed to avoid the pictures online (good for you 'cause I certainly haven't), let me get you up to speed. I pretended to be a volunteer on an olive grove in order to gain the intel I needed to manage a takeover. Only, during my weeks and months in Italy, all I managed to do was fall for the enemy: Giuliana. Gorgeous, strong, wonderful Giuliana. The actual owner of the grove. I've since released my stake on the land—it belongs squarely to her and her family. But my lies kept building.

First was my identity and my reason for being there. But later it stretched as far as staging a fake proposal to help her research avenues to make the grove more profitable. Imagine my surprise to find pictures of that moment splashed across the internet. And her shock when she found out I've been nothing but a liar from day one. I fell in love with her family—the way they treated me with kindness and care—the jokes shared around the kitchen table and during long hours working the grove.
I fell in love with her in the quiet moments in between. I can't make it right, not in the way that counts. So, the best I can do is tell you all about how amazing she is and her plans for the future. I hope you'll feel inclined to help an incredibly hard-working woman achieve her dreams of honoring her legacy, and providing others with the tools to do the same.

Here goes nothing—one of those favors I asked my friends to help with. I insert some of the pictures I'd taken of the grove. Front and center are the farmhouse's before and after, and the link to the website I had my friend design. In the email I'm sending Giuliana is the instructions on how to access her website and my friend's information. Free for her and he'll do whatever she needs. Formatting will tidy up the rest of the article and make it decent for publication but I'm on borrowed time.

Giuliana's worked this land her whole life,

tradition dictating that she wasn't supposed
to inherit. But despite expectations and
societal prejudices, she excels. Her workers
are happy, made up of mostly women (after the
men on her father's payroll left when he died)
and a breeding ground for a program she hopes
to implement with money from a B&B onsite.
It's called agriturismo, and it's a way to get
a feel for Italian farm life while on
vacation.
In turn the profits will be going toward a
scholarship program for women in agriculture
and hands-on mentorship. It will give those
women a chance to seize their own destiny in
the overly male-dominated agricultural field.
It's impressive and it's difficult and I'm
going to help however I can, even though I'm
the last person she wants to hear from.
Giuliana deserves success and being featured
far more than I do. My notoriety and name have
been woefully underutilized. So, I intend to
use whatever platform I have left to amplify
her voice and the voices of those like her:
people who care deeply about community and the
betterment of others.

Beneath that lies the other favor I called in: a fundraiser for
people who would like to donate—not just to Giuliana but to
other female-led farming initiatives in Italy and the United
States. Rich people love nothing more than tax breaks and the
illusion of philanthropy. But it works in our favor now. These
women get what they need and my "friends" get to pat them-

selves on the back for helping their fellow man—or woman in this case.

Pressing send, my email is loosed into the internet ether and I don't know if Giuliana will want to open the article before it posts, or if it'll end up in the trash. But this is something small I could do to atone and make up for my multitude of mistakes. Giuliana deserves more, and I'm going to keep trying to make it up to her in whatever way I can.

I dress for my big meeting with Alan. He expects me to come in and sign my life away. But he doesn't know my mom is coming, or Charlie. I have no intention of going quietly. If I go down, I'm taking him with me. There are other shareholders capable of running my father's company, shareholders that aren't despicable assholes. We've been in contact with a few, and Alan's involvement is looking shadier by the day.

All we need to do is get Alan to admit he's been lying.

Making the trek up the elevator to his office, I try to ignore the sick lurch in my stomach as the floors dip beneath us. He'll know by now that I haven't come alone since the receptionists no doubt recognize my mother.

As for the grizzly old man she's brought with her, well... he's not what I expected. Charlie looks like he'd sooner be doing pro bono work than high-level inheritance and family law. But I like him immediately. He's scruffy with a white beard, kind eyes, and a host of wrinkles beside them. Like a courthouse Santa, only of average girth, and without the sack full of presents.

Alan's secretary tries to protest when we head straight for the office but my mother levels her with a look I'd hate to be on the receiving end of. I thrust the door open with all the courage I can muster. His eyes dart between us, and I realize I've never seen him so nervous.

Alan looked sleazy the last time I saw him—a little questionable. But I've never seen him look cowed before. Alan is smaller, lesser than I remember. Or I'm the one that's changed.

"Matt, nice of you to finally show up. I was worried you might be going back on our agreement."

"A worry that was well-founded, Alan, since I have no intention of signing anything."

Settling into the seat directly in front of him, my mother slides into the one beside me.

"Genevieve," Alan sneers and she scoffs in response, not even bothering with a greeting.

"This is my lawyer, Charlie. He has some questions for you regarding the validity of my father's will and the supposed clause you keep shoving in my face."

Charlie might look like Santa but it turns out he's like a bulldog on a leash—only contained as long as his master commands and then he's ready to rip into the threat.

"We managed to get a copy of the real will, Mr. Becker. Not only has it not been updated since prior to the divorce of Mr. and Mrs. Palmer, but there is no addendum stating that Matteo is in any danger of losing his inheritance."

Alan ignores him, staring me down. "Matteo, huh? Really leaning into the lie?"

"It's not a lie. It's the truest I've ever been to myself. Now, you better start talking or things are going to go very badly for you." Voice shaking with anger, I'm unable to keep the resentment at bay.

Because of this man and his threats, I was sent down a path that cost me everything I care about. Because of this man I've spent the last few months in fear. I will not waver again.

"The will is sealed, the probate not settled. There's no way you got your hands on it."

Alan sounds so fucking smug. I want to wipe that little constipated smile off his face. I still don't know what the fuck a probate is but Charlie assured us it's all in hand. Alan's lying through his teeth.

"You underestimate me, and my mother. Unlike the way you conduct your business she hasn't burned every bridge in this city on her way through."

Alan swallows hard, the cracks starting to show—ones that will spread and shatter the facade of his threats.

"We compared the redacted document you provided with the bonafide will we received and it appears some changes were made. Unauthorized." Charlie's voice is a rough gravel, like Sam Elliot without the drawl. I have no idea where my mom found this guy but he's fucking great.

Leaning forward, I rest my forearms on the desk as I stare my father's old lawyer down, taking in the too-smooth skin and the neck that surgery can't hide before I speak. "You know, Alan, fraud is such an ugly word. And in your position, how far you've climbed..." I chuckle, sick satisfaction burning through me. "It's a long way down."

"I don't like what you're insinuating. You're here to sign stating you understood the repercussions of your actions. Unlike usual you won't be skating by on good looks and your daddy's money. It's time to grow the fuck up."

"That's the thing though. I have grown up. And with that came a lot of reflection. Whether I get this money or not is irrelevant to me. All I care about is seeing you rot for the harm you've done to me and my family."

Alan rolls his eyes at me. "Always blaming someone else for your shortcomings. When are you going to face up to the fact that you're nothing? Without your father's money and his name, you're worthless. You haven't done a single thing of merit in your life and now you never will."

Rage builds in my chest, my lungs tight with the scream of frustration that I want to loose into his face. He's wrong. Alan is wrong about me but I can't give in to my emotions to try and disprove his statement. It's what he wants and what he's bargaining on.

"That's your opinion. One of many that I don't give a fuck about. Now, show me the will or I walk."

"You've already lost, your threats hold no sway." He leans back in his chair and crosses his arms over his chest as if he's reclining somewhere relaxing, unbothered by the scene.

"See, I don't think that's true. If I automatically lost everything, why are you so worried about me signing now? Is it because people are starting to question the validity of my signature as of late? We've been having some conversations with the rest of Palmer Enterprises and things just aren't adding up. If I've lost, why are the board members and police currently in a meeting discussing your misappropriation of funds? Trying to figure out which documents you've forged over the last year?"

And there it is. His eyelid twitches, nostrils flaring despite his attempt at looking casual.

"No, Alan. I think you've misunderstood what we're doing here. It was a chance for you to be open. Honest. To *cooperate*. That clause is nothing but a piece of paper you invented when my antics threatened your bottom line. You were sick of me getting in your way. Even as my mentor and basically interim-CEO you were tired of having to ask for signatures and beg me to join board meetings. When it became clear I wasn't going to let you mold me into what you needed, you wanted to get rid of me. What more foolproof way than to have me give up—no one could blame you then. Italy was a distraction to get me out of your way."

Alan pushes away from his desk, his chair shoved back and spinning into the wall with the force of his movement.

"You're full of shit. You shouldn't have any of this. You didn't *earn* it. You didn't spend night after night up here with your father, sacrificing everything for this company."

Seething, Alan's chest rises and falls with rapid breaths. His words are spit out like they taste bitter and he needs to expel them off his tongue.

"I didn't. But that doesn't change the fact that he *still* didn't choose you. Thomas Palmer chose family over business at the end of the day and it kills you. No matter what you do, you'll never be considered anything but his lackey. The man who did all the dirty work for none of the praise." I rise from my seat as well, advancing on him.

"He should have updated the fucking will. What kind of self-respecting businessman leaves that sort of thing untouched?" Alan shouts now, backing his way toward the door.

"My father knew he couldn't trust you with it. Plus, family law is a little outside your purview. Something we're all glad for now, despite your attempts to fudge things."

"You can't prove a damn thing!"

I know he's made sure of it, or tried. But the forensics people will be on it soon and with the cooperation of the rest of the board it'll be short work.

"You should have forged my fucking signature again, saved yourself this whole scenario."

"You're right," he says. "I just wanted the satisfaction of seeing your face while you did it."

Hubris. They say pride goeth before a fall for a reason. It's Alan's turn to find it out.

"And now it's going to cost you everything."

Alan yanks open the office door and is met by two police-men, biding their time. It took a little convincing for them to let me do my little scene, but they're getting the arrest we promised. There's a bit of a scuffle as he resists at first, but once the first cold cuff is slipped around his wrist and the police start reciting his rights, he goes very still.

Alan stares back over his shoulder at me with hatred simmering on his face and I know the victory won't be all I wanted. Yes, I've called him out and proven what an asshole he is. But he knows how to work the system. Even if he sees time, he'll find a way to whittle it down by cutting a deal with someone.

At least he'll never be an issue for my family again. Turning back to my mom, she has a small smile on her face and gives me a nod of approval.

"You ever considered law, kid? You've got a knack for the dramatics while cutting to the meat of the issue." Charlie sounds impressed and I try not to let the praise get to me. This was the bare minimum I could do to honor what my father built, and fix the mistakes borne from my neglect and disinterest.

"Nah. I can't stand being cooped up in an office. Let's get the hell out of here."

There will be more discussions about business and how things will be run from now on, but the itch is back and I need to get out of this building before I lose my mind. There's no voice this time, though. It's something I've failed to notice the past few days since my last session with Dr. Pritchard. The inner asshole has grown quieter and quieter. As if trying to fix things, trying to do what's right, has finally given it a reason to shut up.

Stepping out of the elevator, our feet slap against the lobby floors. When the automatic doors whoosh open in front of me and hard concrete meets the soles of my shoes, I finally breathe. I've never been so happy to be on a fucking sidewalk. It's over.

Alan has no hold over me anymore.

I'm free.

The article hits the internet like a bomb, and coupled with the news of Alan's arrest and fraud allegations it blows up even more. Palmer Enterprises seems poised for freefall. Stocks aren't looking great and the board members are panicking. I'm so close to being done with it but I can't leave while this mess hangs over me.

I call a meeting, the second I've initiated in days if you count the one just prior to Alan's arrest. Men and women in stuffy suits sit around the oval table in my father's largest conference room, talking. The din of disagreement carries from down the hall but it quiets when I step into the room. When I slide into my father's seat at the head of the table it's so quiet, I can hear the acid gurgling in my stomach.

"Thank you all for joining me. I know there's a lot of turmoil going on right now and I appreciate you taking time out of your day to attend this meeting." Injecting as much authority into my voice as I can, I hope they'll take me seriously. At least this one time.

"I'm sure you all have a lot of questions about the state of the company now that Alan's been arrested. I'll try to touch on the main points first. He's being held for now. Bail is set very high so we're hopeful he won't be able to get out right away. Especially now that his accounts have been frozen for investigation."

My back muscles ache from trying to keep my body still and stop my feet from bouncing against the floor.

"Which leads me into my second point: as of right now Palmer industries is under audit. We will cooperate fully with police and investigators to make sure the full extent of the duplicity is uncovered. While I can't fix what's already happened, I can make sure that we weed out any wrongdoing to minimize further damage to the company."

Dozens of eyes are watching me—trained on me—and I fucking hate it. But it's not forever. I just need to keep it together for a little bit longer, until the meeting and press release are over. I can do this. I have to do this.

"There's been a lot of concern over the company since my father's death and worry over whether I have what it takes to step into his role. Especially now that the 'mentor' who was helping me transition into CEO is behind bars."

Some of them tense, trying not to lean into every word I'm saying, but there's fear in their eyes.

"I'm here to say that I don't have what it takes to take over this company and I'm fully aware of my shortcomings. So, because of that I'll be selling my majority share back to the corporation and it will be distributed between whichever board members remain to buy it out. The board will elect a new CEO from the remaining pool. Personally, I'd like to throw my vote behind Graham Renner, but I know my say doesn't count for much." My mom's inside-man who helped us look into the will and exposed Alan's forgeries would be a far better replacement.

It's at this point that the room erupts again, voices carrying over others. Some argue they can't stay on a sinking ship; others are pleased to have the millstone of Matt Palmer removed from the situation.

Rising from the seat, I clear my throat behind the near-choking top button of my shirt. The tie is like a hand around my neck. *Almost done. I'm almost done.*

They quiet when I hold my hand out.

"I'll be holding a press conference highlighting the same points I just mentioned, and that will be my last measure as my father's heir. We all know Palmer Enterprises is better off without me and I have full faith that it will survive. Thomas Palmer built an empire. It will not fall because of the greed of one man."

I wait one breath, two, for the words to sink in. I see a few nods before leaving the room and the chaos inside of it. It's not perfect. I could have given them some warning but there's been no time. In the long run this is the best solution. They've served on the board for years—some for as long as I've been alive. The business will survive. But I won't if I'm forced to stay inside of it.

Stepping out onto the same sidewalk I'd praised not too long ago; a small podium is set up and a bunch of reporters lie in wait. Flashes of light slash over my face and dance across my vision as I settle behind the microphone. Despite the fact that my hands are balled into shaking fists at my sides, hidden behind the podium, my voice is steady.

My fingernails dig divots into the soft flesh of my palm but I speak with conviction, laying out the same discussion points as in that meeting room.

"I have full belief that Palmer Enterprises will survive this. We are ready to face this blight on our name and eager to cooperate with investigators to make sure this company is again above reproach. My father was one man, a looming shadow, but one man nonetheless. There are countless employees who've worked hard for this company, from the custodians and receptionists, and all the way up to those who worked closely with my father to make it a success. I will not give Alan Becker—*one man* —the satisfaction of destroying what my father and so many others worked hard to build."

Questions are launched at me from all sides but I'm too exhausted to formulate responses. Looking beyond the crowd, I check for my mother's town car and Clyde. I play it off, slathering a smile onto my face despite the cold sweat crawling up the back of my neck.

"No further comment. Any questions can be fielded to the governing board of directors. They are currently hard at work inside. And me... well, we all know Matt Palmer was never CEO material."

A few of them chuckle along with me and their questions shift from business to personal.

"What's next for you, Matt? Another party? Another girl?" one reporter shouts and something inside my belly shrivels. But I spot Clyde, and work my way through the crowd, smile in place.

"I need to take a nap, man. Corporate overhauls are no joke."

I push past shoulders and elbows, surrounded by smothering body heat. In a way this is no different to those parties I drowned myself in before Italy. A press of bodies who want something from me. Something I don't have to give. Cameras go off in my face.

"What about that Italian girl, Giuliana? We saw your article. Was that the real deal? Did the Palmer Playboy finally meet his match?" a young woman yells from behind me and my feet fail me. I'm stuck, my body trapped, my brain begging me to keep going but I'm frozen at the mention of her name.

It was only a matter of time.

I turn to face her, the female reporter impeding my desperate exit. There's two ways I could play this. Matt Palmer could lean into what she's saying, crack another joke and make a smooth exit. But he's gone—left in the skyscraper behind me, the glass coffin of greed and poisonous ambition.

Instead, I give a sad smile with my heart in my eyes. "My match and then some."

Shoving my way through the last of them, I sag into the car. Clyde shuts them out with the thud of the door closing. Tension melts away under exhaustion. It's finally done. My body relaxes after the pressure of the day—the tension and friction keeping me up for two days straight. Somewhere between the financial district and Bryant Park, exhaustion pulls me under. The car rocks me into a state between everything and nothing.

Sometime later Clyde slams his car door. The sound echoing through the concrete parking lot under my mother's building pulls me from my nap. I'm going to sleep for the next week, I swear to god. No wonder my dad croaked under the pressure of it. Thank fuck I don't have to deal with it anymore. My mom and her lawyer will see to it that the *real* will is enacted. The funds my father set aside will be tucked away to gather interest, and when I find my feet again, I'll put it toward something worthwhile.

My mother waits inside, wrapping me up in a quick hug before I pull the tie from my neck and unbutton the suffocating shirt.

"We'll have dinner in an hour or so, okay?" Her voice is gentle, as if she can tell how much of a toll this has taken on me.

"I'm going to lie down for a little first. I passed out in the car on the way here." I give a tired laugh, relief not quite sinking in yet but well on its way.

Kicking my dress shoes off by the door, I flop down onto my bed face first. My phone on the bedside table is going nuts. It has been all day, which is part of why I left it here in the first place. When will the vultures give it a rest?

Some morbid sense of curiosity wants to see how many people have tried to reach me today when they never bothered during the summer. How many "friends" want to connect now that my name's all over the internet and gossip surrounds me again? I scroll through the first few dozen messages and notifications before tiring of it all. I should turn the damn thing off. So I do. The screen turns dark and I settle in for a nap.

I feel like I've barely nodded off when my mom shakes me awake. Eyes burning with fatigue, I know I've had one of those naps where time ceases, and becomes irrelevant. It could be one hour or one day of sleep. Either way my face is creased from the pillow and my hair is a riot of mussed curls.

Wiping the bit of drool from my cheek, I ask. "Dinner time?"

"Actually, there's someone here to see you."

"Mom, I've had enough of people for today. No more reporters, no more answering questions. I'm tired." So tired. Can't she just let me curl into a ball and recover from the whirlwind of the last few months?

I have a broken heart to nurse. It's not only the stress of Alan and the business, and this mess with the press. I lost something big—something I have no right to want. That sort of thing leaves a mark and it'll take a while to get over it.

"Trust me."

I've used that line enough times to know it must be serious, or at least that my mother thinks it'll be in my best interest. She's done a lot for me the last while. I can handle talking to one of her people if it's going to help her.

My mother slips out of the room, the door clicking shut behind her and I take the time to try and make myself more presentable. It's kind of a wash though. The button up, ironed and pressed this morning, is now an array of ridges and wrinkles where I've slept in it not once, but twice. The sleeves are some combination of rolled up and shoved up onto my forearms. My hair has fought the product that kept it contained this morning, curls a halo around my head and I know I look ridiculous.

Whoever it is better not have a freaking camera.

Wiping my hand across my face, I clear the last remnants of

sleep, and steel myself with a deep breath before leaving the sanctuary of my room.

Standing in the living room, staring out at the city, is our guest.

And I feel faint.

My head spins with hope, my heart racing at the possibility.

There's no way. There's no fucking way. She said she never wanted to see me again.

She's so close though it makes my chest hurt. The curtain of dark hair, the soft curve of her waist. I want it to be her so badly and I'm terrified to hope.

But then she turns and I soak her in incrementally. The slant of her eyebrow, the rich warm brown of her eyes. The full lips that I've savored and missed and despaired for. How is she here? In my mother's apartment? In New York?

The harvest is over but I'm sure she has pressing matters back home. Still, my confusion is no match for the wonder at seeing her in the flesh, on my turf, a few steps away.

"*Lia...*" I breathe, fearful that the moment is going to disappear. One wrong move and this will all be a figment of my imagination.

Then my mother clears her throat behind us to let me know we're not alone. "I'm going to head out for dinner and leave you to it."

Mom gives us both a little smile and when I look back at Giuliana, she's got one on her face as well, that little divot of her dimple cutting into her cheek. So fucking beautiful. I drink in the sight of her, parched, desperate. I've never wanted to move as much as I do now. A few steps and I could touch her skin—feel the warmth of it seep into bones brittle and exposed.

How the fuck did I think I'd be able to get over her given time? No measure would do it. Giuliana's crawled under my skin, burrowed so deep into who I am just a second of seeing her pulls me back in. Silence cocoons us in a bubble of everything I want to say but can't. The door shuts behind my mother, overly loud in the room. It becomes unbearable and, in my discomfort, I blurt out the first thing that comes to mind.

"What are you doing here?"

Giuliana's smile drops along with my stomach. God, I'm an idiot. One thing is certain besides death and taxes: I'll find a way to fuck it up. This time it's my inability to say the right thing.

The soft catch of Giuliana's inhale sounds so close and I can't believe she's here, breathing the same air as me. Behind her, the dusk of New York City lights her up like before—my personal goddess come down to earth. It's gorgeous, she's gorgeous, and when she leaves, I'll never be okay again but I don't care. Not when I get to see her now, one more time.

She reaches into her bag and pulls out a bottle, dark green with the *Abundantia* label on the front and my mind is thrust back to that day at the beginning when I joked about my reward for passing the volunteer program.

I wait, scared to breathe as she opens her mouth to speak.

"I brought you this. It's the product of this year's harvest and will be distributed soon but I thought you deserved a taste before it goes out. You did earn it after all."

I take a tentative step toward her and wrap my hand around the glass, the sides of our fingers touching as the bottle changes hands. The need to breathe her in, to nuzzle my face into her neck and clutch her to me, feels like my life depends on it.

She must see it. It's written all over my face, sleep-wrinkled and all.

Giuliana's spiced rum eyes are molten when she looks up at me and I'm trapped in the world of emotions there. "Teo..." she whispers, and I'm on the balls of my feet ready to surge forward if she says the word.

I set the bottle of olive oil down on the nearest surface and step as close as I dare. She bites her bottom lip and my eyes are caught there, on wants and memories, and the tart sweetness of the taste I know awaits. It looks like she might invite it. She's here, after all. Instead, she hits me with cold water in the form of her next sentence, and it opens a chasm of distance I wish didn't exist.

"We need to talk."

ot what I hoped to hear from that delectable mouth, but it's expected, I suppose. Giuliana's had time to think and collect all her anger and pain into what will no doubt be a well-rehearsed speech. She is poised, deliberate, and not one for half measures. Despite her occasional anxiety around pulling things off, she's steady and confident. Giuliana wouldn't be here if she wasn't ready to be.

Still, I want to stall for time and get as much out of this situation as possible before she dissipates. When she leaves back to Italy, she'll take my heart with her.

"Do we have to do this here?" It's stupid. We could talk anywhere. It doesn't matter that we're in my mother's apartment.

The question stumps her—her shoulders deflating a little as if she'd been preparing to launch into the discussion. But she shrugs in agreement.

"I feel strange in my mom's apartment. Plus, you've never been to New York before, right?"

Shaking her head, she looks over her shoulder at the city as if just remembering she's here.

"So, let me take you out somewhere. It can be as private or public as you'd like, but you should get a feel for the city at least once."

Let me show you my corner of the world. Or at least Central Park.

Pulling the strap of her purse closer to her body as if gathering courage, Giuliana nods and follows me out of the apartment. I'm going to burst out of my skin and lose my mind, or fizz into an effervescent haze in the autumn air. She's here. *Giuliana is here with me.*

We don't talk. This silence between us is delicate. One wrong move and it'll all be over.

It's already over.

While not as mean as some of the other things I've said to myself, it's no less devastating. Waiting at the crosswalk, we listen for the beep and tick letting us know we can go. The symphony of New York is such a juxtaposition to what we had in Italy. There's no summer night sounds of bugs and birds—no light breeze ruffling the olive branches and infusing the air with the scent of earth and fruit.

New York wafts the smell of car fumes and too many people. It's hot and cold. The asphalt is warm from the sun but a sharp fall wind sucks between tall buildings and launches directly at us. It teases her aroma around my nose—her summer scent that I'll relish until the day I die and search for in every warm day.

Giuliana looks out of place, not because of the loose strands of her hair dancing in the air or her clothing, which is fine. Jeans, sweater, boots. It's her gaze—trained up and around trying to take in every inch of the city as we walk. Her brown eyes are wide and a sense of excitement vibrates through both of us. Trying to see it the way she might, I consider how it would come across for the first time.

The city is loud and famous, nowhere near the history of Italy but the stuff of legends regardless. When we make it to Central Park, the trees are lit up and glowing with golden sunset. I can't help but find it beautiful. Giuliana must agree because she does a little twirl—a 360-degree view to absorb it all.

And it's that excitement, that thirst for something new on her face that spurs me into action. A horse snickers nearby, drawing my attention to the carriage ride. It's something that always felt stupid and touristy to me but has a certain charm now. Without thinking I grab her hand, tugging her toward the carriage, and hoist her into the seat as soon as the driver gives the okay.

"Teo... I don't know about this."

The nickname does me in. Things can't be all bad if she's still using it. It means something, right?

"This'll give us a way to see a bit of the city and the privacy to talk. Unless you'd prefer to do it in a restaurant or on a park bench?"

The clop of the horse's hooves starts against the road while she considers, and her lips thin into a little line. "Okay. This is fine."

As the horses turn onto one of the paths off the main road, I gather the courage to look at her. I've stalled for long enough. Hopefully the scenery will soften the blow, or at least put her in a merciful mood.

"Now, although I put my foot in it earlier, I really do want to know what brought you here. You said you wanted to talk, but the way we left things..."

It was a fucking mess. Her ordering me away from her life will never leave my memory and it's precisely why I'm confused. Why would she have come? The article was supposed to help. But I don't imagine it's enough to fix everything.

Reaching into the bag she's got nestled on her lap, Giuliana pulls out my journal. That fucking journal I left in the desk drawer in my room. *Her* room, technically. It was only ever going to be mine temporarily.

"*Shit.*" I don't mean for it to slip out but I think of everything I've written in there. From the first day of deceit all the way through to the end, when I'd given everything up for her. I want to say something else, and promise that I can explain everything, but the journal does that for me.

Between the article and that book in her hand my heart is laid bare.

"Did you mean it?" Giuliana asks.

"Which part?" I'm not sure if I'm actually expecting a response but she flips to a page she's got dog-eared and it does something to me, to know that she's read it all.

It fucks me up a little to see Giuliana run her fingertips across the paper, caressing my words the same way I'd done to hers before. As if she's trying to gather some kind of essence of me from pen put to paper.

She clears her throat and reads my words aloud: *"I've finally found something that makes the pain worth it. The one who makes me want to be a better person and who I'll risk everything for."*

Her breath shudders for a moment and she skips ahead slightly.

"When I leave, I'll carry this love home with me like a souvenir of hurt. Because I do love Giuliana. So, she comes first. Everything else is background noise."

Past and present collide in the most potent of ways as my feelings are spoken aloud and yet, I don't say a word. Lost in this moment, time slips away from us with the sun, darkness spreading. Soon, she won't be able to see the words anymore. Soon, we'll be wrapped in night, and it'll be even harder to pretend I'm unaffected by how close we are.

"She's like a drug, in my bloodstream and on my mind, every second of every day. I love her. I've finally fallen and I understand. You want them to be happy above all else. Their needs supersede your own. And Giuliana doesn't need me. No matter how desperately I need and want and love her."

Voice shaking by the end, I could swear Giuliana's getting choked up. Dusk gives way to twilight and the shadows lengthen, robbing me of every detail of her expression.

"Teo..." she sighs.

"I'm so sorry. I'm *so, so* sorry. I will regret it until the day I die."

Her gaze whips up from the journal to my face and I see pain etched there.

"*She's better off.*" Giuliana reads off that line and my chest cracks wide open. All my self-doubt and hatred are out in the open. "Is that really what you think? That I'm better off without you?"

"What place do I have at your side? I've brought you and your family nothing but trouble, and lies, and hurt. I want to say I wish I'd never come but I'm too selfish for that. I don't want to give that up. Those memories are some of the best in my life. So, I'm sorry I fucked up but I'm not sorry I met you." The words are harsh, hoarse coming out around the tightness of my throat and the emotion packing down onto my vocal cords.

"I'm not sorry I love you," I whisper.

Love. Present tense. Because it's not going to change and I need to say it out loud at least once before we part again.

"You hurt me, Matteo. You betrayed me."

"I know."

"Your article and these words can't change that."

"No."

The sky is a wash of blues. From the darkest purple above, to a periwinkle dipped in gold where the sun's surrendered to the horizon, stars peek out from their daytime slumber. Giuliana's face is nothing but dark lines and curves in the evening around us. Her expression is lost to me and so I pay attention to the catch in her breathing and the feel of her body trembling next to mine.

Why are you here? If it changes nothing—if it doesn't matter— why did you come?

I can't ask. I don't want to push her... away.

"But—" she starts, and I swear to god I suck in a breath like

I've been submerged far too long and I've no idea if I'm about to be plunged back under. "It's a start. You hurt me, in so many ways, but reading this..."

She holds up the journal and waves it to and fro before tucking it under her hands in her lap. "How could you possibly think I'd be better off without you? Teo, you make me brave. I'm tenacious, sure, but it's from necessity, not belief. Spite kept me going but *you* gave me a chance to see myself as you saw me. You make me want to believe that I can do it all and deserve it, too, without the need to prove myself."

"Giuliana—" I start but she lifts her hand to stop me, and I wait.

"I'm not good with words. I'm not a writer or a poet; I'm just a farmer. I'm better with actions than words, and my hands are what I use to show the earth love and respect. My hands are how I express myself. Time and strength, passion and pain, all of it shows on my palms and the callouses beneath my fingers, but I realize that you can't see how empty my hands are without yours to hold. So, I'm here. To say the words." Her voice wobbles as she speaks, as it rushes out of her, and she gesticulates with those beautiful hands before they knot together in a worried clutch.

"I"—this time she's the one to stumble and struggle with the words—"I love you too."

Hand shaking, I bring it up to her jaw, spanning the side of her face. I rub my thumb against the soft, hot skin of her cheek. We're suspended in this second of time before we both surge forward.

Lips meet, needy and not enough. Salt against her mouth, I tug her closer to my body and feel the press of her softness and the hard ridges of that fucking journal between us. It's the kind of kiss that stops time. A connection restored. A love acknowledged bursting between us from embers we've harbored all summer to an inferno that rivals the hues of autumn.

I touch every inch of her I can, reverently. Adoration brushed against the edge of her jaw, my fingers trail over the slope of her shoulder and the soft dip at her waist—the one I've been stupidly in love with since that first touch on the Vespa. Sound fades and I'm caught up in the feel of her heat, driving away the rapidly dropping temperature. Her heartbeat thunders, or maybe that's mine, and eventually we realize the carriage has come to a stop.

The driver—bless him—has had the grace not to stop us, just staring out into the street and minding his own damn business. I would too, considering he gets paid based on time and not distance.

Honking cars and music pouring out of a venue nearby filter back into my senses. The light from a nearby streetlamp spills across Giuliana's face, highlighting kiss-swollen lips and the pink tip of her nose. She stares up at me with her heart in her eyes and I would do anything for this woman.

I'd go down on my knees and kiss the ground at her feet if she asked. Even though it's New York so it's fucking filthy.

How do I ask where to go from here? What does this mean?

Sensing my hesitation, Giuliana lifts her hand to my cheek and traces her thumb against my lips. I plant a little kiss against the swirls and ridges there.

"Teo..." Turning my face into her hand, I lean into that touch as if it's going to fortify every corner of my aching heart.

"Yes, love." I whisper, afraid of what comes next and worried this is goodbye. This will be the part of the night where punishment comes to greet me.

But as usual she knocks me off my guard, the same way she's always done.

"*Ti perdono.*" Her voice is sweet, the words of amnesty

sweeter because I don't need to speak Italian to understand. Written all over her face, it's in the touch of her hand against my cheek like a boon.

"Come home, please." She's the light guiding me, and her words are ones I didn't know how desperate I was to hear until this moment. Everything I've wished for is in the back of a carriage, on a corner of the city that's never truly felt like mine.

"Yes."

Epilogue

One Year Later

Harvest comes around so quickly this time. Though, I suppose it makes sense when considering everything we've been doing to ensure its success. Giuliana isn't in the office when I peek my head in. Her empty chair overlooks the grove. Standing there for a minute with my hands on the top of it, I stare out at the place that changed my life.

It looks the same, in the sense that seasons change and fruit grows and ripens before dropping from branches. Rain washes away footprints and colorful birds peck at the ground afterwards. Change is a constant. It's lifeblood and excitement. A tiny yawn breaks my concentration and I look down to find Cora curled up on the seat of Giuliana's chair. It took me about a week to figure out she'd named the damn cat after an olive cultivar, but she was sneaky about it. It wasn't until she'd admonished the kitten and called her Coratina that I realized.

Cuddled into a little ball, Cora gets her fur all over the seat. I know Lia will complain while she wipes the chair down but then leave the door wide open and let the cat right back onto it. Two very headstrong ladies.

On the desk there's a piece of paper, neatly folded in half with my name on the front. Unfolding it, I smile as I trace the handwriting I've become so familiar with.

I miss you, amore. The volunteers are lovely but I can't lie, I'm counting the seconds until harvest is over. As much as my aching body appreciates your hands in the evenings, I can't wait for it to be done so I can curl into bed with you and sleep until I've had my fill. Dawn is pretty, but I'd rather enjoy it from the other side of my eyelids.

My chuckle startles Cora and she gives me the cat version of side eye. I never realized Giuliana isn't a morning person until after we got back from New York. Apparently, I pissed her off every morning last summer by necessitating my little wake-up calls when she'd much rather have stayed in bed until the very last minute.

Want to sneak off with me once the party is in full swing?

Oh, she has no idea how much I'd love to escape with her again. We can't be late though, not like last time. This year Giuliana has to give a speech and I get to stand by her side and look pretty. Pulling a pen from the holder on the desk, I scratch my reply onto the paper.

You can count on it. I'll see you at our spot around sunset? After a shower lol

Cora gets a little scratch behind her ear before I head out to see to my own harvest duties. Isabella knows and the plan is in motion. After things wind down for the evening, she'll be heading into Gravina with Chiara to give us a little privacy. I just have to survive the heart palpitations until then.

Joining countless others in the rows, my mechanical picker sends vibrations down my arms. Ripe olives cascade onto the netting, hitting the ground with a soft thud as they skid and collect. Sunlight bakes my body, leaving a trail of sweat down my back. I move with a confidence I couldn't have fathomed last year.

Matt Palmer was soft-handed, arrogant, and lost.

I'm thankful to say I am no longer any of those things. Though Giuliana might disagree on the arrogant front, I *know* I've been humbled by this whole experience. I doubt I'll ever truly be tamed though.

Catching her eye as she walks among us, I survey the progress we've made. We share a secret smile and she gives me a nod—one that lets me know she saw my response on her letter. My thoughts race to that night on the hill.

No, never fully tamed.

By late afternoon my entire body is an ache and my arms are shaky from holding the machine up all day. I'm covered in dust and sweat. We—the workers and the newest batch of volunteers —all head up toward the big house once it's done. Taking turns, we scrub our hands and gather around the stone courtyard. When we run out of room the crowd spills over onto the grass around the house.

Glasses of sparkling liquid are passed around. The aroma of good food wafts from the house, reminding all of us how strenuous the day has been and how starved we are. But, there's something else to do first. Giuliana steps up onto a chair, tapping against her glass with a tiny fork to get everyone's attention.

"I'd like to take the time to thank you all for your hard work over the season. This place functions and flourishes because of people like you and I am so grateful. I know everyone is hungry. We've got a spread of food coming soon. But I had to say this before the night devolves because of the music and drinks."

The crowd laughs, tension from the day already dissolving, and I stare up at her with wonder. Even with a dirt smudge across her forehead and her hair tumbling from the bun she's tried and failed to secure all day... Giuliana is the most exquisite creature I've ever laid eyes on. Hanging on her every word, I'm tethered to the honeyed tone of her voice. I can't wait until that voice is wrapped around my name.

And her legs are wrapped around your waist? The voice jokes. It's not wrong—not in the slightest—and it makes me chuckle a little. Because yes, I'd love for her to be wrapped around me. It's been a busy week mostly spent apart. I've missed her and her body.

"It's been a whirlwind of a year. Besides officially kicking off our volunteer initiative, we've also established a scholarship program and partnered with a nearby farm to source fresh ingredients to ensure the best for our B&B. There's even been some talk of trying to convince Nonna to turn our kitchen into a restaurant, but I'm sure after a long day of cooking like today she'd scold me for saying so."

More laughs this time from people acquainted with Isabella, all fully aware of how well she'd take to being coerced into anything. My eyes scan the crowd trying to find her but she's likely still inside getting everything ready.

"Guests have visited the grove this year from all corners of the world, but it's *you*. It's every one of you that makes this possible. My father and his father and all those who came before have poured their love into this land and I'm so proud to be able to say we're doing the same. So please, raise a glass as we toast to this new beginning and fresh iteration of the dreams of our predecessors."

I walk over to the sign we've got covered—the one that's going to go over the road at the entrance. It took almost all year to complete but it had to feel right. Harvest was the best time for it. My hand wraps around the fabric, ready to pull it off as soon as I get Giuliana's cue. The crowd raises their glasses, waiting.

"To the past. To *Abundantia,* and to the future…" Giuliana's voice rings out, clear and sure.

"To *Rinascita!*"

Tugging the fabric away, it flutters off of the sign with a swish. Burned into the wood is the new name—a vow as much as a brand. It's a message to all who enter and to those of us who know what lies beneath it. *Rinascita* is forgiveness in the face of love. It's letting go of grief and loss and fear to take charge of our own destinies. The name represents the rebirth of possibility. This land is Giuliana's but it's my home as well, and will be for the rest of my life. Our lives, if I have a say in it.

Cheering in celebration, we tip the crisp liquid into our mouths, bubbles fizzing along our throats on the way down. I manage to grab a few bites before sneaking away into the house to shower. After sloughing the dirt from my body under the hot spray, I dress and slip into my old room—now a sort of office for me.

The door creaks a little as I ease it shut, and I rush to slide the desk drawer open, reaching inside. A new journal—a Christmas gift from Giuliana, and beside that…

I sit and start writing, one sentence to clear the nerves and mark it down as real.

Tonight's the night.

Our bedroom door is shut when I tiptoe out. The patter of water from the shower and Giuliana's soft humming sounds from our ensuite. That shaft of light I stared at far too often creeps from under the door. I only have a few minutes head start so I'll have to make it count.

Grabbing the basket Isabella prepared for me, I give her a kiss on the cheek in gratitude during the one minute she stands still. She tuts me away, turning back to all her guests with a smile, and I rush out the back door and up the hill.

The sun is dipping toward the horizon, not quite blazing her last but it'll be here soon. I lay out the candles around the base of the tree and down in a little trail from the blanket. It's small, subtle. Not what a Palmer would have done, but then again, I'm not a Palmer. I've never really fit into that skin—that person.

Tapping my pocket for the fifth time since I left my old room, I breathe a sigh of relief at the hard square bumping against my leg at the movement. Giuliana strides up the little trail, her eyes large as she takes it all in. There's a hesitancy to her smile—a need to ask questions—but she holds off and I'm glad. I'm a fucking mess and if she distracts me right now, I might implode.

"Amore?" It's soft, a little breathless, and I love how she's found her own nickname for me. After I've teased her with so many different ones.

Holding out my hand for her to take, I shudder when she slips her palm against mine. Her fingers thread between my own and the grip is tight, reassuring. Raising her hand to my lips, I pray my voice will be steady and my palm's not too clammy and cold. My heart beats hard against the cage of my ribs—it roars, barely contained.

"Lia..." I kiss the back of her hand, savoring the fresh scent of her body wash and the softness of her skin under my lips. I've grown spoiled and accustomed to it. I try my best to soak it in now and make sure I never take it for granted that I'm beside her, touching her skin.

"I'm so proud of you."

She beams up at me at my words, that dimple displaying her joy and it warms me to know that I've pleased her.

"This past year with you has been the best of my life. You're the most amazing woman I've ever met and you've made me a better man—a better person. I'm in awe of you. When you walk into a room I can't look away and when you leave, I trace every corner looking for you. My days begin and end with you."

Taking a deep breath, the air rattles inside my lungs as nerves impact my ability to keep my cool.

Don't fuck this up. Don't fuck this up.

It's the most important moment of my life up until now and I'm praying I make it through this without incident.

"I think I've loved you since the first moment you yelled at me. Sitting there shaking on that Vespa, I watched you in amazement and every rational thought I had melted into nothing. You've knocked me off kilter the same way ever since. I feel you with me even when you're gone, in the little letters you leave or the strands of your hair that cling to all my clothing."

Giuliana laughs but I can see the moisture gathering in her eyes and glistening in the flickering candlelight. Her hand grips mine and I know she's just as affected as I am. Patting my pocket again, I slide my hand inside—trying to be subtle about it. It's almost as hard as trying to catch my breath when all I want to do is capture her mouth in mine.

All I want to do is lose myself in her.

"When I left here, I was a shell of a person and I resolved myself to a life without you but now... now I can't bear the thought of us ever being parted. You own me, body and soul, and it's for that reason I beg you..."

Stepping back slightly, I sink onto my knee and her tears tip over, down her cheeks. She raises her hand to her lips, as if she can hold in the gasp escaping regardless.

"Lia, I will love you until my body gives out. I will wipe your tears and tickle you until you can't breathe. I will hold you through the bad and celebrate the good. All I ask... is that you do me the honor of being my wife." My own tears choke me now. The words are a strangled plea by the end and I flick the box open to reveal the ring.

The same one from all those months ago—stuck in that desk drawer along with all the secrets she uncovered. It was the real deal then and now. I just didn't realize it. But this ring is as much a part of our story as this grove is.

"Yes," she sobs, "*Yes.*"

Giuliana lets go of my hand so I can slide the metal onto her finger and I surge up to kiss her. Hands tangling in my hair, I spin her in a circle, our kiss broken. Her laughter against my lips is the most divine thing I've ever tasted. I kiss away every tear, tiny pecks across her eyelids and down her cheeks. And then place a sweet kiss against her mouth.

"I love you," she says when we pull apart.

"I love you too. Always."

Pulling her left hand from my hair, Giuliana glances over my shoulder to admire it and I watch her features shift as she realizes.

"Is this?"

"Yes, just resized to fit. I knew it was yours from the moment I saw it at that jeweler's, and I've been holding onto it ever since. It didn't feel right until now: the grove's rebirth. It's our new beginning, and what better way to mark it?"

Joy shines through her smile and radiates through every fiber of my body as my mind screams at me. *She said yes. She said YES!*

"What better way indeed." Her smile takes on a little edge, mischief tucked into the corners. "Now, I hope this blanket isn't just for show."

Both looking around, we wait with bated breath to tell if

there's any other sound nearby. There shouldn't be. Isabella is under strict orders to keep people from the area. Though not for this reason, I suspect. Backing Giuliana up to the blanket, both of us sink onto our knees and I give her a deep kiss before speaking again.

"This blanket... this blanket's sole purpose is for your comfort as I worship every inch of you."

"*Worship?*"

"*Sì, Santa Giuliana.* Patron Saint of Reformed Playboys." Kissing down her neck, I ease her onto her back, and settle between her knees. My hand caressing her thick thigh.

"Reformed?" It's a sigh, pleasure catching at the back of her throat.

"Mostly."

Sharing a laugh, her mirth sputters to a halt when my thumb grazes the curve of her bare hip—one of those sensitive spots.

"Well, it seems like you still have some work to do, Matteo de Palma, to prove yourself worthy."

I slide her dress up, my hand wrapping around the soft give of her breast as I press against her heat. The layers of clothing we'll soon lose burn between us. As much as it pains me, I pull away. Parting her thighs and kissing my way up them, I'm ready to show my adoration. My answer is muttered against her soft flesh.

"Oh, I think you'll find my reverence up to standard before the night is through. Until then I remain your most devout admirer."

Tugging her underwear down, I savor her. Every hitch in her breathing, every moan washes over me as she burns through her first orgasm under the fiery sunset. And later, after I sink into her and we lose ourselves, I hold her against my chest. The stars blink above us, navy silk interspersed with silver. An owl hoots in the distance and beyond that we can make out the music of the party, still in full swing.

The air smells of harvest and her. God, I wish I could bottle this night—this sensation—so I can pull it out and savor it whenever I miss her. Our hearts beat hard against each other. With our limbs entangled and breathing as one, I know in my soul that I'm home.

ACKNOWLEDGMENTS

Thank you to my wonderful family. My husband who gave me the space and understanding to write this book despite everything going on around us. Matteo's anxiety and depression look a lot like my own sometimes and having someone as kind and wonderful as you, Tyler, helps me get through the hard days so I can enjoy all the amazing ones with you. I love you.

To my parents and sister, thank you for always believing in me. I feel your love even from so far away. Every meme in the group chat, every comment, every video call means the world to me. I am what you made me. To my in-laws, thank you for being so supportive and excited for me, and never letting me forget that this is real and I'm living it. Thank you for making me feel loved always.

My friends and everyone I know who showed up to support Playing For Keeps and this book, thank you for your excitement, for celebrating these milestones with me, and making every day I see you all a day that's better.

We did it! Again. I cannot believe I bamboozled Britt into publishing a second book of mine. Lake Country Press has been phenomenal to me and I am so appreciative of Britt and Bryan for all their hard work, encouragement when I wanted to burn this manuscript and my laptop, and the many laughs over the past two years. The community they've built and the authors within it are so amazing and I feel so lucky to know you all.

This book would not have taken shape without my amazing and generous CPs and beta readers. Ashley, Ana, Nichol you three have stuck with me through so much and I wouldn't have kept at it back in the day if not for your encouragement. From the ReyloCreatives Server until now, I couldn't ask for better critique partners or friends. Elle, thank you for letting me scream about this story and for brainstorming with me on Discord for hours over voice and chat. Your belief in this project helped me see the potential and I'm lucky to know you. I'm so excited to get to hold your books soon!

Juliet, it has been an absolute joy getting to work with you on this, and to have you indulge my Dramione brainrot. Kirsten, you keep me sane. Kat, your comments give me life. I'm so happy LCP brought us together and gave me new friends. Thank you for sprinting with me, thank you for talking me down and bolstering me when I needed it.

Thank you to Clare, Ashley Merdalo, and Gloria for beta reading this and helping me polish it into something readable (and hopefully enjoyable). Gloria was gracious enough to help me with the Italian aspects of this book, any inaccuracies are my own.

Tara, you are a blessing and this book wouldn't be half as good without the time and effort you put into reading and giving me constructive feedback. I appreciate you and thank you (and I know anyone reading this book does as well because it was a mess before you dove in to save me).

Thank you to my friends in the 321Write Server for cheering me on, sprinting with me, and being a space in which I feel excited to be part of the writing community.

Vivian, you've knocked it out of the park as usual. I'm so glad I got to work with you on cover art for one of my books again. Playing For Keeps and I Think Olive You are going to look so stunning side by side!

I owe thanks to Taylor Alison Swift... this book was written almost entirely while listening to Taylor Swift and considering this book was three times as hard to write as Playing For Keeps was, I owe a lot of my fortitude and excitement to her music. Cruel Summer is the song of this book—it captures the vibes of wanting what you can't have and only a limited amount of time in which to feel that passion. August featured heavily as well though this book sipped away like a bottle of extra virgin olive oil drizzled onto focaccia bread. Plenty of other songs make little appearances in easter eggs so small you'll probably miss them, but just know that her music was as much fuel for pushing through as it was inspiration.

Last, but not least, thank you to every reader who has supported me. Whether that be support for my fanfics, Playing For Keeps, or I Think Olive You. None of these stories would exist without you there to (hopefully) enjoy them. Writing is solitary and knowing that there's someone to receive what I've written on the other end of this is what keeps me going. Thank you for making this dream of mine a reality.

ABOUT THE AUTHOR

Wife. Fangirl. Disney lover and belter of show tunes. Overall ball of anxiety. As a teen, Tristen escaped into her mother's trove of historical romance books and hasn't resurfaced since. Exploring new worlds through reading also fostered a hankering for travel. When she's not working or writing about two idiots falling in love, she is researching and visiting as many different places as possible. Tristen was born and raised in South Africa but now lives in Maryland with her husband and their ever-growing book and board game shelves.

You can connect with Tristen here:
www.tristencrone.com

ALSO BY TRISTEN CRONE

Playing For Keeps

I Think Olive You

Coming Soon...

Under Locke & Key